Readers' praise for THE UNQUIET BONES

Thoughtful and curious, surgeon Hugh is an engaging character who feels totally real. – Rikki B. USA

Absolutely loved the book and cannot wait for the next one. One of the best medieval genre novels I've read in years. More of the same please – soon! – David C. UK

I enjoyed the setting, the period, the very realistic characters and the dry wit. – Donna B. USA

I enjoyed the story, and the insight into life in 14th century Britain. A lovely way to learn history – I'm looking forward to the sequel. – John H. UK

I read all of it in one go; it's quite the best medieval mystery I've read in a while. I teach medieval history, so it's always nice to read something by someone who actually knows what they're talking about. Can't wait for the next one! – Sarah T. USA

The first chronicle of Hugh de Singleton is a great read. – Richard A. UK

I found your novel a most enjoyable read and a rewarding venture into the history of Bampton in the company of real and entertaining characters. Should I find myself in the UK again I will definitely stop for a peek at St Beornwald's. – Anne Marie C. Ireland

A wonderful story, which could have been ghost-written by a true 14th century surgeon. I'm looking forward to reading more of his work. – Jill M. USA

A great read – appreciate the detail – and the glossary. I hope you have more to follow! – Ross D. Australia

As a retired nurse I enjoy reading the history of medicine. This book fed my hunger and left me wanting more. I am sending a donation to help save the beautiful old church in the story. – Patricia N. USA

This is an outstanding book and I found it impossible to put down. I shall look forward to the next chronicle with eager anticipation. – Roger F. UK

The first chronicle of Hugh de Singleton was first rate all the way. Amusing, educational, interesting, clever, and realistic all rolled into one fantastic piece of work. I am eagerly awaiting the second. – Annie E. USA

Just a few lines to say how much I have enjoyed reading *The Unquiet Bones*. It is going on my 'keeper shelf' with my other favourite medieval mysteries. I hope this book is the first of many. – Sue G. UK

An excellent first novel. The plot is well thought out and moves along nicely, with enough in the way of twists, turns, and red herrings to keep the reader interested. – Gary M. USA

What an outstanding first novel! Great plot, easy to read ... I've read all the Cadfael books and *The Unquiet Bones* exceeds them all. Can't wait for the next book in the series. – Peter S. UK

Excellent debut of a fine new protagonist ... the author shows a firm grasp of history. We can cheerfully hope that this will be the first of many. – Suzanne C. USA

I have never written to an author before but I really feel I must thank you for *The Unquiet Bones*. I have so enjoyed this book. I am a great fan of medieval whodunits and this must rank as one of the best. – Roger G. France

All in all this was a great first novel and I will purchase any others forthcoming from this author. – Ruth I. USA

The book contains fascinating insights into medieval surgery. *The Unquiet Bones* is a delight to read and I'm looking forward to the next installment. – Chris P. USA

I have just finished *The Unquiet Bones* and I loved it – a breath of fresh medieval air. – Annie C. USA

You've created a real sense of place, coupled with characters a reader can like and be interested in. Hugh is a great hero and I look forward to more of his adventures. – Maria H. USA

It was a wonderful read; I can't wait to see where Master Hugh's adventures will take him. – Travis B. USA

The first chronicle of

Hugh de Singleton, surgeon

MELVIN R. STARR

MONARCH
BOOKS

Oxford, UK & Grand Rapids, Michigan, USA

Copyright © 2008 Mel Starr.
The right of Mel Starr to be identified as author of this work has
been asserted by him in accordance with the Copyright, Designs
and Patents Act 1988.

First published in the UK in 2008 by Monarch Books
(a publishing imprint of Lion Hudson plc),
Wilkinson House, Jordan Hill Road, Oxford OX2 8DR.
Tel: +44 (0)1865 302750   Fax: +44 (0)1865 302757
Email: monarch@lionhudson.com
www.lionhudson.com

Reprinted 2009.

ISBN: 978-1-85424-885-5 (UK)
ISBN: 978-0-8254-6290-0 (USA)

Distributed by:
UK: Marston Book Services Ltd, PO Box 269, Abingdon, Oxon
OX14 4YN;
USA: Kregel Publications, PO Box 2607, Grand Rapids, Michigan
49501.

Unless otherwise stated, Scripture quotations are taken from the
Holy Bible, New International Version, © 1973, 1978, 1984 by the
International Bible Society. Used by permission of Hodder &
Stoughton Ltd. All rights reserved.

This book has been printed on paper and board independently
certified as having come from sustainable forests.

British Library Cataloguing Data
A catalogue record for this book is available from the British
Library.

Printed and bound in Malta by Gutenberg Press.

Acknowledgments

On a June afternoon in 1990 my wife and I discovered The Old Rectory, a delightful B&B in the tiny village of Mavesyn Ridware. Tony and Lis Page, the proprietors, became good friends. Nearly a decade later Tony and Lis moved to Bampton, and Susan and I were able to visit them there in 2001. I saw immediately the town's potential for the novel I intended to write.

Tony and Lis have been a great resource for the history of Bampton, for which I am very grateful.

Dr John Blair, of Queen's College, Oxford, has written several papers illuminating the history of Bampton. These have been a great help, especially in understanding the odd situation of a medieval parish church staffed by three vicars.

When he learned that I had written an as yet unpublished novel, Dr Dan Runyon, of Spring Arbor University, invited me to speak to his classes about the trials of a rookie writer. Dan sent some sample chapters to his friend, Tony Collins, Editorial Director of Monarch Books at Lion Hudson plc. Thanks, Dan.

And thanks go to Tony Collins, my editor Jan Greenough, and the people at Lion Hudson for their willingness to publish a new author with no track record.

Before trying my hand as a writer I spent thirty-nine years teaching history. The experience gave me a greater respect for the teachers and professors who struggled to instill some wisdom into my own youthful mind. Thanks to:

Jack Gridley, eighth grade teacher of extraordinary skill and kindness.

Celestine Trevan, who demanded clear, concise writing in her high school English classes.

Dan Jensen, whose enthusiasm for teaching history was infectious, and who also pounced on bad writing.

And many others too numerous to list here.

Mel Starr
Ascensiontide 2008

For Susan
Proverbs 12:4a

For further information visit the author's website:
www.melstarr.net

Glossary

Angelus Bell: Rung three times each day; dawn, noon, and dusk. Announced the time for the Angelus devotional.

Bailiff: A lord's chief manorial representative. He oversaw all operations, collected rents and fines, and enforced labor service. Not a popular fellow.

Bolt: A short, heavy, blunt arrow, shot from a crossbow.

Burgher: A town merchant or tradesman.

Bylaw: A community assembly. The term applied to the meeting and to the laws and regulations passed.

Candlemas: February 2. Marked the purification of Mary. Women traditionally paraded to the church carrying lighted candles. Tillage of fields resumed this day.

Capon: A castrated male chicken.

Cautery: To sear with a heated metal tool. Generally used to seal a wound.

Chamberlain: The keeper of a lord's chamber, wardrobe and personal items.

Chauces: Tight-fitting trousers, often of different colors for each leg.

Childwite: A fine for having a child out of wedlock.

Christmas Oblation: An offering due to the church at Christmas.

Church of St Beornwald: Today the Church of St Mary the Virgin in Bampton, in the fourteenth century it was dedicated to an obscure Saxon saint enshrined in the church.

Coppicing: The practice of cutting trees, especially ash and poplar, so that a thicket of small saplings would grow from the stump. These shoots were used for everything from arrows to rafters, depending upon how much they were permitted to grow.

Cotehardie: The primary medieval outer garment. Women's were floor-length, men's ranged from thigh-length to ankle-length.

Cresset: A bowl of oil with a floating wick used for lighting.

Demesne: Land directly exploited by a lord, and worked by his villeins, as opposed to land a lord might rent to tenants.

Deodand: An object which caused accidental death. The item was sold and the price given to the king.

Dexter: A war horse; larger than pack-horses and palfreys. Also, the right-hand direction.

Ember Day: A day of fasting, prayer, and requesting forgiveness of sins. Observed four times per year, on successive Wednesdays, Fridays, and Saturdays.

Epiphany: January 6. Ended the twelve-day Christmas holiday. Celebrated the coming of the Magi to worship Christ.

Extreme Unction: "Last rites." A sacrament for the dying. It must not be premature. A recipient who recovered was considered as good as dead. He must fast perpetually, go barefoot, and abstain from sexual relations.

Feast of the Assumption: August 15. Marked the day Mary was supposedly carried to heaven.

Fewterer: Keeper of the lord's kennel and hounds.

Furlong: A bundle of strips of land, of different tenants, but generally planted with the same crop.

Garderobe: The toilet.

Goodrich Castle: Rebuilt in the thirteenth century. In Herefordshire, near the southern Welsh border. Came to Gilbert Talbot through his mother, Elizabeth Comyn.

Groom: A lower-rank servant to a lord. Often a teen-aged youth. Occasionally assistant to a valet.

8

Haberdasher: Merchant who sold household items such as pins, buckles, hats, and purses.

Half-virgate: Fifteen acres.

Hallmote: The manorial court. Royal courts judged free tenants accused of murder or felony. Otherwise manor courts had jurisdiction over legal matters concerning villagers. Villeins accused of homicide might also be tried in a manor court.

Hayward: A manorial officer in charge of fences, hedges, enclosures, and fields. Usually a half-virgater or mid-level villager, he served under the reeve. Also called a beadle.

Heriot: An inheritance tax paid to the lord of the manor, usually the heir's best animal.

Hocktide: The Sunday after Easter; a time of paying rents and taxes. Therefore, getting out of hock.

Horn Dancers: Men wearing deer antlers who danced in the town marketplace at Michaelmas. Probably an ancient pagan hunting custom.

Hypocras: Spiced wine. Sugar, cinnamon, ginger, cloves, and nutmeg were often in the mix. Usually served at the end of a meal.

King's eyre: A royal circuit court, presided over generally by a traveling judge.

Kirtle: The basic medieval undergarment.

Lammas Day: August 1, when thanks was given for a successful wheat harvest.

Leech custard: a date paste topped with wine syrup.

Leirwite: A fine for sexual relations out of wedlock.

Lettuce: Bitter-tasting wild lettuce was sometimes added to soups, but was best known for its sedative and narcotic effect, especially when going to seed.

Marshalsea: The stables and associated accoutrements.

Maslin: A bread made from a mixture of grains; commonly wheat and rye or barley and rye.

Metatarses: Small bones of the foot.

9

Michaelmas: September 29. The feast signaled the end of the harvest. The last rents and tithes were due.

Ninth hour: 3 p.m.

Oxgang: About thirty acres. The term was more commonly used in northern England. See "yardland."

Palfrey: A riding horse with a comfortable gait.

Pax Board: An object, frequently painted with sacred scenes, which was passed through the medieval church during services for all present to kiss.

Phlebotomy: The letting of blood in the treatment of disease.

Pollard: To cut a tree back to produce dense new growth.

Quadrivium: The scientific university studies – arithmetic, geometry, astronomy, and music.

Rector: A priest in charge of a parish. He might be an absentee, and hire a vicar or curate to serve in his place.

Reeve: The most important manor official, although he did not outrank the bailiff. Elected by tenants from among themselves, often the best husbandman. He had responsibility for fields, buildings, and enforcing labor service.

Rogation Sunday: Five weeks after Easter. A time of asking God to bless the new growing season, accompanied by a parade around the boundaries of the village.

St Andrew's Chapel: An ancient chapel a few hundred yards east of Bampton dating to before the Norman conquest.

St Catharine's Day: November 25. St Catherine was the most popular female saint of medieval Europe. Processions were held in her honor on her feast day.

St Crispin's Day: October 25.

St Stephen's Day: December 26.

Scrofula: A swelling of lymph nodes on the neck.

Sixth hour: Noon.

Solar: A small private room, more easily heated than the great hall, where lords often preferred to spend time, especially in winter. Usually on an upper floor.

Squab: a young pigeon about four or five weeks old.

Subtlety: An elaborate dessert, served between courses (removes) of a meal. Often more for show than consumption.

Sumptuary laws: Laws designed to regulate expenditure on lavish clothing and food.

Suturing: Stitching a wound closed.

Tenant: A free peasant who rented land from his lord. He could pay his rent in labor, or more likely by the fourteenth century, in cash.

Terce: The canonical service at 9 a.m.

Third hour: 9 a.m.

Toft: Land surrounding a house, in the medieval period often used for growing vegetables.

Trepanning: Removing a circular section of the skull, usually to relieve headaches. It sometimes worked!

Trivium: The literary university studies – grammar, rhetoric, and logic.

Valet: A high-ranking servant to a lord. A chamberlain, for example.

Vicar: A priest who serves a parish but is not entitled to its tithes.

Villein: A non-free peasant. He could not leave his land or service to his lord, or sell animals without permission. But if he could escape his manor for a year and a day he would be free.

Wear the willow: "Weeping" willow was a symbol of sorrow. To wear the willow was to grieve. People did actually wear a sprig of willow to indicate their sorrow.

Week-work: The two or three days of work per week owed to the lord by a villein.

Whitsuntide: Pentecost; seven weeks after Easter Sunday.

Yardland: Thirty acres. Also called a virgate. In northern England often called an oxgang.

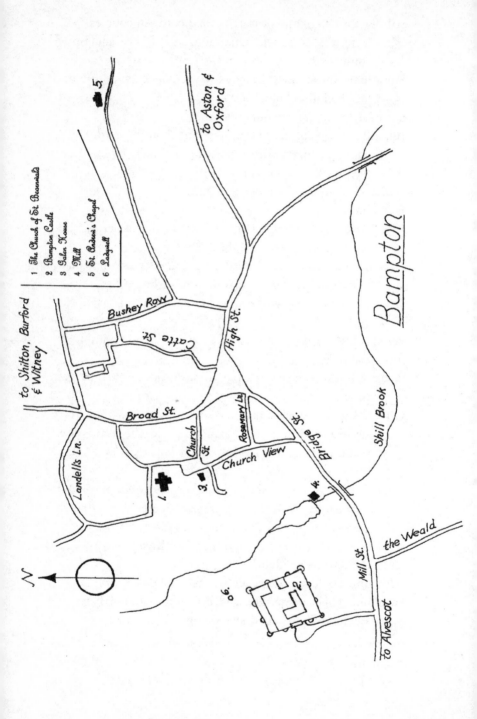

Bampton

1 The Church of St. Beornwald
2 Bampton Castle
3 Salem House
4 Mill
5 St. Andrew's Chapel
6 Ladywell

Chapter 1

Uctred thought he had discovered pig bones. He did not know or care why they were in the cesspit at the base of Bampton Castle wall.

Then he found the skull. Uctred was a villein, bound to the land of Lord Gilbert, third Baron Talbot, lord of Bampton Castle, and had slaughtered many pigs. He knew the difference between human and pig skulls.

Lord Gilbert called for me to inspect the bones. All knew whose bones they must be. Only two men had recently gone missing in Bampton. These must be the bones of one of them.

Sir Robert Mallory had been the intended suitor of Lord Gilbert's beauteous sister, Lady Joan. Shortly after Easter he and his squire called at the castle, having, it was said, business with Lord Gilbert. What business this was I know not, but suspect a dowry was part of the conversation. Two days later he and his squire rode out the castle gate to the road north toward Burford. The porter saw him go. No one saw him or his squire after. He never arrived at his father's manor at Northleech. How he arrived, dead, unseen, back within – or nearly within – the walls of Bampton Castle, no one could say. Foul play seemed likely.

I was called to the castle because of my profession: surgeon. Had I known when I chose such work that cleaning filth from bones might be part of my duties, I might have continued the original calling chosen for me: clerk.

I am Hugh of Singleton, fourth and last son of a minor knight from the county of Lancashire. The manor of Little Singleton is aptly named; it is small. My father held the manor in fief from Robert de Sandford. It was a pleasant place to grow up. Flat as a table, with a wandering, sluggish tidal stream, the Wyre, pushing through it on its journey from the hills, just visible ten miles to the east, to the sea, an equal distance to the northwest.

Since I was the youngest son, the holding would play no part in my future. My oldest brother, Roger, would receive the manor, such as it was. I remember when I was but a tiny lad overhearing him discuss with my father a choice of brides who might bring with them a dowry which would enlarge his lands. In this they were moderately successful. Maud's dowry doubled my brother's holdings. After three children Roger doubled the size of his bed, as well. Maud was never a frail girl. Each heir she produced added to her bulk. This seemed not to trouble Roger. Heirs are important.

Our village priest, Father Aymer, taught the manor school. When I was nine years old, the year the Black Death first appeared, he spoke to my father and my future was decided.

I showed a scholar's aptitude, so it would be the university for me. At age fourteen I was sent off to Oxford to become a clerk, and, who knows, perhaps eventually a lawyer or a priest. This was poor timing, for in my second year at the university a fellow student became enraged at the watered beer he was served in a High Street tavern, and with some cohorts destroyed the place. The proprietor sought assistance, and the melee became a wild brawl known ever after as the St Scholastica Day Riot. Near a hundred scholars and townsmen died before the sheriff restored the peace. When I dared emerge from my lodgings, I fled to Lancashire and did not return until Michaelmas term.

I might instead have inherited Little Singleton had the Black Death been any worse. Roger and one of his sons perished in 1349, but two days apart, in the week before St Peter's Day. Then, at the Feast of St Mary my third brother died within a day of falling ill. Father Aymer said an imbalance of the four humors – air, earth, fire, and water – caused the sickness. Most priests, and indeed the laymen as well,

14

thought this imbalance due to God's wrath. Certainly men gave Him reason enough to be angry.

Most physicians ascribed the imbalance to the air. Father Aymer recommended burning wet wood to make smoky fires, ringing the church bell at regular intervals, and the wearing of a bag of spices around the neck to perfume the air. I was but a child, but it seemed to me even then that these precautions were not successful. Father Aymer, who did not shirk his duties as did some scoundrel priests, died a week after administering extreme unction to my brother Henry. I watched from the door, a respectful distance from my brother's bed. I can see in my memory Father Aymer bending over my wheezing, dying brother, his spice bag swinging out from his body as he chanted the phrases of the sacrament.

So my nephew and his mother inherited little Singleton and I made my way to Oxford. I found the course of study mildly interesting. Father Aymer had taught me Latin and some Greek, so it was no struggle to advance my skills in these languages.

I completed the trivium and quadrivium in the allotted six years, but chose not to take holy orders after the award of my bachelor's degree. I had no desire to remain a bachelor, although I had no particular lady in mind with whom I might terminate my solitary condition.

I desired to continue my studies. Perhaps, I thought, I shall study law, move to London, and advise kings. The number of kingly advisors who ended their lives in prison or at the block should have dissuaded me of this conceit. But the young are seldom deterred from following foolish ideas.

You see how little I esteemed life as a vicar in some lonely village, or even the life of a rector with livings to support me. This is not because I did not wish to serve God. My desire in that regard, I think, was greater than many who took a vocation, serving the church while they served themselves.

In 1361, while I completed a Master of Arts degree, plague struck again. Oxford, as before, was hard hit. The colleges were much reduced. I lost many friends, but once again God chose to spare me. I have prayed many times since that I might live so as to make Him pleased that He did so.

I lived in a room on St Michael's Street, with three other students. One fled the town at the first hint that the disease had returned. Two others perished. I could do nothing to help them, but tried to make them comfortable. No; when a man is covered from neck to groin in bursting pustules, he cannot be made comfortable. I brought water to them, and put cool cloths on their fevered foreheads, and waited with them for death.

William of Garstang had been a friend since he enrolled in Balliol College five years earlier. We came from villages but ten miles apart – although his was much larger; it held a weekly market – but we did not meet until we became students together. An hour before he died, William beckoned me to approach his bed. I dared not remain close, but heard his rasping whisper as he willed to me his possessions. Among his meager goods were three books.

God works in mysterious ways. Between terms, in August of 1361, He chose to do three things which would forever alter my life. First, I read one of William's books – *Surgery*, by Henry de Mondeville – and learned of the amazing intricacies of the human body. I read all day, and late into the night, until my supply of candles was gone. When I finished, I read the book again, and bought more candles.

Secondly, I fell in love. I did not know her name, or her home. But one glance told me she was a lady of rank and beyond my station. The heart, however, does not deal in social convention.

I had laid down de Mondeville's book long enough to seek a meal. I saw her as I left the inn. She rode a gray palfrey with easy grace. A man I assumed to be her husband escorted her. Another woman, also quite handsome, rode with them, but I noticed little about her. A half-dozen grooms rode behind this trio: their tunics of blue and black might have identified the lady's family, but I paid little attention to them, either.

Had I rank enough to someday receive a bishopric, I might choose a mistress and disregard vows of chastity. Many who choose a vocation do. Secular priests in lower orders must be more circumspect, but even many of these keep women. This is not usually held against them, so long as they are loyal to the woman who lives with them and bears their children. But I found the thought of violating a vow as repugnant as a solitary life, wedded only to the church. And the church is already the bride of Christ and needs no other spouse.

The vision on the gray mare wore a deep red cotehardie. Because it was warm she needed no cloak or mantle. She wore a simple white hood, turned back, so that chestnut-colored hair visibly framed a flawless face. Beautiful women had smitten me before. It was a regular occurrence. But not like this. Of course, that's what I said the last time, also.

I followed the trio and their grooms at a discreet distance, hoping they might halt before some house. I was disappointed. The party rode on to Oxpens Road, crossed the Castle Mill Stream, and disappeared to the west as I stood watching, quite lost, from the bridge. Why should I have been lovelorn over a lady who seemed to be another man's wife? Who can know? I cannot. It seems foolish when I look back to the day. It did not seem so at the time.

I put the lady out of my mind. No; I lie. A beautiful woman is as impossible to put out of mind as a corn on one's toe. And just as disquieting. I did try, however.

I returned to de Mondeville's book and completed a third journey through its pages. I was confused, but 'twas not de Mondeville's writing which caused my perplexity. The profession I thought lay before me no longer appealed. Providing advice to princes seemed unattractive. Healing men's broken and damaged bodies now occupied near all my waking thoughts.

I feared a leap into the unknown. Oxford was full to bursting with scholars and lawyers and clerks. No surprises awaited one who chose to join them. And the town was home also to many physicians, who thought themselves far above the barbers who usually performed the stitching of wounds and phlebotomies when such services were needed. Even a physician's work, with salves and potions, was familiar. But the pages of de Mondeville's book told me how little I knew of surgery, and how much I must learn should I choose such a vocation. I needed advice.

There is, I think, no wiser man in Oxford than Master John Wyclif. There are men who hold different opinions, of course. Often these are scholars whom Master John has bested in disputation. Tact is not one among his many virtues, but care for his students is. I sought him out for advice and found him in his chamber at Balliol College, bent over a book. I was loath to disturb him, but he received me warmly when he saw 'twas me who rapped upon his door.

"Hugh... come in. You look well. Come and sit."

He motioned to a bench, and resumed his own seat as I perched on the offered bench. The scholar peered silently at me, awaiting announcement of the reason for my visit.

"I seek advice," I began. "I had it in mind to study law, as many here do, but a new career entices me."

"Law is safe... for most," Wyclif remarked. "What is this new path which interests you?"

"Surgery. I have a book which tells of old and new knowledge in the treatment of injuries and disease."

"And from this book alone you would venture on a new vocation?"

"You think it unwise?"

"Not at all. So long as men do injury to themselves or others, surgeons will be needed."

"Then I should always be employed."

"Aye," Wyclif grimaced. "But why seek my counsel? I know little of such matters."

"I do not seek you for your surgical knowledge, but for aid in thinking through my decision."

"Have you sought the advice of any other?"

"Nay."

"Then there is your first mistake."

"Who else must I seek? Do you know of a man who can advise about a life as a surgeon?"

"Indeed. He can advise on any career. I consulted Him when I decided to seek a degree in theology."

I fell silent, for I knew of no man so capable as Master John asserted, able to advise in both theology and surgery. Perhaps the fellow did not live in Oxford. Wyclif saw my consternation.

"Do you seek God's will and direction?"

"Ah... I understand. Have I prayed about this matter, you ask? Aye, I have, but God is silent."

"So you seek me as second best."

"But... 'twas you just said our Lord could advise on any career."

"I jest. Of course I, like any man, am second to our Lord Christ... or perhaps third, or fourth."

"So you will not guide my decision?"

"Did I say that? Why do you wish to become a surgeon? Do you enjoy blood and wounds and hurts?"

"No. I worry that I may not have the stomach for it."

"Then why?"

"I find the study of man and his hurts and their cures fascinating. And I... I wish to help others."

"You could do so as a priest."

"Aye. But I lack the boldness to deal with another man's eternal soul."

"You would risk a man's body, but not his soul?"

"The body cannot last long, regardless of what a surgeon or physician may do, but a man's soul may rise to heaven or be doomed to hell... forever."

"And a priest may influence the direction, for good or ill," Wyclif completed my thought.

"Just so. The responsibility is too great for me."

"Would that all priests thought as you," Wyclif muttered. "But lopping off an arm destroyed in battle would not trouble you?"

"'Tis but flesh, not an everlasting soul."

"You speak true, Hugh. And there is much merit in helping ease men's lives. Our Lord Christ worked many miracles, did he not, to grant men relief from their afflictions. Should you do the same, you would be following in his path."

"I had not considered that," I admitted.

"Then consider it now. And should you become a surgeon, keep our Lord as your model, and your work will prosper."

And so God's third wonder: a profession. I would go to Paris to study. My income from the manor at Little Singleton was £6 and 15 shillings each year, to be awarded so long as I was a student, and to terminate after eight years.

My purse would permit one year in Paris. I know what you are thinking. But I did not spend my resources on riotous living. Paris is an expensive city. I learned much there. I watched and then participated in dissections. I learned phlebotomy, suturing, cautery, the removal of arrows, the setting of broken bones, and the treatment of scrofulous sores. I learned how to extract a tooth and remove a tumor. I learned trepanning to relieve a headache, and how to lance a fistula. I learned which herbs might staunch bleeding, or dull pain, or cleanse a wound. I spent both time and money as wisely as I knew how, learning the skills which I hoped would one day earn me a living.

Chapter 2

I left Paris and returned to Oxford in 1363, at Michaelmas. Trees were beginning to show autumn brown, reapers were completing their labors in the fields as I passed, and horn dancers pranced in the marketplace.

I understood that Oxford might be a poor place for an untried surgeon, there being many others who followed the profession there, and physicians as well. But I felt at home in no other place but Little Singleton, and there would be no custom for me there in such a small village. I shudder to think all I might have missed had I set up my shop in Ashford or Canterbury, as I was tempted while passing through those towns. Of course, I may have missed much by not remaining in one of those places. Who can know? I believe I have served God's will, but have wondered occasionally if God's will might be variable.

I found lodging on the upper floor of an inn, the Stag and Hounds, on the High Street; an establishment where I had often supped in my student days, but not by choice. The rent of such a location was sixpence each month – more than I could afford, but I wished to hang my sign in a visible, well-traveled place. I unpacked my meager possessions, aligned my surgical instruments, hung a board above my window with my name and profession emblazoned on it, and waited for patients.

Much of the next week I spent realigning my scalpels, razors, and forceps. There was little custom. A mother brought in her child, a lad of seven years or so, who had fallen from a wall and dislocated his elbow. With some tugging and much screeching, I put it right, fashioned a sling, and sent them on their way. Fee: twopence. For the most part I stayed in my room, fearing to be out when a supplicant might call.

From my window I was distractedly watching the bustle on the High Street when opportunity found me. A gentleman and two grooms rode through the throng toward St Aldgate's. As they passed the inn a cat darted across the street just before them. The horse of the first groom started, then bucked and wheeled, scattering pedestrians like fallen leaves. His rider did not lose his seat, but neither did he quickly regain control. As the horse spun, he wheeled against the noble. I heard a shouted curse over the neighing horse and bawling crowd, and while I watched a great stain of blood spread from the noble's thigh to his calf, and dripped from his stirrup. The groom's horse had kicked the aristocrat, and badly, from the look of it.

I gathered some instruments and threw them into a leather bag, made certain I had thread and bandages, and bounded for my door.

Someone in the crowd must have noticed my sign and told the other groom of it. As I hastened down the stairs I met him coming up, taking the steps two at a time. He brushed me aside without slowing.

"Out of my way, lad," he gasped, and charged on up the stairs.

"Who do you seek?" I called after him. I was sure I knew the answer to that.

"The surgeon who lives above."

"That's me. I saw your master hurt."

"Then come," he cried, and preceded me down the staircase as rapidly as he had come up, two at a time. I thought I might add a fee for setting a broken leg, but he arrived at the landing unmarred.

I should have recognized Lord Gilbert. I had seen him once, a year and more before. But the lady with him had distracted me. He was a solid man, squarely built, square in the face. He wore a neatly trimmed beard just beginning to show gray against reddened cheeks. His face was lined from years of squinting into the sun from horseback. It was a handsome face, in a blunt fashion.

At the moment my interest in him was professional, not social. With aid from bystanders, he had dismounted. I knelt over his leg, which flowed blood freely from a gash six inches long, halfway up his thigh. His chauces were torn open, so the wound was clearly visible.

He sat on the cobbles, his legs stretched before him, his solid body propped on his hands. There was no grimace on his face or quiver to his voice.

"Are you the surgeon?" he asked, nodding toward my sign.

"I am."

"Can you repair this dent I've received, or should I seek another?"

I probably seemed young to a man whose future ability to walk, whose life, even, might be in my hands.

"I can."

"Best get on with it, then," he replied.

I felt first round the wound to learn if the bone was broken. When I was satisfied it was not, I chose two onlookers to assist Lord Gilbert, whose name I did not yet know, up the stairs to my room. I sent the still-puffing groom – the other had a frozen grip on the three horses, including his own recalcitrant beast – to the inn for a flagon of wine while I followed the grunting baron and his helpers up the uneven stairs.

Once in my surgery, I directed the injured man to lie on my bed, then cut away the ripped fabric from the wound. The groom arrived with wine, and I washed the wound. Lord Gilbert winced but slightly, then bade me sternly to proceed. I threaded a needle and began to stitch the gash, careful to do my neatest work and keep my patient as free from pain as possible, which was not actually possible. I made twenty stitches, more than might have been necessary, but when I saw he bore it well, I thought a neatly healed leg might, in future, be good advertising for my skills.

I tightened and knotted the last suture, then stood to stretch my aching back.

23

"Do not walk over much on that leg for four days, and do not ride a horse for three weeks," I told Lord Gilbert, who, while I spoke, was tentatively stretching his injured limb. "In three weeks I will remove the stitches."

"And I can ride then?" Lord Gilbert demanded.

"I do not advise it. A wound so deep as this will need careful treatment. A young man heals quickly. Were you but a squire I might say yes, but you seem a man of thirty years and more." He frowned and nodded. "So my advice, for proper healing, would be to keep from a horse for a month." He grimaced again.

"Will you dress this now?" he asked, and nodded toward his leg.

"No. I follow the practice of Henry de Mondeville. It was his observation that a dry wound heals best. Do not cover the wound. I will lend you chauces of mine to see you through the streets and home, but when you are at home you should leave the leg uncovered. Watch if the wound produces pus. If such be white and thick, there is no great harm, but if the pus be thin and watery, call for me at once."

"Nothing more, then?" he asked.

"No, m'lord. I have finished."

Lord Gilbert pulled his good leg under him and the groom rushed to help him stand.

"Help me down to the inn," he said, pointing to the stairs. My room was above a cheap establishment intended to serve students, not nobles. Its soup was thin, its meat was gristle, and its ale sour. I ate there often.

"I will wait there. Find a litter to swing between two horses. I will go home that way."

From my chest I drew chauces with which Lord Gilbert might cover himself. He drew them on and hobbled to my door to descend to the inn. I wanted to follow, for a pint of even bad ale seemed a good idea, but thought he might consider my continued presence an affront, or a bold request for payment. I assumed I would be paid, though the man had said no word about it.

Nearly an hour later I heard footsteps at my door, followed by a manly thumping on its panels. It was the groom who had first sought me. He held out a small purse.

"Lord Gilbert will have you receive this for your service to him. If this is not sufficient, he will make up the difference when you visit him to remove the stitches. I will call for you in three weeks to take you to him. God be with you."

"And with you."

The groom turned and tumbled down the stairs in the same fashion he'd done an hour earlier. Lord Gilbert must be a man, I thought, who does not like to wait.

When his back was turned I emptied the purse into my hand. It held ten silver pennies! And the man was willing to pay more. I resolved to eat well that day, and not at my landlord's table.

The following two weeks brought little business. A woodcutter sheared off two toes with his axe. I could do little but clean and dress the wound, and advise him to be more careful. Certainly he appreciated the advice.

I tried to seem busy when Lord Gilbert's man called for me twenty days later. "I am Arthur, here to fetch you to Lord Gilbert Talbot. You sewed him up a fortnight and more ago."

I followed him down the stairs to where he had tied two horses in the street. I thought that polite of Lord Gilbert; don't make the surgeon walk. But when we crossed Castle Mill Stream and put the town behind us, I realized the horse under me was more than good manners.

"Where are we going?"

"To Lord Gilbert," Arthur replied. That was helpful.

"And where might he be found?"

"Oh... You don't know? In Bampton, at the castle there," he answered.

I'd heard of the town, that was all. "How far must we travel?"

"Fifteen miles... Perhaps sixteen."

25

I settled myself as comfortably in the saddle as I could. I had not ridden a horse for many years. I knew that by the time I returned to Oxford in the evening I would be sore in the nether regions. Perhaps, I thought, I should volunteer to walk home.

The first thing I saw of Bampton was the spire of the Church of St Beornwald rising above the fields and forests surrounding the village. The spire was visible before we reached Aston, more than two miles distant. We passed an ancient chapel dedicated to St Andrew, and entered the town on the High Street. I felt at home already. Does every English town have a High Street? At the center of town we took the left fork and followed Mill Street to the bridge across Shill Brook.

I attracted a good deal of attention as we rode through the village. Strangers in small towns tend to do that. The town and people seemed prosperous enough. I even saw a few houses made of stone, although most were wattle and daub, with thatched roofs.

Bampton Castle is an impressive structure, all the more so when one views it for the first time. A curtain wall twenty feet high and six feet thick surrounds one of the largest castle yards in all the realm, for the wall is 360 feet long on each of its four sides. At each corner are round towers three stories high, with arrow loops at each level. Four more towers stand on the sides, and a gatehouse in the west wall permits entry. To the northwest of the castle, near a turf close, is the famous Lady Well, whose waters are of miraculous reputation.

Lord Gilbert's chamberlain showed me to the solar, where I found my patient. The wound was healed well. There was no pus and, according to my patient, never had been. Some physicians prefer a wound to issue white – laudable – pus, but I hold with Mondeville that, although white pus is much to be preferred over watery, stinking pus, no purulence at all is best.

It was but a matter of minutes to remove the sutures.

26

The seam across Lord Gilbert's thigh was neat and straight. Not, unfortunately, in a readily visible location so as to proclaim my skills. Word of mouth in this case would have to suffice.

"Remember, no riding for another week," I reminded him.

Lord Gilbert puffed his cheeks skeptically, glanced at my bag, and said, "I have two villeins in need of a surgeon's care. Will you see them before you go?"

Clients! Of course I would see them.

The first man brought to me was a simple case. He had a large, fleshy wart on his neck. He had tried the usual remedies: rubbing with the skin of a bean pod; touching the wart with a knotted cord, then burying the cord; rubbing with a slug, then impaling the slug on a thorn bush. These had been unsuccessful. If a wart disappears after such treatment it is, I am convinced, mere happenstance. Such a wart would have faded anyway. I tied a bit of string tightly around the base of the wart, and gave the man another.

"If the wart does not wither and fall away in two weeks, loose the string and have your wife tie this other on, and tightly."

The ploughman nodded understanding, but turned away with a skeptical expression on his weathered face. This cure was effective, however. I saw the fellow some weeks later, and he was free of the growth. Blood is cut off to the wart. It shrivels and dies and falls away.

The second man I was to see was more seriously afflicted. Arthur showed me to his hut and waited uneasily at the door. The fellow was a large, beefy man, with a broad back and legs made strong following a plow. His brow was crevassed in pain. His wife hovered, fidgeting, near the bed, which sagged beneath his weight.

"He has a stone," Arthur said by way of introduction. The villein nodded agreement.

"Had one before," he explained through clenched teeth. "Two years past... at Candlemas. I drank from the

Lady Well and the blessed virgin interceded for me. The stone passed after a week or so. But this... since Lammas Day I'm barely able to rise from my bed."

Nearly two months. This stone was too large to pass. It would become larger, more painful, and weaken the man to an early grave. Well, not all that early. He appeared to be about forty, although the illness might influence his features. He would not expect to live many more years.

"Lord Gilbert's man said he'd send you. Can you do aught for me?"

"I can remove the stone. But such surgery is dangerous. You might not live."

"I cannot live in such torment as this. I would rather see God this day than live another hour as I have these past weeks."

"I will speak the truth – that may happen. And if not today, then tomorrow or next day."

"But if I live, the pain will be gone?"

"Aye."

Alfred glanced at his wife. Her pursed lips indicated the decision she would make. But he turned from her and said, "When will you do this?"

"Today. Now, if you are determined."

He peered at his wife again briefly, then sighed, "I am."

I had seen a lithotomy performed once, in Paris. That patient did not survive. But he was near sixty years old, and my instructor assured me that many times he had performed such surgery successfully. I was eager to try my skills, and to relieve the man's suffering. But I will tell no lies: I was anxious both for my patient and for my reputation should I fail. Lord Gilbert's sound leg would not balance a new corpse in St Beornwald's Churchyard. It troubled me to think that I was as concerned for my reputation as for my patient's life, but that was the truth of it. This attitude began to change when I came to know the people of Bampton well. It is difficult to look clinically upon a patient who has been a friend for a year or two.

28

I heard a voice at the door of the hut, and turned to see Arthur approach through the haze produced by the smoky hearth.

"A message from Lord Gilbert; will you be long here? He would have you join him for dinner."

Six hours had passed since I ate a crust of bread and drank a half-pint of ale to begin the day. The knot in my stomach might have been hunger as well as apprehension for what I was about to do. If I accepted Lord Gilbert's invitation, I could put off the surgery. I accepted.

Arthur led me to the castle yard, through the inner gatehouse to the hall. Tables erected in a "U" shape now occupied most of the room. Trenchers and loaves of bread – white bread! – sat, one at each place, on the cloth. Twelve places were set around the tables. I passed a hand over the nearest loaf: yet warm from the oven!

Arthur left me in the hall. As he passed out one door, my dinner companions entered through another.

She was among them: the beauty I had seen on horseback a year earlier. You may wonder that I would remember and recognize her after a year. If you had seen the lady, you would wonder no more.

Lord Gilbert saw me standing alone, probably looking as awkward as I felt, and spoke to his companions. "Ah, here is the surgeon who has put me back together. Master Hugh de Singleton; my wife, Lady Petronilla; my sister, Lady Joan." I heard other names vaguely, obscured as they were by the lovely Joan – sister, not wife, to Lord Gilbert.

I remember little of the meal. I ate well: even love has seldom been able to suppress my appetite. She smiled at me once. I spent most of the meal trying not to be obvious about her charms and their influence on me. This was most difficult between removes, for there was no food then to occupy my eye or thoughts.

Lord Gilbert placed me beside a guest, Sir William Fitzherbert, but two places removed from himself at the high table. I was cognizant of the honor.

"Are you able to relieve my villeins?" Lord Gilbert asked, between the first and second removes. I told him what I had done for the first, and what I proposed for the other. I did not think it the proper time or place to explain the procedure in detail, however.

"I pray you succeed. Alfred has been in torment for months, and he's no good to me as he is."

"He may die," I warned.

"So may we all," Lord Gilbert laughed.

"The surgery may not succeed."

"Alfred knows this?" Lord Gilbert frowned.

"He does."

"Yet he desires you to proceed?"

"He said he would rather see God this day than live longer with his pain."

Lord Gilbert toyed with a crust from his trencher: "Well, it must be his choice. Will you need assistance?"

"Some strong lads to hold him quiet; four, I think. Some hot water, ale, and a flagon of wine."

"Wine? Will not ale suffice? A man may be made as drunk on ale as on wine."

Lord Gilbert, I was to learn, is a bit miserly. Ale is cheap, wine is expensive.

"To wash the incision. Do you remember how I cleansed your wound?"

"Ah... yes. Well, you shall have your wine."

I caught one last glimpse of Lady Joan Talbot as she left the hall for her chamber and I departed the room through the entry hall to make or mar my reputation.

Lord Gilbert acted quickly on my request. I had but stepped through the door of Alfred's hut when four men arrived: two valets I had not seen before, and the two grooms who had accompanied Lord Gilbert to Oxford. Arthur had a flagon of wine and another of ale.

"Cicely is heating water. She'll send a girl 'round with it as soon as she can."

"Cicely?" I asked.

30

"My wife, Master Hugh. She be in charge of Lord Gilbert's scullery." I caught just a faint note of pride in Arthur's voice.

I took from my bag two pouches: one contained willow bark, ground fine; the other held hemp seeds and roots, also crushed fine. The willow and hemp I mixed freely with the ale. Lord Gilbert's ale was of good quality; Alfred drank the mixture with relish. Willow and hemp can relieve pain. In the surgery I was about to do, there would be great pain, willow and hemp or not.

I explained to my four assistants what I was about to do, and where I intended to do it. Not in the dim hut: I would need all the light I could get, for where I planned to work the sun did not shine much. One of the valets went quite pale when I finished my instructions.

I asked for the toft behind Alfred's hut to be cleared and for his bed to be taken there, with him in it. I got him maneuvered across the bed with his kirtle pulled up and his buttocks pointed toward the sky. He must have been mortified to be made to assume such a position, and in great need to do so willingly.

A girl, blushing at the sight of Alfred – or what she could see of him – brought the water and I set to work. One man seized each of Alfred's arms and legs, as I had instructed them. I will spare you details of the procedure and list the events of Alfred's surgery in rudimentary fashion.

I asked his wife for lard, and with it greased several fingers. These I must then insert in Alfred's rectum until I felt his bladder. With luck, I would also feel the stone.

God was with me, or with both of us, for I found the stone immediately. It was large, and so easy to locate. No wonder that he could not pass it, and that it caused him such torment. Using my finger, I worked the stone down to the neck of the bladder. Alfred grunted several times, but bore the pain stoically.

I took several deep breaths to steady myself for the hazardous work I must now do. I used the hot water and a fragment of linen to wash Alfred's private parts, then bathed the area in wine. There is no precedent for this, and I know most consider it a waste of good wine. But it seems to me that, if washing a wound with wine aids healing, washing the skin with wine before a wound is made might do so as well.

I made an incision between Alfred's rectum and scrotum, and deepened it carefully, trying to avoid damage to the complex plumbing in that place. I wanted to cut no deeper than necessary, so several times probed the incision with my finger, to see if I had got to the bladder yet. Alfred twitched and gasped a few times, but gave his captors no serious struggle.

This was good, for just as I felt the stone through the wound, the valet holding Alfred's left leg shuddered, rolled back his eyes, and dropped to the ground. Alfred's wife, who had been standing apprehensively in the door of the hut, rushed out. But rather than tend to the fallen man, she took his place at Alfred's leg and attached herself to it like a leech.

I used a tiny razor to slice into the bladder and pried out the stone with a finger. Alfred gasped again. Reader, you would, also. Most would probably scream. I suspect I would have. Alfred had lived with pain for so long that additional distress seemed to torment him little.

All that remained was to once again wash the incision with wine, and sew him up. I made few stitches. Alfred needed no more pain, and where I was working Alfred was unlikely to show off my handiwork. Four stitches would work there as well as ten.

The fallen assistant came out of his swoon as we rolled Alfred to his back and replaced his bed in the hut. I left instructions with his teary-eyed wife, washed my bloodied hands in what remained of the warm water, and departed the house. I have rarely been so glad of leaving a place.

"Lord Gilbert would see you before you return to Oxford," Arthur told me as we walked across the castle yard. It was now past the ninth hour, and gray clouds hung low in the autumn sky. It would be dark before I would see the High Street and Oxford. But when a lord wishes to see me, I usually make time for him.

We found Lord Gilbert in the solar, sitting with his wife before a small fire. It was a picture of connubial bliss. I hoped to insert myself into a more modest version of such a scene one day, but to that point had made no progress toward the goal.

"You have done with Alfred, then? Did the surgery go well?" Lord Gilbert asked.

"I am optimistic. I left him resting without pain. Not much pain, anyway."

"Good... good; well done. I have directed a room be prepared for you. It is too late to pack you back to Oxford tonight. We will share a light supper shortly. I will send John for you. John!" he called to his chamberlain. "Show Master Hugh to his chamber." John did so.

The room was light and airy, or as airy as a room of stone walls can be. The chamber was off the great hall, and lit by several narrow windows of glass. I had rarely slept behind glass before, so this would be a special experience to me. I lay back gratefully on the bed; John had to thump heavily on the door to wake me two hours later.

A light supper, Lord Gilbert said.

There was parsley bread and honey butter, cheese, pea soup, a pike, a duck pie, a capon, cold sliced venison, and a lombardy custard.

When I had eaten my fill and was rested and satisfied, Lord Gilbert steered the conversation to my profession. I see now what he wanted, but at that moment I had no clue to his direction and so was caught off guard. I had been off guard for most of the meal; Lady Joan was in attendance. She was silent while Lord Gilbert questioned me about medical and surgical practice. But when the conversation lagged, she spoke.

"Where did you train, Master Hugh?"

Her joining the conversation so disconcerted me that

33

I nearly choked on the capon leg upon which I was at the time gnawing. "Uh... Paris, m'lady. And Oxford."

My conversation with Lady Joan was ended as soon as it began. Lord Gilbert retrieved the end of our parley he had momentarily dropped, and Lady Joan returned to her fish, peeling white flesh from bones with dainty fingers.

"You are, no doubt, engaged in your profession at Oxford?" he asked. It was a question, not a statement. I might have answered, "yes," to salve my vanity. Then my vanity might have been intact, but my future laid in ruins. It was not the first or last time I found that uncomfortable honesty was a tree which might bear agreeable fruit.

"No, Lord Gilbert. I am new to my profession, and new, as a surgeon, to Oxford. My clients are few."

"Ah. Well..." I saw him smile, and wondered why my lack of patronage should bring him pleasure. "There would be work for you here, in Bampton. The village has no physician, only a barber who draws blood from the ill. But he has not your skill. A house of mine in the town is empty – several houses, to be truthful." He frowned. "The recent plague has left many empty dwellings. But the town has yet enough citizens that a surgeon would find himself regularly occupied."

Lord Gilbert told me he would show me the house in the morning. I told him I would think on the offer and give him an answer then. Truth is, there was little reason not to accept his offer. Should clients prove few in Bampton, I could move back to Oxford, where I would be no more unemployed then than now. Meanwhile it seemed unlikely I could have less custom in the village than in Oxford. But I did not want my services to seem too easily acquired. Hard won is most relished.

The house Lord Gilbert showed me in the morning was a substantial dwelling, two stories high, of solid timber construction, wattle and daub. The roof was newly thatched, probably before the tenants perished in the returning plague two years before. It sat among others like it, on

34

Church View, but three doors from St Beornwald's Churchyard. The site was ideal for one who sought business in his trade. Most of the population would pass the house at least once each week on the way to church.

Arthur had brought along the key. Lord Gilbert stood back to allow him to twist it in the lock and push open the heavy door. It had been undisturbed for many months, and the hinges squealed in displeasure. Hinges seem to be like many people; unhappy at their lot in life and determined to protest when called to duty.

Inside, the house was dim and dusty. But I saw the possibilities: my private room on the upper floor, a dispensary and kitchen on the ground floor. There was but one hair in the soup. The rent on such a house would be more than my thin purse could countenance. I explained this frankly to Lord Gilbert

"I have no income from this house at all now," he replied. "So I will make you a bargain – four shillings a year, to commence at the beginning of the new year. You will have six months to improve your state before the first rent is due." We struck the deal with a handshake. I borrowed a horse from the castle marshalsea, rode to Oxford to retrieve my few possessions, and returned to Bampton as night closed on the village.

John had sent two girls from the castle to clean the dusty place, and I found a coney pie still warm on the table. I was home.

In the next weeks I treated village inhabitants for sprains and scalds, tumors and broken bones, fevers, cuts, dislocations, swellings and eruptions. My location was propitious for attracting custom. Many town residents had borne afflictions for years with no treatment, and word soon traveled to neighboring villages that a competent surgeon resided in Bampton. I was on my way to prosperity.

Lord Gilbert suggested another benefit of my situation on Church View Street. My failures had but a short

35

distance to travel to the churchyard. Lord Gilbert has, at times, a ghastly sense of humor.

I was fortunate that but one patient went to the churchyard in that first month. The woman had suffered a cancerous tumor on her cheek for two years. I excised what I could of it, but the malignancy had traveled to her jaw. She perished on St Crispin's Day.

Now you will understand why I was called to the castle to inspect the bones pulled from the sludge of the cesspit. I had more dealings with bones than anyone else in the town. But my expertise in osseous materials seemed hardly necessary. Word of the find spread through Bampton promptly, and all knew these must be the bones of the missing suitor, Sir Robert Mallory, or his squire.

They were not.

Chapter 3

Digging up a cesspit is not work for the squeamish. It is not done often. Some never do it. But Petronilla Talbot is a particular woman. She demanded the removal of sludge every year or two, and Lord Gilbert knew better than to argue the point. Besides, he could direct others to do the job.

The cesspit had been added to the castle years after its construction was complete. The garderobes were attached to the wall like a giant chimney, with the cesspit at the base of the structure.

Four villeins were assigned to dig, haul up buckets, and cart off the filth. Uctred was assigned the work of hauling up the bucket when the unfortunate man appointed to work in the pit had filled it. He was then to dump the contents in a waiting cart, and send the bucket back to be refilled. When Uctred dumped a bucket, he saw the bones. The man in the pit had seen nothing. It was too dark where he worked.

Swine, he thought, until another bucket came up containing the skull. That is when Arthur was sent to bring me to the castle. I had only a few minutes earlier removed a large splinter from the palm of a plowman whose plow shaft had shattered as he turned over a rock. But when Thomas called I was unemployed and so went straight away to see the curious remains recovered from the cesspit.

I found Lord Gilbert and his reeve, John Holcutt, standing over the small pile of bones. "Ah, Hugh, see here. What do you make of this? I fear we have found poor Sir Robert."

I could see no reason at the moment to disagree with him, but I wondered how a man last seen leaving town on a horse might be discovered in a cesspit. And what of his squire? Might two sets of bones be revealed?

I knelt to study the skull at my feet and felt a gnawing apprehension that Sir Robert was yet missing. I kept my uncertainty to myself. Each new bucket of sludge generally brought with it more bones. As the pit was emptied, a nearly complete skeleton lay on the cobbles between the castle and the marshalsea. As new bones rose to the light of day I cleaned them, and the putrefying flesh which adhered to some of them, in a tub of water and laid them out. Each new bone justified my first suspicion.

The bones were mostly free of flesh and gristle. Decomposition was advanced. The jaw was barely affixed to the skull. At the back of the skull a small patch of fair hair clung to decaying scalp.

"What color hair had Sir Robert?" I asked.

Lord Gilbert studied the skull as I turned it in my hands. "Very much like that," he nodded. "A dark blonde, with a flash of red in the sunlight."

"How tall was Sir Robert?" I asked.

"Quite tall. He had two inches on me," Lord Gilbert replied. That would have made Sir Robert five feet nine or ten inches tall.

"These are not Sir Robert's bones," I told the onlookers. Lord Gilbert's jaw dropped. "The hair color may suit, but these are the bones of a woman, I think. See how delicate is the skull. And a young woman, a girl, as well. The teeth are not yet beginning to rot, and I see no evidence of wisdom teeth erupting. This is the skeleton of someone barely five feet tall, perhaps less."

"But... there are no women or girls missing in Bampton," Lord Gilbert spluttered.

"Well, there is a lass missing from somewhere. Perhaps no one knows of it yet. But I assure you, these bones never held Sir Robert aright."

Lord Gilbert called Thomas de Bowlegh and Hubert Shillside to the scene. Father Thomas is one of three vicars of the Church of St Beornwald. He spoke the sacrament over the bones in the dying light of a gray autumn day.

Hubert Shillside, prosperous freeholder and the town haberdasher, is also the town coroner. He quickly assembled a jury of prominent citizens, inspected the bones in the fading light, and in consultation with his peers pronounced a probable homicide. No deodand could be found, nor could a perpetrator be identified.

Lord Gilbert made arrangements with Father Thomas to have the bones interred in the churchyard next day. I thought this hasty. A closer inspection in better light might yield some clues to identity, or the cause of death. I approached Lord Gilbert with a request that the bones be transferred to my dispensary for examination next day. They had been unburied for many months – at least, not buried in hallowed ground. One or two more days would matter little. Lord Gilbert's response took me aback.

"No! I'll not deny Christian burial to... to... to whoever has died in my castle."

"Did she die in your castle?" I asked.

"How do I know?" he snapped. "I don't... we don't even know who she – it – is, much less where or how she died."

His vehemence surprised me. I wondered why he wished the bones out of sight so soon. I confess to a moment of suspicion. "You make my point readily. Study of the bones in good light tomorrow may yield answers to those questions."

Petronilla stood silent, listening to our debate. "It seems a small thing, Gilbert, to allow Master Hugh [I never completed my doctor's degree, so could not properly be called "doctor," although I was a practicing surgeon] a day or two to learn what he might. It will be of no difference to this soul," she glanced down at the bones, "and God has waited for her to be buried in consecrated ground. He will not begrudge another day or two."

Two against one will generally win the day, even against a knight who fought bravely at Poitiers alongside Edward, the Black Prince.

Uctred and his companions had by this time completed their malodorous work. Lord Gilbert reluctantly assigned him and another the work of boxing up the bones and conveying them to Galen House, which name I had given my abode in honor of the great physician of antiquity.

I did not sleep well that night, with a box of bones below me on a table. I tell myself now that my wakefulness was due to curiosity, that trying to sleep over what remained of a corpse was no cause of my insomnia. The truth lies somewhere between, as is often the case.

Behind Galen House was a small walled toft. The house blocked the rising sun to the east, but the diffused light there was better than the pale beams filtered through the small windows of the house. In the morning I dragged the table, box and all, through the door into the toft and set to my work.

Many small bones of feet and fingers were missing, Uctred and his fellows being not so thorough as they might have been. But the great bones – arms, legs, ribs, and most of the spine – were accounted for. And the skull. In this better light I could see that fragments of ligament and flesh held the mandible to the skull, and most of the vertebrae were yet connected. How long, I wondered, would it take for all flesh and connective tissue to dissolve? Would this happen slowly or quickly in a cesspit? Instinct told me that decomposition would occur rapidly in such a place, but I cannot verify this assumption. Such observations were not part of the curricula in Paris.

I assembled the bones, one by one, on the table. I had observed dissections and studied skeletons, so I could compare this human frame with others I had seen. I was more convinced than before that it was female. And young. The bones were small, and light. I visualized a young, delicate girl. Perhaps I romanticized. But I was right. More of that anon.

Would not the person who did such a murder expect the bones to be found? Perhaps not. Lord Gilbert was unusual in his sanitation habits, and then due mainly to the diligence of his wife. Most nobles, to the gratification of villeins to whom the task would fall, never evacuated their castle cesspits. Human remains in such a place might never be discovered. Bad luck, for someone.

There was another question. How did this young woman die? I peered at the bones again, all of them, turning them over, one by one, in my hands.

I nearly missed it – the scratch on the third rib – for traces of flesh and some skin remained on the bone. But I had no doubt of what I saw. A knife had glanced from that rib, and gouged out a fragment of bone as it passed on its way to her heart.

Who was she? Did she know her attacker? From where did she come to be here, in Bampton? Why should I care, or need to know?

Because someone was dead. Made in the image of God; a child of His. I felt bile rise from my stomach, and it was not because of the putrid flesh yet attached to the bone I held.

I walked south on Church View, turned right across Shill Brook, passed the mill, and entered Bampton Castle yard. Wilfred, Lord Gilbert's porter (he whose horse had spooked in Oxford on the High Street some months before), greeted me at the gatehouse. He'd been promoted. Or perhaps Lord Gilbert thought he worked more effectively on foot.

"I would see Lord Gilbert. Tell him I have news of the bones."

Wilfred was at his post at the gatehouse when the bones were found, so had not seen them as they were brought from the cesspit. But he knew of them. By dawn this day all the town would know. By the morrow Oxford would know – those who care about such things, or have nothing better to speak of.

Wilfred was a tall man, who could walk quickly without appearing to do so. Moments after he entered the inner

41

gatehouse, he reappeared. "Lord Gilbert will see you," he puffed, "in the solar. The chamberlain awaits you and will take you there."

I told Lord Gilbert what I had learned. "You have no doubt of murder?" he queried.

"None. She was killed, and put in your cesspit to hide the crime."

"Would it not have been easier," Lord Gilbert wondered aloud, "for her slayer to have buried her in the country hereabouts? There is much uncultivated land now, since the plague. This place was once called Bampton in the Bush for its wild situation. The bushes are reclaiming what was once theirs, I have so few tenants and villeins to work the land."

"I have considered that," I replied. "Were I the killer, I would seek the easiest, most secure place to dispose of the body. Why would your castle be more convenient, or more secure than, let us say, the nearby forest?"

Lord Gilbert scratched the stubble on his chin. It was an affectation I had seen before when he was lost in thought. "Perhaps whoever did this evil was more familiar with my castle than with the surrounding country."

"Perhaps," I agreed.

"Or," he scratched again, "she was killed here and to remove the body would risk discovery."

"Do folk enter the castle grounds without someone, Wilfred or Arthur or John, or you, knowing of it?" I asked.

"No. Except, perhaps, at market time. The town is overrun at the Feast of the Assumption. We sometimes find folk wandering through the gate, usually so drunk they think themselves at the inn. And, of course, some poor reside in the forecourt huts."

"But such as these," I asked, "do not pass the inner gate?"

"Not any more! Wilfred is scrupulous about his duties, as well he might be. He fears yet I will put him in the fields for his defective horsemanship." Lord Gilbert chuckled: "Wilfred will be a loyal servant for all that."

42

"So if she was killed inside the castle, the deed was done by someone who did not arouse suspicion for being here."

"I do not like to think of that," Lord Gilbert admitted. "I fear she was done to death in my castle."

"I agree."

We remained silent with our thoughts for a moment, then Lord Gilbert put voice to my reflection.

"She was smuggled in, then?"

"Aye. But could that happen if she was unwilling?"

"If she was given a potion?" Lord Gilbert mused aloud.

"Possible. But would it be easier to enter the grounds with a supine body, or with one awake and alive?"

"I see your point," Lord Gilbert attacked his chin once again. I began to fear he would draw blood. "Someone connived with this girl to get her past the porter." He pursed his lips. "There is likely but one reason for that."

"I think so," I agreed. "An assignation gone wrong. Will you commission your bailiff to find the killer?"

"I cannot. He died the week after Rogation Sunday. I have not yet appointed his replacement. John expects to receive the position, but I mistrust his ability in that post.

"This death is a stain on my name," he continued. "For such an evil to befall a lass under my roof! Master Hugh, I would have you search out the assassin."

I was speechless. "But m'lord... I have no skill in such work. I do not seek out the unseen. I deal with things visible. I am but a surgeon, not even a physician."

"Who brought the girl to my castle?" he asked. "John Holcutt, perhaps?"

"You think so?" I was surprised at the suggestion.

"No. The reeve is a good man. But do not even good men sometimes shelter malignant thoughts?"

"They do," I agreed. "Even our Lord Jesus was tempted, as the apostle tells us."

"May not evil thoughts become deeds if unchecked?" Lord Gilbert asked.

"They may."

"Then you must seek out a murderer for me. We are agreed, I think, that one who frequents the castle has done this. I might choose that man, unwittingly, to seek out the murderer. I believe all my servants incapable of such a crime, yet I am certainly wrong."

"I will do as you ask," I sighed. "I held the girl's bones in my hands and felt sorrow, and anger, too. Who was this lass? And what did she do to merit such a death? Did she laugh, and love? Was she a wife and mother? I think not, for I believe she was too young, but would she have become such? I would know the answers to these questions, as you would, m'lord. But I will tell you straight, I fear my ignorance of such probing as will be required will undermine my endeavor. And perhaps a clumsy question may give warning to the killer."

"Perhaps. But I have observed you at your work this past month. It may be you underestimate your abilities. Where, then, will you begin?"

I thought for a moment: "I think the first work must be to discover who the victim is... was."

"Sensible. How will you do this?"

"I must think on it. She was not from Bampton, you are certain of that?"

"Aye," he nodded agreement, pulling again at his chin.

"My guess is that she came from a village close by. She did not arrive here alone, I think, and if she came from some great distance, why?"

"You will need a horse," Lord Gilbert declared. "I will direct John to have the marshalsea keep a horse ready for you. Whenever you are free to visit another town in your search, call here for the beast. When will you begin?"

"Today," I shrugged. "No one has done anything foolish or dangerous recently, so my skills are not presently required."

"You could visit Aston, and Cote, today, and return before nightfall."

44

"I know Aston," I remarked. "A reasonable place to begin."

"A horse will be ready within the hour. I shall notify Thomas de Bowlegh. We will bury the remains tomorrow."

"I would not," I answered.

"Oh?"

"If God grants grace to my labor, and I find the girl's family, they will want her close by. And perhaps further study will yield another clue to this mystery."

"Hmmm... yes. As you wish. And Hugh," he said as I turned to go, "do keep me acquainted with the progress of your search."

"And if there is no progress, must I inform you of that, as well?"

"You are wrong to disparage your competency."

"I esteem your opinion. I will return for the horse when I have dined and viewed the bones again."

Chapter 4

I returned to Galen House and took a maslin loaf and a cold capon breast to the toft where I had, perhaps unwisely as I think back on it now, left my table and its bony burden. I worked my way about the table while I ate, seeking some new knowledge. None readily appeared. I washed down my meal with ale purchased from the baker's wife, who brewed tolerably well.

After several loops of the table I was no wiser. I set my cup on the cobbles and decided to make one more thorough inspection of the bones before I set off for Aston and Cote. I began with the skull. Had I started at the feet, I might have been home before dark.

I will explain. The skull told me nothing but what I already knew. This was a young person, surely female, who had yet no wisdom teeth, although on close inspection, the rear of the jaw showed just the beginning of a tooth erupting. The long bones and the scarred rib yielded no further clues. At last I reached the feet, and the few small bones which were recovered. There I found what I sought. This girl had broken her foot. Which foot I could not know. One of the metatarses showed sure evidence of a fracture, now poorly healed. This was not much of a clue, but how many maids have broken a foot?

My outlook improved with the discovery. I returned to the castle with more optimism than when I had left it two hours earlier. I exchanged greetings with Wilfred and set off across the yard to the marshalsea. I did not get there; not straight away.

As I rounded the base of the southwest tower, I came face to face with Lady Joan Talbot. There was no one I would have preferred to meet face to face. This was not, however, a meeting for which I was prepared. I fear my wit did not impress the lady.

"Uh, good day, m'lady."

"Good day, Master Hugh. Do you seek my brother?"

"No. I've come for a horse."

"Do you ride for pleasure, Master Hugh?"

"No, m'lady. I am on your brother's business."

"Oh? What business is that?"

"You know of the bones found yesterday?" She nodded. "Lord Gilbert will have me investigate this matter. I am off to visit villages in the shire hereabouts to see if a young woman has gone missing."

Lady Joan's brow furrowed. "You are sure it was a woman found in the... waste pit?"

"Aye. I have no doubt. And I know how she died."

Lady Joan caught her breath and stepped back. "Oh?"

"A rib bears a deep gouge where the knife which killed her glanced from it on its way to her heart."

She blanched, then spoke softly. "Then I wish you good fortune in your search."

I thanked her for her good will, doffed my cap, and bowed in what I thought was a graceful sweep of arm and body. I think I overdid it. I heard her giggle softly as she glided on across the castle yard.

I know I am not a handsome fellow. Women do not compete for my attention. But neither do small children run and hide when I appear. I am as tall as Lord Gilbert, although he has thirty pounds on me. He is a warrior. I would not say that I am scrawny; slender would be more apt. Well, some would say I am scrawny. I prefer to think of my form as wiry.

My nose is a trifle large for the adjacent geography, but I have always thought that lends character to a face. To a masculine face, anyway. It seems to depart my brow properly, but then takes a right turn, as if my nostrils were trying to direct my attention to some event on the dexter side. It is inherited. My father viewed the world across a nose of similar size and bearing. My father was also bald. I know that my thick brown locks will soon vanish. I hope I may find a wife before that happens, although I am not sure I want a wife who thinks more of what is atop my head than what may be in it.

Although I am the son of a landed knight – all right, not much land – I hold no manor. Our stations were too far apart for me to hold dreams of holding Lady Joan.

I had seen her rarely in the month I'd lived in Bampton. I heard it spoken about the town that shortly after Sir Robert's disappearance, she journeyed to Exeter, and there spent the summer with her cousin, Lady Alice Boteler. She returned at Michaelmas, at near the same time my employment in the town began. Village gossips soon had it that the visit to Exeter was a failure, its purpose being to introduce m'lady to available young gentlemen of the appropriate station.

Numerous reasons were given for this miscarriage: Lady Joan was too opinionated, she was too demanding, she was shrewish, she thought too highly of herself. Whether any of this was true, I knew not. But no one ever spoke of her appearance as the cause of her failure to find a husband, if indeed she sought one.

I watched her walk across the castle yard and was reminded again that a wife would be a good thing to have. Any man would think the same, whatever his rank, when he beheld Lady Joan, coming or going.

Mooning over the unobtainable would not get me to Aston or Cote, although as it turned out, I might have remained in the castle yard, for all the good a horseback ride did me that day. Thomas must have recalled my riding skills, for he had the marshalsea prepare for me an elderly gelding of wide back and gentle demeanor.

"Bruce, we calls 'im," the stableman told me. "Lord Gilbert rode 'im at Poitiers, he did. Took a bolt in the haunch, but never so much as flinched. Lord Gilbert didn't know as he'd been hurt 'til battle was over."

The stableman held the horse's head and scratched his forelock while I mounted. Four hours later Bruce and I

48

ambled through the gate with barely enough light to see that Wilfred had not yet swung it shut nor dropped the portcullis. Waiting for my return, he said, as I greeted him.

No one, male or female, was missing from Aston or Cote. Not missing for unknown cause, anyway. There were so many missing from plague that the old woman who spoke to me in Cote suggested that the families who remained might petition their lord to remove to Newbridge or some other town less decimated by disease.

I planned to visit other villages to the east of Bampton the next day, but this was not to be. Shortly after I rose from my bed, before I completed my morning wash – I know many consider this an unnecessary affectation – there came a pounding at the door of Galen House.

I opened it and peered into the gloom. Before me stood three men, two of them carrying a litter upon which a fourth was lying. Motionless.

The door-thumper removed his hat and explained their mission. The man on the litter was his father. They were foresters in Lord Gilbert's lands to the northwest of Bampton. At dusk the evening before, they had felled a last oak for the day. The man on the litter had not seen it coming his way as it dropped until it was too late. A large limb had caught him across the head as he ran, leaving him unconscious, and leaving a dent in his skull as well as a laceration. He had regained consciousness briefly, complained of headache and nausea, then, after they got him to his wife and hut, he'd passed out again. And this time remained comatose. I motioned for them to bring him in. Fortunately I had thought to repackage the bones and move my dispensary table to its rightful place. The sight of a surgeon's table strewn with bones might put off even the most needy client.

"Put the litter on the table there."

I lit two more candles – one was already burning – and inspected the wound. It was depressed to the depth of my finger and yet oozing blood.

49

"Can you do aught for 'im?" the son asked, his cap still grasped tightly before him.

"Perhaps. You would have done well to have brought him to me last night."

"'E woke up for a span. 'Is wife wanted us to bring 'im in, but 'e said 'No.' Worried 'bout t'expense, y'see. So when he went down again we thought 'twas but for a minute, like. But he hasn't wakened yet, an' seems to me he ain't breathin' right."

He wasn't. I told the son and the other bearers I would do what I could, but I was not optimistic. For what I must do I wanted no spectators. I sent my patient's three companions to wait in the street. The injured man remained comatose, which was good. He would feel no pain, nor thrash about.

I heated water and shaved the indented part of the skull, and a circle around it, then bathed the wound with the last of my wine. I used the scalp laceration for the cross-stroke, and made two vertical incisions at either end. This created two flaps of scalp which I could fold back to reveal the fracture.

I caught my breath when I saw the extent of the damage. The fracture was a finger's length in diameter, and included four large bone fragments and many small splinters. I employed a probe to lift the largest piece, and in the gathering light from my eastern window I peered beneath it.

I was cheered to see that the damage was not so severe as the broken skull would have it appear. I saw no great rupture of dura mater encompassing the brain. There was much coagulated blood under the break, but that could be teased out, with time and care.

So I took my time and was careful. Three hours later I had cleaned the smallest bone splinters from the wound, positioned the larger pieces in a convex curve to match the undamaged portion of skull, and sewed up the "H" flap of scalp. My back ached and sweat ran into my eyes, but a sense of accomplishment overwhelmed my discomfort. The man might not survive, but he had not died on my table. At least, not yet. And I had given him a chance to live.

I packed ground moneywort over the wound, wrapped the woodcutter's head in several layers of linen strips, then called to his son and friends. They had remained standing, motionless, since the moment I sent them out, and it was now past the sixth hour. I had seen them through the window several times while I worked.

"Take him home carefully. It will be his life should he receive another blow on the head. He must not rise from his bed for a week. After seven days he may rise but to eat and care for himself. No labor! In a fortnight he must return to have the wound inspected and have the windings changed."

"He will live, then?" asked the brother.

"He may. I cannot pledge. The fracture was severe."

"When can he return to work?"

"Perhaps a month. Certainly it will not be safe to do so sooner."

"What is your fee?"

A wage for men like these might be two pence per day. I asked for four pence, brain surgery being somewhat more skilled employment than woodcutting and, from the stiffness of my back, nearly as arduous.

"I've but t'uppence. He'll bring two more in a fortnight. If God wills an' he lives."

Fair enough, I thought. Success should be worth more than failure.

I was weary from the morning's labor, and had no heart for another unfruitful journey through the autumn countryside. I had used much white archangel and moneywort to staunch the bleeding of the woodman's scalp, and knew a meadow north of town where I might replenish my supply.

The afternoon I spent gathering plants; white archangel, lady's mantle, clover, moneywort, and betony. All these

51

I did not find in the same field, but since the plague much land lay fallow. Brief journeys from meadow to meadow supplied all my needs. I hung my gathered medicines from beams in the dispensary to dry.

I sat and contemplated this room as the day died. Tomorrow I would resume my search. Tonight I would enjoy the quiet reward of a day lived well, work well done, and the pleasure of searching God's forest and field for the tools he has provided whereby we may be healed of our afflictions. I concluded the day with maslin, a haunch of cold mutton, and a pint of the baker's wife's ale. Life was good.

The Angelus Bell awakened me early next day. It does so every day. Before the sun was over St Andrew's Chapel I bid Wilfred good morning and found Bruce snoring contentedly in the marshalsea.

I rode northeast this day, to Yelford and Hardwick, then all the way to Witney. Plague had reduced the first two villages so I spent little time there. No one had gone missing.

Witney was grown large as Bampton, and plague had reduced it but little. Witney required more time. My task was to learn what I could, as thoroughly as I could, as quickly as I could. I decided on two strategies; seek an innkeeper, and approach an old woman or two. If such as these knew of no person mysteriously absent from the town, it was likely all its inhabitants could be accounted for. Two hours later an innkeeper and three grandmothers could recollect no missing citizen.

I returned to Bampton through fields brown with autumn, forests golden, as frost worked its designs. A pity, I thought, to be on such a morbid mission when beauty surrounded me. But this also reminded me of death. Leaves and stems were dying, as would I, some day. Would my death bring some brief glory to the world, as did the dying foliage?

Some deaths bring no radiance. To die young, or of some festering disease, this is an infamous way to meet

52

God. Even the slaughter of battle may bring with it an aureole of dignity. I had chosen to spend my life battling against ignoble death – against wasting disease and injury. But now I found myself in a struggle against the calamity of murder, the death of the young. I felt unequal to the assignment. My feelings would nearly prove accurate.

I did not seek for a missing girl next day; 'twas Sunday. At the third hour, bells from the tower of the Church of St Beornwald called the faithful to matins and the mass. They called the unfaithful as well. I suppose the congregation included some of each.

Lord Gilbert did not attend. He and his family worshipped in a private chapel in the castle, but most others in the town could be expected to be present. Before plague struck, the nave was barely large enough to contain the parish. Now there was room enough and to spare.

Father Thomas led the two other vicars in procession around the church, blessing altars and congregation, and sprinkling holy water on both. A clerk led the prayer of confession and read the scripture for the day from St Paul's epistle to the Galatians: "And let us not grow weary while doing good, for in due season we shall reap if we do not lose heart. Therefore, as we have opportunity, let us do good to all, especially to those who are of the household of faith."

"Do not grow weary in doing good." I thought this a word from God, for I was already grown weary of wandering the countryside searching for a girl who might be missing from some place of which I had never heard a hundred miles away.

My mind was so occupied that I neglected the prayers for the living and the dead. Father Thomas sang the mass well, and as I had some little training to do the same, my thoughts returned to the service in time to venerate the host and kiss the pax board. We shared the holy loaf, and as always after mass, I departed the church determined to live better, and in particular, to discover a name for a missing girl. I should attend mass twice each day. Although, come to think of it, there are lords who do for whom the practice seems without benefit.

I am always ravenous when mass is done. Although some break their fast before the sacrament, I hold with those who do not. After the midday meal of a Sunday, it is Lord Gilbert's custom to invite tenants and yeomen to bring bows to the castle forecourt for practice at the butts. He provides a cask of ale to ensure good attendance, and a prize for the most competent marksman. As the award, usually two pence, is not granted until the last competition, those who rewarded themselves already with Lord Gilbert's ale seldom stagger home with any coin.

Monday found me unoccupied, so I journeyed to the north again, to Curbridge, Minster Lovell, and Brize Norton. A woman had disappeared from Minster Lovell seven years earlier, but the gossip who told me of this was convinced her disappearance had to do with a band of Italian wool buyers who passed through the area a few days before her husband awoke to a cold bed. And the woman was twenty-six: too old to be the skeleton in my dispensary.

I did not mount Bruce again until Wednesday. I had an earache and a boil to deal with on Tuesday. Truth to tell, the child's ear was not the only thing in Bampton which ached. My hindquarters were unaccustomed to days spent in a saddle. A day practicing my profession provided sorely needed respite.

On Wednesday I rode through Black Bourton, Alvescot, and Shilton, all the way to Burford. Burford was as large as Bampton, so I tried the strategy I had used at Witney: grandmothers and innkeepers. The second crone stopped my search.

The old lady narrowed her eyes when I asked if anyone was missing from the town. "Who wants to know?" she asked guardedly.

"I am the surgeon from Bampton," I announced. If I expected this news to impress her, I was disappointed. She

54

stood, a basket of turnips pressed against a hip, and waited for more information.

"A body has been found near Bampton. It cannot be identified, and no one from the town or nearby villages is unaccounted for. I am acting as Lord Gilbert Talbot's agent to put a name to the corpse."

"The smith's girl went missing in early summer. A week after Whitsuntide, it was. Folks thought she'd run off with her lad, but he come back a day later, said he'd took a cart of oats to sell for his father. Moped around for weeks, he did. Still looks like devil's got him by the ankles last time I saw 'im."

"What was the girl's name?"

"Margaret."

"How old was she?"

The old woman screwed her face in concentration. "She were born afore my John died o'plague... maybe seventeen, eighteen years old."

"Where can I find her family?"

"Just her father, Alard. Mother died seven, eight years back. His smithy's down by the river, just across the bridge. Lord Thomas won't let him set up on town side 'cause o' fire."

I found the smith easily enough. The man stood outside his hut and cast a practiced eye at Bruce's gait as I crossed the river and approached. He seemed surprised as I drew up before him. Evidently he had seen no flaw in Bruce's pace which would dictate a need for his services.

"You are Alard, the smith?" I asked by way of greeting. The question was rhetorical. One look at his forearms was enough to assure me of his trade, whatever his name.

"Aye," he replied, unmoving.

"I am told you have a missing daughter."

His back stiffened and his eyes, once dull, flashed.

"Aye. Four months now. Who are you? Have you news of her?"

I identified myself and told the smith the reason for

my visit. But I did not tell him everything. If Lord Gilbert's skeleton was this man's daughter, he did not need to know yet where she was found or her condition when discovered.

"Had your daughter any injuries... broken bones?" I asked.

"Nay... She were a strong lass. Wait; when she were small she'd follow me about the smithy near all day. Could hardly get my work done for tumblin' over her. Tried to pick up my sledge once. She were but seven or eight years old. 'Twas too heavy for her. Dropped it on her foot. Swole up an' turned black for two weeks an' more, but she were up an' runnin' again in a month or so. Troubles her now and again."

"She limps?" I asked.

"Aye, a bit, when t'weather turns."

"She may have broken a bone in her foot," I remarked.

"Aye... so I thought," he shrugged.

"When did you last see your daughter?"

The smith's shoulders slumped as he thought back to the summer. "'Twas soon after Whitsunday."

"Had she given sign that she might run off?"

"Nay. She were quiet, though, seems to me as I think back on it. Thought at first as she'd run off with her lad, but they'd no reason to do that. Tom's a good lad. His father has a yardland near Shilton of Lord Thomas. Tom'll come to it, as he's oldest." He paused. "Margaret were my youngest... all I had left. Her brother died at Poitiers, an' two sisters gone when plague come first time."

"Why did you think she might have run off with her lad?"

"He were gone, too. I went to see his father when I heard t'boy were gone. Tom'd gone off with a cart of oats to sell. Came back next day an' seemed confused as t'rest of us."

As he spoke the smith's demeanor drooped with his shoulders until I feared he might fall. He seemed to want to talk of the girl, yet paid a terrible price for doing so. News of his daughter's death would collapse him even more, but I thought it better to disclose what I knew than await a recovery of his distressed spirit, only to strike him down again.

"The dead girl, found in Lord Gilbert's castle, had suffered a broken bone in her foot," I told him.

The smith sat heavily on a sack of coals. "Which foot were it?" he asked.

"I cannot tell. I know only that one of her feet received a blow which broke a bone."

For all his distress, the smith retained a keen mind. He saw the meaning of my answer. "She's but a skeleton, like, then."

"Aye. That is so."

"How did she die?" he whispered.

I told him of the gouged rib, but could not bring myself to tell him where she was found.

"We've not buried her. We thought, when we discovered who she was, her family would want to do that."

"Aye."

"I have her at my house, in Bampton. Galen House. Will you send someone for her, or would you have me send her with one of Lord Gilbert's men?"

"Nay. I'll come for her tomorrow. I can borrow a cart."

I told the smith where to find Galen House, bid him good day until the morrow, and left him sitting grief-stricken on the sack of coals.

I made my way to Bampton Castle early next morning to report my discovery to Lord Gilbert.

"The broken foot settles the matter, I'd say," he remarked when I told him the news. I nodded agreement.

"Now you must discover who has done this. And soon. I wish to have this matter cleared before I go to Goodrich for Christmas."

"I know not where to begin," I protested.

"You have begun well already. Now you need but to conclude. A job well begun is near done... so wise men say."

"I sometimes wish wise men would keep their thoughts to themselves," I muttered.

Lord Gilbert chuckled. "I wish to leave for Goodrich in three weeks, after St Catherine's Day and the procession. Find the killer in our midst by then, or I must return here on winter roads to do justice when you do find the man."

Chapter 5

Alard, good as his word, arrived with a horse and crude cart at the sixth hour next day. Together we lifted the box of his daughter's bones to the bed of the cart. Alard could have done the work alone, but I felt it a last service I could perform for the girl. Surgery is a service for the living. I have no skills to aid the dead. Had I a wish to serve the dead, I might have taken holy orders. But what use was a priest now to Margaret, only child of Alard, the smith? To pray her out of purgatory? What priest would concern himself with a smith's daughter? If she had not done the work to position herself for heaven, no priest or monk was likely to bother now. A wealthy father might endow a chapel where monks might pray for her soul. Alard the smith could not. So would she remain in purgatory, with no prayers to set her free? Did not our Lord himself say that it was more difficult for a rich man to enter heaven than for a camel to pass through the needle's eye? Margaret was not rich. Would she then gain her soul's rest more easily than Lord Gilbert? Lord Gilbert could endow a chantry for himself. Would this propel him past Margaret to the gates of heaven? I puzzled over these thoughts as Alard turned the cart and drove north past St Beornwald's Church and out of the town.

Lord Gilbert had assigned me my next task. That's what nobles are best at – assigning work to others. They would say in their defense that someone must organize society. I suppose that is so.

After a midday meal I wandered back to the castle. I had no reason. I did not need to see Lord Gilbert again. I saw no path open to me whereby I might discover a killer, but I look back now and think I must have believed proximity to the place of crime might provide some fresh interpretation. It did, to my chagrin.

My presence in Bampton Castle was so regular that

59

no one paid me any attention as I wandered the castle yard and forecourt. I studied the garderobe tower, as I had done the day I was summoned to inspect the bones, and several times since. The garderobe tower had been added to Bampton Castle as an afterthought, some years after Aymer de Valence, Lord Gilbert's grandfather, had received permission from King Edward II to fortify his house in Bampton. So the tower stood outside the wall, attached to it. But there was no danger of an enemy battering it down to gain entry to the castle. Its only openings were those inside the tower, at each level of the castle, and the opening outside the tower, at the base, now closed with wooden planks, from which Uctred and his companions were at work when they discovered the bones.

Could one man lift those planks? If so, Margaret's bones might have entered the cesspit there. It seemed to me unlikely that a killer would try to stuff a body through a garderobe. I walked across the muddy yard to inspect the cover more closely. It was near two paces long and as high as my waist, and little more than an inch thick. Its maker had nailed planks together against two backing boards. I bent my knees, pushed my fingers under the cover, and strained at the planks. It resisted, then broke free. With little effort I had the cover ankle-high in its vertical tracks in the tower's foundation stones. A whiff of the cesspit below persuaded me to let it drop back to its place. One man might lift the cover and push a corpse through the opening. But more likely, it seemed to me, two would be required for the task.

This did not answer my question; it merely raised another. Did the girl's body enter the cesspit here? Certainly more people had access to the outside of the garderobe tower than to the inside. But this also meant possible witnesses to such a deed. Would a killer risk discovery here in the castle yard?

While I pondered this new discovery, my attention was diverted. A farm cart, loaded with hay, entered the castle forecourt, proceeded with Wilfred's blessing through the gatehouse, then made its way across the castle yard to the marshalsea.

A stableman appeared from a darkened stall and together he and the carter pitchforked the load of hay to an empty corner of the stable.

I watched this activity because I could think of nothing else to do. I did not intend to eavesdrop on their conversation as the men worked. Indeed, they said little, concentrating on their labor. But as they finished their work the stableman addressed the carter.

"You can leave t'cart right here. Unhitch t'horse an' put 'im in yon stall. You've got a nice soft bed of hay there t'keep you warm tonight. An' if you ask at t'kitchen 'round back, they'll have a loaf an' more for your supper."

I approached the stableman as the carter strode off to the kitchen. "You'll be wantin' Bruce, then?" he asked.

"No. About the hay... Is that fellow," I nodded toward the departing carter, "a villein of Lord Gilbert's? I've not seen him before, I think."

"Nay. He's Sir Geoffrey Mallory's man, from Northleech."

"Must Lord Gilbert buy hay from Sir Geoffrey?"

"Aye, an' oats as well. You'll remember how't rained so in t'spring? Hay an' oats rotted in t'fields."

I knew that harvests this year had been poor due to the cool, wet weather early in the season, but my occupation required of me little thought about agricultural vicissitudes. So long as I had patients who could pay my fees, I did not concern myself with crop yields. When the price of bread rose, then I gave attention to the harvest. In the past months this I had begun to do.

"Then Lord Gilbert is forced to buy fodder?"

"Aye. Well, not yet, like, but if he waits 'til winter price'll go higher. Hill country over to Northleech drains better, so they wasn't so bad off as us. Got enough an' to sell."

"So Lord Gilbert is buying now. Is this his first purchase?"

"Nay. See t'loft there?" I peered into the dim stable. The loft was filled with hay. "This'll be fourth, fifth load."

"All from Sir Geoffrey?"

"Nay. Got a load of oats from up north. One o'Earl Thomas Beauchamp's tenants. Back in t'spring it was, just after Whitsuntide. Lord Gilbert saw trouble comin', the hay bein' so poorly an' oats little better."

Whitsuntide? A cartload of oats? My mind was unsettled for a moment, then I made the connection. Margaret's lad.

"The oats; did Lord Gilbert send a man for the load?"

"Nay. A lad came with nine sacks. All his cart would carry."

"Did you help him unload?"

"Nay. T'smith was here an' we had horses to shoe. Lad said as how he'd take t'sacks to loft. Strong young fella. Didn't need no help. Went right up t'ladder with 'em easy as you please."

"You watched him unload?"

"Just the first sack... t'make sure he could manage. Farrier was workin' on Lord Gilbert's best dexter. He's a mean 'un. Took me an' Uctred to hold 'im."

"Did the lad return to his home that night?"

"He stayed. Slept on t'straw there like this fella'll do." He nodded in the direction of the kitchen. "Left next mornin' soon as light t'see t'road."

"I shall need Bruce tomorrow," I told him.

There seemed too many coincidences. The bones, their location, the missing girl, the sale of nine sacks of oats, and the timing. Perhaps that was all it was: coincidence. But to learn if that was so, I must return to Burford.

I walked from the castle with a warm sun at my back. I had no urgent need to return to Galen House, so I stood on the bridge over Shill Brook and watched the wheel of Lord Gilbert's mill turn slowly.

What if Margaret and her beau had quarreled? What if the argument had become violent? What if, in a fit of rage, the youth struck and killed her? What if he then took her body to Bampton Castle under the oat sacks? Would he not risk discovery in unloading? Would a distressed young killer think of that? Why not dispose of the body in some forest between here and Burford? There were too many questions. Tomorrow I would return to Burford and seek answers to these riddles. Some of them, anyway.

Bruce seemed eager to take me on my journey, perhaps because I always rode him at an easy pace to spare my rump the unaccustomed abrasions. Or perhaps he grew bored staring at the walls of his stall.

As Bruce shambled along the path north to Shilton and Burford, I observed the countryside more closely than I had on my first journey. Lord Gilbert's remark about unused, vacant land was accurate. There were many oxgangs of meadow now growing back to woodland. At several places the forest was coppiced, but not so regularly as it would have been before the plague. I saw few travelers on my way, although there might have been more in the summer. Certainly there were many places where a body might be hauled from the road into a wood or overgrown meadow and never seen again, until the beasts of the forest had rendered it nothing but bones moldering in the moss and bracken.

I wanted to speak to Alard again, but before I spoke to him I hoped to find the crone with the basket of turnips who had sent me to him. There were things I wished to know about Margaret Smith that Alard might not wish to tell me. And other things he might not know, considering the possible relationship between a man and his daughter.

I rode Bruce up and down the High Street and cross-lanes of Burford until folk began to peer at me with furrowed brows as I passed them for the third or fourth time.

I tried to remember what the old woman was wearing, but it was nothing unusual enough to recall. A plain brown cloak and gray wimple, which might once have been white: the habit of every woman her age in every village in England.

I gave up my search, crossed the bridge over the Windrush, and reined Bruce to a stop before the smith's hut. I saw no smoke from his chimney. To my shout there was no response. The town mill was but fifty or so paces upstream along a path which wound through the willows. I went there seeking news of the smith's whereabouts.

"He'll be at t'churchyard, won't he," the miller answered, "buryin' his Margaret."

I remembered seeing a small knot of people in the churchyard as I passed it – several times. Death and burial are common enough that I did not associate this interment with the bones I had puzzled over. I decided not to wait for the smith's return, but mounted Bruce and made my way back across the river and up the sloping High Street. I turned Bruce east into Church Lane as mourners passed out of the gate. Alard led the procession. Near its end was the old woman I sought.

I dismounted and followed the old woman to her house, leading Bruce by the halter. The house was wattle and daub, like most in the town, and showed signs of neglect, as did its owner. The thatching of the roof was thin, and chunks of daub had fallen from the walls, exposing decaying wattles. A widow's home, I thought.

I tied Bruce to a fencepost and approached the door. It opened before I could raise my hand to knock. The woman saw me standing before her and started back so violently that I feared she would fall.

"Oh – you've nearly made me drop me eggs!" she exclaimed.

The woman clung to a basket. From the rear of the decaying house I heard hens clucking. They were apparently a source of income, perhaps along with turnips her only source of cash.

"Forgive me. I had no wish to frighten you. Do you remember me?"

"Aye. You asked of Margaret, the smith's girl, a few days back."

"I did, although I did not know her name until you told me. I would ask a few more questions about her."

"I promised these eggs to the vicar before noon. Father Geoffrey likes his eggs fresh." The woman's house was but three streets from the church and vicarage.

"Will you return when your errand is done?"

"Aye, straight away."

"I'll wait."

The woman kept her word. I spent the time observing the house and street. It was a duplicate of hundreds I had seen across England, and France, too, in my travels there. The streets were similar, but the stories of the people inhabiting them all different. The crone; was she a widow? Never wed? Children? Grandchildren? Had she loved and laughed once? The crinkled skin about her eyes said "yes," but the downturned corners of her mouth revealed sorrow in her life. As I mused, the wrinkled eyes and downcast mouth rounded the corner and limped toward me.

I had not noticed her hobble as she walked away. Now she returned shuffling, nearly halting each time her left foot struck the ground. When she came closer I could see a grimace, too, when her weight shifted to her left foot. Her condition aroused my medical curiosity.

"You walk with pain," I observed when she approached.

"Aye. Since Easter last I've suffered."

"What is the cause?" I suspected the disease of the bones. She was of the age for it. It was unlikely her diet was rich enough to cause gout.

"It's me toe. Swole up an' red. 'At's right, you be t'surgeon from Bampton. 'Eard of you."

I wondered what she'd heard, but decided it could not have been too bad, as with her next breath she asked if I might examine the offending digit.

I followed her into her house, but the light there was

65

too dim to properly diagnose either wound or injury. I carried a bench out to the sunlight, bade her sit upon it, and knelt before her to remove her shoe. I could see the swelling through the cracked, ancient leather, and heard her giggle softly behind her hand as I took her ankle to pull off the shoe. The giggle concluded with a gasp as the shoe abraded her toe.

Her pain was due to a badly infected ingrown toenail; one of the worst I've seen. The wonder is she could walk at all.

"Can you do aught for me?" she asked.

"Aye. But not now. I've no instruments with me."

"Instruments?" She said it as a question, with a trace of alarm in her voice.

"You have an ingrown toenail. I must trim it back, and remove some putrefied flesh from about it."

"Can't you put somethin' on it – a poultice, like?"

"I could, but that would serve only temporarily. The swelling might subside for a day, and the pain with it, but it would surely return. It does little good to treat pain. I must treat the cause of the pain."

"I see; sore toes is much like other sorrows God's children must endure."

The old woman did not look like a philosopher, but surviving sixty or seventy years of the assorted trials common to mankind must turn all but the most shallow to contemplative thought now and again.

"I will return tomorrow to treat you. Can you find a flagon of wine?"

"You wants your pay in wine?" she said incredulously.

"No... no. I will bathe the wound in wine, to speed healing."

"Wound," she said limply.

"A small incision only. But I must tell you that we must do all we can to aid healing. You are not a young woman. The young heal more quickly than the old. And

66

wounds of the extremities in the old heal even more slowly. I do not know why this is, but I have observed it so."

"What fee, then, do you ask?"

"Some information. Is that reasonable enough?"

"Aye, if I got it."

"If you do not, perhaps you can get it for me when I return tomorrow."

"If I can. What you want t'know?"

"Perhaps we should go inside to talk. Here, I'll help you stand."

I assisted the woman to her feet. She leaned heavily on me as I helped her into the dim interior of her hut. She sat heavily on the first bench we came to. I went back for the other outside.

"The smith's girl... Margaret. Had she other suitors than Thomas of Shilton?"

"Oh, la, she were always popular with the lads. But I don't know as you could call all who gave her a look suitors."

"What would you call them?"

"Pleasure seekers, maybe."

"Were they likely to find it with Margaret?"

"Couldn't say. Rumors 'bout town said maybe yes, maybe no. But folks didn't gossip much 'bout Margaret 'cause they didn't want to explain theirselves to her father, if you take my meanin'."

"Then she was an attractive girl?"

"Oh, aye. A beauty. Could've had most any lad hereabouts, but she seemed set on Tom."

"'Seemed,' you say?"

"Oh, she'd flirt with the lads some. You'll not credit it now, but I were pert when I were a lass. I seen her with men a time or two, an' I remember how it was." Her eyes, once fixed on mine, wandered over my shoulder to the window. "A villein's daughter has little to look forward to. So a little harmless dalliance wi' the boys... it's 'bout all she's got."

"Harmless?" I asked. "Is it always? Does dalliance sometimes lead to serious matters?"

"Aye, it does that." She pursed her lips. "I could tell you stories..."

"Of Margaret?"

"Oh, no. I were thinkin' of times long past, though there be folk hereabout younger'n me who'd remember well enough."

"So Margaret's flirting with other young men was not so serious as to lead them on, or cause Thomas to be jealous?"

"Well, I can't say as what'd cause a lad to be jealous. Margaret was that pretty, I guess a fellow'd get anxious whenever she spoke to other lads."

"You think Thomas of Shilton the jealous sort?" I asked.

"Can't say. He don't live in town, 'course. Seems a quiet lad. I probably heard him speak a time or two, but I couldn't recognize his voice were he callin' outside the door this moment. Not very helpful, eh? What you want to know all this for?"

"Lord Gilbert Talbot has charged me with finding Margaret's killer."

"Oh!" She sat up straight, eyes wide. "You think her Tom mighta done it, or one of t'others she'd trifle with?"

"I know not what to think," I answered. "Perhaps you can help me. Can you find answers to my question by tomorrow, or should I wait another day or two?"

"I got friends who know what I don't," the woman smiled. "An' I don't wanna live with me toe a day longer than I got to. You come back tomorrow. I'll have somethin' for you, if there's anythin' to be knowed."

"Don't forget the wine."

I intended to speak also to the smith that day. But I was of two minds. Should I interrogate a man, who two hours earlier had buried his daughter, about her friends and activities? Should I wait until the morrow, when my presence in the town would be bandied about? I'd ridden up and down the streets often enough that many saw me. A stranger in such a place is likely to create questions anyway, particularly one who seems to wander the streets aimlessly. The smith lived on the opposite bank of the river Windrush, but gossip would carry that far soon enough.

I turned Bruce north when I reached the High Street and crossed the bridge. As I approached the smith's hut, I saw a wisp of smoke rise from his forge. Bereaved or not, a man must earn a living.

I heard the rhythmic pounding of his hammer before I dismounted. I had to speak his name twice before Alard laid down his hammer and turned to me.

"Oh. You have news? I must finish this hinge before it cools." And he turned back to his work. A few more skilled blows, and the work was done.

"Now, then, you said as you'd tell me soon as you learned what befell my Margaret…" He left the phrase dangling, not as a question, but as an acknowledgment of either my competence or his faith.

"I did, but I do not know that yet. I am here to learn more of her, that I may solve this puzzle."

"What good will that do? Know what you will of her… won't tell who killed her," he said with bitterness in his voice.

"It might. I think most who are murdered are done to death by someone they know, not some stranger or unknown thief on some deserted byway."

Alard shrugged. "Then ask what you will."

"Had Margaret any other suitors?"

"You mean more than Tom? Aye, she was one who caught men's eyes. Like her mother." He crossed himself.

"Any in particular?"

"None as had a chance with her. She'd set her cap for Tom Shilton."

"Did the others know that?"

"Yer askin' did she lead lads on, like?"

Alard was no fool. He saw the answers I sought before I asked the questions. "Yes, that's what I wish to know."

Alard looked down at the hammer dangling from his right hand. "We had words 'bout that. A few times."

I thought, from his manner and tone, that Alard and his daughter might have visited the subject more than a few times. I said nothing, waiting for him to continue on his own.

"She liked the attention, y'see. 'Twas Tom she'd chosen. Most other lads hereabout knew it. Didn't stop 'em as thought the matter weren't settled."

"Did Margaret give them reason to think 'the matter weren't settled'? Is that what you had words about?"

"Aye." He hesitated. "Told her as it wasn't right, leadin' lads on. She'd laugh an' say 'twas but a lark. I told her they might not see it that way."

"Any young men in particular who thought they might have a chance with her?"

Alard paused and contemplated his hammer again. "'Bout all of 'em, I suppose. Maybe John, the miller's boy," he bent his head toward the mill, just in view upstream, "was most taken with her."

"What kind of fellow is he?"

"Oh, he'll do well. Inherit the mill with but a small fine to the Earl. His wife'll not want for bread nor ale."

Spoken like a true father. I asked again, phrasing my question differently. "What of his appearance? Tall? Short? Handsome? Ill-favored?"

"Oh... well, not so handsome. Short, stocky fellow. Some lasses might not care for his looks, but he'll get more appealin' to his wife as the years pass an' the family grows an' he provides."

"Are there girls who are interested in him?"

"I suppose. I think Theobald's daughter – he's in trade, wool merchant – would have him."

"Would have him, or wants him?"

Alard smiled thinly. "All right... wants him."

"What did the merchant's daughter think of Margaret?"

"They wasn't close. Her bein' of a different station. She didn't much like it that the smithy's daughter could dress plain an' get more attention than her in fine clothes."

I thought my next appointment should be with the miller's son. I bid Alard farewell, took Bruce by the reins, and led him up the path along the river to the mill.

The creaking and grinding machinery drowned out my call, so I walked through the open door and found the miller at his work in the dusty interior. He peered through the haze at me, trying to place me among his circle of acquaintances. He held up a finger to indicate a brief delay, then resumed his work. When he finished he pushed past the sacks of flour recently ground and made his way to me.

"I am Hugh de Singleton, surgeon of Bampton. You know of the fate of Margaret, the smith's girl?"

The miller motioned me to follow him out the door to the relative quiet of the yard. "Aye... woeful thing."

"Did you know her well?"

"Watched her grow up."

That did not answer my question, but I could see that the miller thought it did. I was to learn that he was a man of few words.

"I've heard she was likely to marry Thomas of Shilton."

"So it's said."

"Had she other suitors?"

"Nay. How am I to know?"

"I heard your son was interested."

"More the fool he."

"Oh... Why do you say so?"

"Always puttin' on airs. Nose in the air. A smith's daughter, mind you. Thought she was too good for my John... or most o' the rest 'round here."

"But not too good for Thomas Shilton?"

"Even him."

This was a surprise. "How so?" I asked.

"He's to come into a yardland an' hopeful of another. She probably thought he was as good as she could catch. But she made 'im work for it."

"Work?"

"Followed her about like a slave, he did."

"So you'd not have been pleased had she set her cap for your John?"

"Nay. I suppose a babe or two would have shifted her mind... but there are those it don't."

"Is your son about? I would speak to him before I go."

"Nay. Gone to Swinbrook."

"Does he return today?"

"Tomorrow."

"Tell him I will call."

The miller stared at me, unblinking, and said, "Why?"

"I should have explained. Lord Gilbert Talbot has charged me with the discovery of Margaret's killer, as her body was found on his land."

"My John had naught to do with anything like that."

"I do not suspect him. But perhaps he may know something of Margaret's friends or activities which might point me to the guilty party."

The miller shrugged. "I'll tell him you will call."

Chapter 6

Bruce knew the way home and would have broken to a trot had I not held him back, so eager was he for oats and a warm stall. I was eager for my own warm hearth. Well, it would be warm after I renewed my fire. I had learned much this day. Whether it would lead me to a killer or was but gossip, I could not know. Such is the way with knowledge; we cannot know when we acquire it when, or if ever, it will be useful to us.

I was pleased to see the spire of the Church of St Beornwald rise above the nearly naked trees when I neared Bampton. The spire is impressive for a town the size of ours but not, perhaps, as graceful as some others. It is solid and substantial, like the villagers who worship under it.

It was near dark when I left Bruce at the castle and made my way to my own door. I lit a candle, built a small fire of the few sticks of wood remaining to me, and made a supper. Days were short. Nights were long. I should have slept well in preparation for a return to Burford, but I did not. Rather, I lay in the dark and reviewed what I had learned. But I could find no pattern.

As soon as dawn gave light I was at the castle gate. I had forewarned Wilfred the evening before, so he was prompt in releasing the bar and swinging open the gate. The marshalsea had Bruce ready. I swung my bag of instruments over his broad rump and set out for Burford once again.

I had seen several forests along the road to Burford which in the recent past had been coppiced, then left unattended; due, no doubt, to the reduced number of laborers available for the task. As I passed one of these thickets but a few miles north of Bampton, I heard a rustling in the grove and saw through the leafless saplings a sow and two of her offspring, which had thus far escaped the autumn

73

slaughter, rooting for acorns in the fallen leaves. The sow raised her head suspiciously as Bruce and I passed, but determined that we were no threat and went back to plowing the forest floor with her snout. Her passage through the coppiced woods was clearly marked, and I idly scanned the upturned leaves as Bruce ambled past the scene. The pigs were soon lost to my sight, but as I turned to the road before me, I caught from the corner of my eye a flash of color which seemed out of place in an autumn wood.

I halted Bruce, and turned him to retrace our path. I peered into the grove, and there, a hundred feet into the forest, among the upturned leaves, was a patch of blue. I dismounted and made my way through the thick-grown pollarding to the object. One sleeve of a blue cotehardie lay above the fallen leaves where the rooting pigs had left it, and was thus visible from the road. I swept away more leaves with my hand, and uncovered the garment, stained and dirty, but whole. I lifted it from the mold for inspection. It was a gentleman's cotehardie. A sumptuous one. It was cut short, in the fashion worn by young men who wished to show a good pair of legs. It was of dark blue velvet, woven in a diamond pattern, and lined with light blue silk. The long sleeves were cut in dags, ornamented with a trim of yellow velvet, and embroidered with gold thread. Even through its filthy condition, it proclaimed its owner a young man of pride and station. Its chiefest flaw, besides the earth and leaves accumulated on it, was a small slash, about two inches long, at the front of the garment. Dirt and mold clinging to the cotehardie obscured a dark stain about the tear. Only later did I discover this discoloration.

I found a fallen limb and used it to scrape about in the leaves, but found nothing more. I saw on closer inspection that the cotehardie might be dirty, but it was not worn or frayed. Indeed, other than the filth, it seemed nearly new. Its owner would not have discarded it in these woods intentionally. I thought for a moment that I might clean it and use it for my own. This idea I dismissed immediately. The

74

garment was far above my station. I would seem foolish to observers who knew me. Perhaps in London I might wear it – or even Oxford – and be thought a young lord. But in Bampton people would snicker behind their hands at my presumption. And sumptuary laws, though mostly ignored, forbid a man of my quality wearing such a garment. I resolved to show the cotehardie to Lord Gilbert. It had an unusual pattern. Perhaps he would know its owner. I slung the cotehardie across Bruce's muscular withers, where it remained for the day, and continued my journey.

The November sun was well up over Burford's rooftops when I reached my patient's cottage. The door swung open before I could find a convenient fencepost to which to tie Bruce.

"I remembered the wine," the woman said by way of greeting.

I would have returned a salutation but did not know her name. I had been more interested in the information she could provide, and the condition of her toe, than the woman herself. I view this now as a flaw in my character, but it was a flaw I took steps to rectify when I understood it. I asked her name.

"Edith, Edith Church... account of I live behind the churchyard."

"Well, Edith, I have brought my instruments. Shall we begin?"

"Aye. Sooner the better. I've had no sleep for days for the ache in me toe."

I dragged her table out into the sunlight in the toft at the rear of her cottage. Neither of us desired spectators, which, if I performed the surgery at her front step, her shrieks would likely attract. I warned her that the procedure would be painful.

Edith peered at me beneath narrowed brows. "I've borne seven children – four yet livin' – naught you can do to me toe will teach me anything about affliction."

I could not argue with her logic, so got her on the

table and went to my work. She was as good as her word. She stifled a groan or two, and twitched as I incised the offending toenail. That was all. I completed my work quickly, bathed the toe once more in wine, then helped the old woman to her feet.

"Do not wear a tight shoe until you see all redness depart from the wound. This might be two or three weeks."

"Hah! Tight shoe? I've but one pair of shoes, tight or no. Will you dress it now?"

I seem to make a habit of explaining my surgical philosophy to patients. It is usual practice, I know, to dress a wound or incision, so I am required to explain why, in most situations, I choose not to do so.

"The wound may yield pus for a few days. Dab it clear, but do nothing to restrain the flow. If the pus turns clear and watery, and releases a putrid smell, send for me instantly."

"Why so?" she asked.

"Because that will likely signify gangrene."

Edith put her hand to her mouth. "What'll you do then?"

"I must then amputate the toe... but I think that unlikely. Walk little, keep the wound clean of the filth of the streets, and raise the foot on a stool when you sit. I believe then all will be well." So it was, for when Edith sent for me a few days later, it was not to discuss her toe.

I helped Edith hobble into her cottage and sat her in what was clearly her accustomed bench before the fire. The house was once grander than now. It was built with a fireplace. I drew up a stool, lifted her foot to rest upon it, then placed the remaining bench before her.

"Now my work is done. Yours begins. What have you learned?"

"'Twasn't easy, gettin' round town w'me toe as 'twas." She waited, seeming to expect some agreement from me that her share of our bargain had been most arduous. So I agreed.

"Like I said, Margaret was never short of admirers. An' she seemed to admire 'em right back. Folks I've talked to say as her Tom didn't seem to mind over much. Told some as how 'twas a kind'a honor, bein' chose by one as had as many choices as she'd want."

"So Thomas Shilton was not the jealous sort?"

"Not regular. But they did have a quarrel, him an' Margaret."

"I suppose most lovers do, once in a while," I replied. "When was this quarrel?"

"Some time past. In t'spring. A week or so before hocktide. Or maybe 'twas after hocktide. 'Bout then."

"What was this quarrel about – do you know?"

"Another man," Edith replied.

"How did you learn of this?" I asked.

"It was me friend, Muriel. Her husband's a wool merchant, you know." I didn't, but I remembered hearing of the wool merchant's daughter. "She was at the river, comin' back from t'mill. Margaret an' her Tom had spoke to her when she walked by the smithy. Reckon her pa wasn't there, 'cause when Muriel got 'cross the bridge she heard 'em yellin' at each other."

"Did she hear what was said?"

"Muriel's hearin' ain't good. She's of an age for that." The same age as Edith, I guessed.

"She did hear Tom say as to how she was bein' a fool. He said, 'He's a gentleman. He'll not take up with the likes of you.'"

"Some screechin' from Margaret next, but nothin' she could make out. Not for want of tryin', I'd guess." Edith grinned and put a finger beside her nose. "Muriel likes a good story."

"Then why did she not tell you of this before?"

"Well..." Here Edith looked away for a moment. "I don't get to see her much any more."

I waited. I thought the woman too needy for conversation not to tell me more.

"Her man don't like it. Wants to buy me eggs an' cabbages himself. I can get more from others than from him. He's tried to put the guild on me."

"The grocers' guild? He's a wool merchant."

"That kind stick together. They don't like folks as horn into their business. Even widows with but four eggs a day to sell."

"Would Muriel speak to me about this?"

"Oh, aye. You'll not get her to stop. So long as Theobald, that's her husband, ain't about."

"He's a hard man?" I guessed.

"Flint. An' a miser, as well."

"Where is Muriel likely to be at this hour?"

"At home. Where she should be, anyway. House behind the shop. Her man'll be countin' his pennies at his business."

"Where is that?"

"On t'High Street. First merchant you'll see past Church Lane."

I thanked Edith for her discovery and led Bruce back to the High Street. I found the merchant, as Edith predicted, in his shop attending his accounts. I knew no way to assure myself that he was there than to enter and feign interest in a purchase. After a reasonable time spent fingering his wool, I headed south on the High Street, then led Bruce east, around behind the block of timbered, thatched shops.

The merchant's daughter answered the door. I understood then the miller's conclusion. She was a plain girl, who had enjoyed a few too many of the offerings of her mother's kitchen. She was not ugly, but she would attract little attention if standing near a beauty – which all assured me that Margaret, the smith's daughter, was.

The girl's mother peered at me over her daughter's shoulder, and invited me in when I mentioned Edith. Muriel asked about the surgery, and nodded approval when I announced likely success. I think she would have listened to

78

a complete retelling of the procedure had I not diverted the flow of her conversation.

I will spare you the particulars. She confirmed what she had told Edith, but had no more for me. It was clear from her glistening eyes and enthusiastic delivery that she wished she had. The daughter sat silent during the conversation; as quiet as her mother was voluble. I remember wondering at the time if she would remain so as the years passed, or if there was some curious work of nature that loosened a woman's tongue about the time of the birth of her second child. I decided not, as I have known talkative women not yet wed, and a few – a few, mind you – silent to old age.

I managed to escape the wool merchant's wife before the sun was over the church spire. I had two more visits to make this day: I must see the miller's son, and ask Thomas Shilton about the gentleman who had attracted Margaret's interest – and perhaps more.

I found the miller's lad assisting his father. One glance, and a few minutes' conversation, went far to explain Margaret's lack of interest in the young man as a suitor. He was shaped like the barrels which contained the flour the Earl's mill produced. He ate well, I decided, from the largesse he skimmed from the tenants who brought their grain to the mill to be ground. I explained that, many months earlier, Margaret and Thomas Shilton had been seen – and heard – arguing on the mill-side bank of the River Windrush. Had he heard them?

The youth glanced over his shoulder at the mill wheel. Its labored groans were accompanied by the sluicing of water off the wheel. "Not likely to hear much, workin' about the mill," he replied. Nor had he seen the couple at any time during the early summer.

The track leading back past the smithy to the bridge curved through thick gold and brown autumnal vegetation. The forge was invisible but for a wisp of smoke above the low trees. I heard Alard's hammer ring but allowed Bruce to amble on toward the bridge. I decided I could learn no more on the north side of the river.

The hamlet of Shilton is but two miles south of Burford on the road to Bampton. I had ridden Bruce through its single street often enough in the preceding days that I might be considered a regular visitor. Always before I had continued on my way, but not this time. I saw a woman at the village well and asked of Thomas. She pointed me toward a house at the south end of the village.

"But you'll not find 'im there," she added. "He's got the oxen for the day. He'll be ploughin' a furlong."

Villagers in a place like Shilton leased strips of land in several locations surrounding the town. Together these parcels might amount to perhaps thirty acres: a yardland. I led Bruce to the appointed home and knocked at the door.

The house was one of the larger of its type in the hamlet. Like the rest, it was made of wattle and daub, with a thatched roof, but this one, unlike a few others in the village, was in good repair. At the rear, filling most of the toft, was a cultivated plot, now barren, which had evidently produced the year's supply of carrots, cabbages, and turnips.

A woman in a flour-dusted apron answered my knock and directed me with pointed finger over the small rise at the southwest corner of the hamlet where, she said, I would find her husband and son and the team of oxen the villagers owned collectively.

I tied Bruce to a sapling and set off for the designated field. The ground was soft with recent rain, but not mud. Ideal for plowing. The two men looked my way as I crested the hill, but continued their work. The older man led the team, the younger held the plow expertly in the furrow. I met them at the end of the long, narrow field, where they would turn the team.

The field they plowed had been fallow. Sheep droppings indicated the use to which it had been put for the past year. Now the manure was being turned into the soil to improve the wheat which would be planted there in a few days.

"Are you Thomas?" I asked the younger man.

"Aye... as is he." He nodded toward his father.

I introduced myself and my mission, and asked if he knew that Margaret, the smith's daughter, had been buried in Burford churchyard the day before.

"Aye." His eyes dropped to the freshly turned earth at his feet. "Knew of it."

Thomas Shilton, the younger, was a large man, just grown to his full size, which was considerable. He was half a head taller than me, and heavier than Lord Gilbert. Twenty or so years of hard work and adequate food had produced a man of broad shoulders, strong arms and legs, and straight back. The stubble on his chin indicated that he was needing to shave more regularly now. His hair was fair, and matted in the wind which blew across the field.

"I am told that, early in the summer, you argued with Margaret on the banks of the River Windrush."

"There, and other places," he answered with a sardonic smile.

"You argued with Margaret often?"

"Aye. She were easy to dispute with."

"Yet you wished to marry her, I am told."

"I did," he said softly.

"She had some, uh, other qualities?"

Tom smiled sheepishly, then said, "She forgot a dispute right readily."

"You argued about another man, I was told."

Tom seemed to think that, as I knew the source of their disagreement, my words required no comment. He stared at me, then studied the fresh earth at his feet once again.

"Who was it that caused your discord?"

"I do not know the man," he replied with some heat.

"How is it that Margaret could be... uh... associated with someone you would not know?"

"He was not of this place."

"From where, then? Burford?"

"Nay. She wouldn't say. Farther, I think."

"It is rumored that he was a gentleman."

"So she said."

"Did she think a gentleman would take up with a smith's daughter?" I asked.

"'Tis what I asked her," he replied, shifting his weight from one foot to the other.

"And what did she answer?"

"She laughed. Said as how I might find out."

"How did you learn of this other fellow?"

"I'd been pressin' her to have the bans read. She wouldn't agree. Back about St George's day she changed her mind. Said as we'd have the bans read soon... but by hock-tide she'd turned cold again. Perhaps I pressed her over-much. She told me I wasn't the only man as wanted her. I knew that. But I told her she'd not do better than me. I'll have my father's yardland, an' the Earl's reeve has promised another soon's I can pay the fine an' the lease."

"What did she reply to that?"

"Laughed at me. Said as how some men had many yardlands."

"So you thought by that she meant a gentleman?"

"Not just then. I said as how I knew no one who had more than three yardlands. A man can't work more'n that. She said as how some men needn't work their own lands; have others do it for 'em."

"That's when you decided she spoke of a gentleman?"

"Aye. I told her she was a fool." He looked away, across the unplowed portion of the field, and watched a flight of geese as it appeared over the bare-limbed oaks of the forest beyond. "That were a mistake," he sighed.

"How so?"

"Margaret didn't like to be told there was aught she couldn't do."

"Is that when the shouting began?"

"Shouting?" he questioned, brows furrowed like the field behind him.

82

"You were heard across the river."

He smiled to himself once again. "Margaret could make herself heard some distance when she wished it."

"When did you last see Margaret?"

"That were t'last time. She yelled somethin' 'bout a gentleman always keeps his promise, an' went off up t'riverbank to the smithy."

"You didn't follow?"

"Nay. I knew Margaret well enough to know I'd best be on my way. She'd cool in a few days an' see more clearly. So I did think."

"But she disappeared before you saw her again?"

"Aye. Near two months."

"She was last seen the same day you took a cart of oats to Lord Gilbert Talbot, in Bampton."

"Aye. Returned next day. Found her father at t'door."

"'At's right," the father joined in. He had been standing silent beside the oxen during my conversation with his son. "Alard thought as how she'd run off w'Tom, 'specially as Tom wasn't about. I tried to tell 'im where Tom'd gone."

"You heard nothing of her after?"

"Not 'til Alard came through t'village on his way to Bampton t'bring her home. He told us you'd found her murdered."

"Yes. Her state allows no other conclusion."

"What state was that, then?" Tom asked through pursed lips.

I told him only that her body had been found and gave evidence of murder. The youth looked down at his feet again – and large specimens they were, too.

"Had Margaret spoken to you of any enemies? Did she fear anyone?"

"Nay. She had disagreements from time to time. No enemies. None in Bampton, anyway."

"You had an argument with her and later you went to Bampton."

Tom's jaw dropped. I could see that the thought that

83

he might be suspected in Margaret's death had never occurred to him. Either that, or he was shocked and frightened that his guilt had been found out. He protested innocence, and his father vouched for his truthfulness. The youth spoke of his reasons for desiring Margaret for a wife, among which were her health, her likely fecundity, her reputation for hard work won at her father's forge, and even her appearance. He did not mention love, but such emotion is trivial compared to the important issues of survival, work, and heirs.

I left the two men staring at my back as I climbed the hill back to town and Bruce. Thomas Shilton seemed to me the most likely suspect in this unhappy death, yet he seemed incapable of such a deed, and the fondness he felt for Margaret was revealed in his voice, his manner, and the empty expression in his eyes.

I do not know how to read a face or posture. The things hidden behind a man's eyes remain a mystery to me. I have been trained to deal with visible wounds, not the invisible.

The wind had risen during the day, and now propelled thick gray clouds from the northern horizon. I wrapped my cloak about me as the wind blew Bruce and me toward home. Bare trees swayed in the gale, dancers rooted to one place, in graceful motion nonetheless.

I passed the woods where, earlier in the day, I had found the cotehardie. I wished to be home, out of the blast, and safe from the sleet or snow I thought likely before morning. But my curiosity was too strong. I had yet an hour before darkness. I tied Bruce to a sapling while he gazed at me with a wounded expression. He wished to be home and out of the storm as much as I. Cotehardie in hand, I penetrated the underbrush. It took a few minutes of casting about before I found the place where the cotehardie had lain.

The wind was quiet here, its gusts broken by the forest. As I studied the ground, and kicked through the leaves searching for more clothing, I heard from the distance a dull thud. Then, a few seconds later, another.

It was difficult to tell, with the wind and dense vegetation, from which direction the sounds came. And when I determined the source, it was not an easy matter to work my way through the undergrowth and coppiced saplings toward the sound.

I came to a place where the coppiced trees thinned to an older growth of forest just as a final thud brought the sound of a falling tree crashing through the branches of its still-standing neighbors. I had heard the sound of an axe laid against a tree – woodcutters were at their trade.

I followed the sound of axes lopping limbs from the fallen tree and found three men at work in the gloom of a gathering twilight. One of the three was conspicuous for the white cap he wore, which marked him from his companions in the dim light. It was the man whose skull I had repaired, who I had told to remain in bed for a week, and to do no toil for a month. Here, but seven days later, he was at his labors.

One of the three took that moment to rest on his axe – no doubt they had been employed at their task all day – and saw me approach. He spoke to his fellows and they ceased their labor to observe me as I picked my way through limbs cast off from trees felled earlier. My patient seemed to recognize me first – not that he could have remembered the time he spent in my surgery – and he spoke as I neared the group.

"You've come for your t'uppence, then?" he asked.

"No. You've a week before I want to see the wound and change the wrapping. You were to remain in bed until tomorrow. This," I looked past them to the fallen oak, "could kill you. Your condition is brittle, and will remain so for many weeks."

"Aye... so you told 'em," he nodded toward his companions. "But," he continued, "if I do not my share of the work I'll not have fare to last t'winter. Then me an' my household may starve. I take a risk, whether I work, or no."

I saw his point. Left to his choice, I think I would have done the same. "Do you suffer... from the wound?" I asked him.

"Aye," he shrugged. "Now an' again."

"When?"

"If I turn me head, quick like, or bend to me feet, then rise... mostly times like that."

"That's to be expected. You feel no other constant affliction?"

"Aye... me left hand an' leg is weak, like."

"Let me have a look." I approached and peered at the bandage I had wrapped about his head. The wound seemed to be healing well, with little oozing to discolor the fabric. "I must change the wrap in a week."

"I'll bring yer pay," he muttered.

I considered the man's station, and my own diminished supply of firewood, and struck a bargain. In a week's time he would bring twopence worth of firewood to me, in payment of the portion of my fee still due. In concluding this agreement I nearly forgot my mission, but another of the woodmen cast his eyes toward the cotehardie I held in my left hand and returned me to my senses.

I held the garment out before me and asked if they'd seen anyone wearing it. They hadn't. I thought an explanation in order, so told them of the discovery. I left them with the admonition to seek me if they found more clothing. I did not think it a promising possibility that they would do so. I thought it more reasonable that they would wear what they found, or sell it, be it beyond their station, like the cotehardie. As I took leave of them I caught, in the shadows, an exchange of glances which suggested they knew more about the blue cotehardie than they wished to divulge.

It was dark before I found Bruce, and sleet pelted my back before I left the animal at the castle and made my way back across Shill Brook to Galen House. I don't remember

86

my supper that night. Whatever it was, it was cold. I ate, and crawled into a cold bed, hoping the woodmen would not long delay delivering the promised firewood.

Chapter 7

Sleet turned to an early snow, heavy and wet, during the night. The gale from the north continued to rattle my shutters even after the thin light of dawn penetrated the cracks between them. I had carefully banked my fire the previous morning, but there was not a coal left to reignite the blaze, and little wood for fuel when I managed to start it anew. I hoped the woodman would soon resolve his debt.

I had in my larder the remains of a maslin loaf I had purchased from the baker two days before, the heel of a cheese, and a small keg of cider. Of such was my noon meal. This simple fare seemed a banquet, for this day was Sunday and I ate no breakfast, as was my custom. Other than attendance at mass, I spent the day reading my copy of the Gospel of St John, beside my meager fire. There was no archery practice to observe because of the miserable weather, and no other reason to venture out. The town was silent.

Wretched as the weather was, the next dawn I could no longer hesitate. I garbed myself in my heavy cloak and, the blue cotehardie over my shoulder, made my way to the castle. This journey was becoming tiresome, especially on such a wet, cold, gray morning. I could be sitting before my fire, such as it was, keeping warm, waiting for paying patients. Instead I prowled the country for Lord Gilbert, to his benefit, not mine.

No, I decided, that was not entirely correct. It was Lord Gilbert who gave me my position, and he charged little enough rent for my lodging. And justice – would that not benefit all of God's creatures? It would, if I, or anyone, could deliver it.

I hesitated at the bridge over Shill Brook to consider these thoughts and admire the stream as it made its way down from the mill between snow-covered banks. There is beauty in even the harshest of things, although it is difficult to appreciate esthetics if one's feet are wet with congealing slush, one's stomach is nearly empty, and one's back is bent under a heavy load – as was, I suspect, the case with the old man who crossed the bridge behind me, heading toward town and the market square under a large sack of something I expect he hoped to sell.

Wilfred greeted me with a puzzled expression, due, no doubt, to the elaborate cotehardie I had hanging from my shoulder. John was called, and the chamberlain took me to the solar. I was barely in time. I had heard hounds barking with excitement as I approached the castle. Lord Gilbert had guests, and was about to go hunting. If he and his friends succeeded, a stag would be added to the fare at their table this evening.

"What, then, Hugh? You have news?" Lord Gilbert spoke to me, but his attention was given to his chamberlain and sartorial preparations for the hunt.

"I found this yesterday." I held the cotehardie before me. "Have you seen a gentleman wearing such a garment?"

Lord Gilbert peered over his shoulder, then, eyes wide, turned to me and grasped the cotehardie. "How came you by this?' he asked as he inspected the stained fabric. I told him of the foraging hogs, and the accidental uncovering of the cotehardie.

"It is Sir Robert's," Lord Gilbert declared softly. "Some harm has come to him… as we feared. He would not have discarded this for the heat, or forgotten it in such a place as you describe."

I agreed with his assessment, showed him the small slit in the front of the garment, and told him then of the woodcutters and my charge to them. "But I have other news as well, regarding Margaret… the girl found in your cesspit."

"Ah… have you found a killer in our midst?"

"No. Not yet." I told him of my interviews in Burford.

89

"Hmm. I believe the suitor the most likely assailant," Lord Gilbert grunted. "He had cause and occasion."

"This is so," I agreed. "But this is little enough to hang a man."

"Perhaps," Lord Gilbert frowned.

"If we hold our peace," I added, "some other fact which now escapes us may be introduced which will assure an accurate charge, either against Thomas Shilton, or another."

Lord Gilbert scowled in my direction. "You suggest we do nothing, then?"

"I do… for now. Although there seem to be grounds for suspecting Thomas, I do not wish to be party to a trial on such tenuous evidence."

"You think the fellow guilty?" Lord Gilbert challenged.

"I am of two minds. The circumstances point to him above others, but I have met him, and cannot view him as capable of such as was done to the smith's daughter."

"Perhaps you are too trusting."

"Perhaps. But I view that as a better fault than being too cynical."

"Hmm. Perhaps. You have done well. I will trust your judgment in the matter. But what," he held out the cotehardie, "of this?"

I suggested he dispatch men to search the woods where I found the cotehardie.

"I shall go. The hunt can wait."

"What of your guests?"

"They may come, as well. Sir John knew Sir Robert… although I cannot say they were friends. He may find this quest an interesting diversion from pursuit of a stag."

Lord Gilbert commanded, and it was done. A short time later four horses and twelve men gathered at the gatehouse. I was pleased to see Bruce among the horses. His presence meant, I presumed, that I would not walk. I am no aristocrat, but I would not go to the search afoot with the commons.

Among the villeins and tenants gathered for the search, I recognized Alfred. He touched his hat and bowed as if I were a duke.

"How do you do?" I asked. "Are you well?"

"Oh... aye. I can do a day's work well as any man. Though, mind you, 'tis well I'll walk today." He nodded toward the horses, stamping their impatience near the gatehouse, blowing steamy vapor into the cold morning air. "I am not suited yet to ride a horse." He chuckled at his own expense.

"That will pass. It has been, what, five weeks since the surgery? I think by Candlemas your restoration will be complete."

"'Tis well enough as is. For that I am much in your debt."

"You must thank God also. He it is who gave me the skills to aid you. He is the Lord of healing, for when we poor surgeons have done our best, recovery is in His hands."

"Aye. That I do. Every day."

Lady Petronilla and Lady Joan appeared at the entrance to the castle screens passage and walked toward the assembly. Richard, Lord Gilbert's two-year-old son, toddled along in their wake, accompanied by his nurse.

"Master Hugh will guide us," Lord Gilbert nodded toward Bruce. The old horse had caught some of the sense of excitement, and stamped his forefeet with as much enthusiasm as he was able. "Lead on, Master Hugh."

I managed to mount with some grace. I was becoming accustomed to the solid platform Bruce provided. I glanced toward the women to see if I was observed. I was. The fair Joan dipped her head in acknowledgment. I smiled – raffishly, I hoped – however, I do not do raffish very well. I have never been accomplished in courtly uncourtliness. One must, I think, be born to it.

I turned my attention to Bruce and the open gate. As I did I caught, from the corner of my eye, the broad face of

Lord Gilbert, his gaze fixed upon me. He had certainly observed my wandering eyes. Well, he must know that Joan had caught more eyes than mine, and in his presence as well. I led the troupe out the gate, across Shill Brook, and north on the road toward Shilton and Burford.

I found the coppiced woods, where Lord Gilbert exercised the rights of nobility and directed the search. This investigation was made more difficult by the crusty layer of sleet and snow now covering the fallen leaves and forest floor.

The band of searchers swept north, then south, penetrating with each sweep deeper into the forest. As we drew away from the road I began to hear the dull thuds of distant axes. This sound grew louder, then abruptly stopped.

Lord Gilbert's crew was a noisy bunch, breaking through thickets, scattering leaves and snow with poles broken from coppiced stumps, and shouting back and forth across the advancing line whenever an object of interest appeared. I theorized that, between blows, the woodcutters heard our approach and decided to pursue their work in some other part of Lord Gilbert's forest.

Then, through the trees, which were beginning to open as we left the coppiced area and drew closer to native growth, I caught a glimpse of white against the gray and brown background of thick oak trunks. My patient, I guessed.

Lord Gilbert was in the midst of the pack of searchers, wet to the knees – as were we all – when I approached him.

"What, then, Hugh? Have you found something?"

"No. Listen – " He stopped his exploration of a hummock of leaves and snow, which he had been vigorously prodding with the point of his sword.

"I hear nothing," he replied after a brief silence.

"That's it; did you not hear the woodcutters a short time ago? They have ceased their work."

Lord Gilbert caught my meaning. "Heard us, have they?"

"No doubt."

"You think they may have knowledge of this matter?"

"I do... but they will hesitate to say so. They might have found other garments and fear an accusation of theft."

"They have no doubt vanished," Lord Gilbert shrugged.

"I think not. I saw one observing us through the trees but a few moments ago. If we go around that copse," I pointed to a thicket to the south of our search, "we may come up behind the fellow. He'll not see us coming, or hear us, if that lot," I nodded toward the search party, "persist in the noise."

They did persist, and but a few minutes later we rounded the copse and found our quarry hunched behind the stump of a great fallen oak, watching with rapt attention the overturning of the forest floor.

"Good day," Lord Gilbert announced our presence behind the fellow in a booming voice. Lord Gilbert was well-practiced at a booming delivery. Most nobles are.

The man jumped and turned so quickly, his feet left the ground. His head, I thought, will ache after that move, for the man was indeed my patient.

"Why, it is Gerard, my forester," Lord Gilbert exclaimed in a friendly tone. "You see us engaged in a search of the forest," Lord Gilbert continued conversationally, as if unaware that his greeting had nearly caused the man's heart to fail him. "Perhaps you may assist us." Lord Gilbert's tone shifted slightly at this last remark. The message was clear: "You had better assist us, if you can."

Gerard stood silent, shaking, from cold, or fear, or both. I thought he might remember more if he feared less, so I sought to allay his concerns. "I showed you a cotehardie on Saturday," I said, and pointed to the garment swinging from Lord Gilbert's left hand. Lord Gilbert still held his sword in his right hand. Certainly this contributed to

93

Gerard's unease. "Have you remembered finding any other clothing in the woods hereabouts since then?"

"Nay... no clothes."

I detected his meaning, and I think Lord Gilbert did as well, for he turned quizzically to me as I spoke again. "What, then? Have you found other than apparel?"

The woodcutter looked about him as if he sought some refuge, or a path of flight through the forest. "What, then?" Lord Gilbert echoed. His voice had gone to booming again.

"A... a dagger, m'lord."

"A dagger!" The booming intensified, doing the woodman's headache no good, I thought. "Why did you not tell Master Hugh of this Saturday?"

"I did not ask him," I interceded. "I asked if he had found other clothing. Had you?" I turned to Gerard and tried some booming myself. Not being practiced, I was not so proficient as Lord Gilbert. "The truth, now!"

"Nay... nothing... just the dagger."

"Show us," Lord Gilbert demanded, "where you found this dagger. And where is the weapon now?"

The woodcutter nodded in the direction of the search party, the raucous exploration drawing ever nearer. "Over t'the coppicing."

"Show us," Lord Gilbert ordered.

Gerard peered about him once more, then turned and led toward the searchers and the road. Lord Gilbert's men quieted as first one, then another, saw us approach, following a stranger with a bandaged head. The forester strode through the line of searchers to an area already covered – not far, I saw, from the general area where I had recovered the cotehardie.

He stopped twice to get his bearings, then walked in a serpentine pattern, scanning the ground before him and to either side. A few more twists and turns and he stopped. By this time the entire search crew, gentlemen and villeins, had stopped their work to follow, either bodily, or with their eyes, our progress through the fringe of coppiced woods.

94

"Here," he said finally, pointing to the ground.

"You are sure?" Lord Gilbert asked.

"Aye. We was cuttin' poles from the coppice. There." The forester pointed to a stump where half a dozen poles had been sliced from the new growth.

"We was draggin' t'poles away an' seen somethin' shine. 'Twas a dagger. Right there it lay."

"Where is it now?" Lord Gilbert returned to booming.

"Walter it was who saw it first. He's got it."

"Walter? Was he one of those who brought you to me with a smashed head?"

"Aye, me son."

"Was he cutting wood with you just now?"

"Aye."

"Where will we find him?"

"We didn't know who t'owner was... didn't know 'twas important." The woodcutter's voice wavered as he spoke.

"Calm yourself, man," Lord Gilbert responded. "But I'll have that dagger. Where is your son?"

"He'll have gone home."

"Alvescot?" Lord Gilbert asked.

"Aye."

Lord Gilbert turned to me. "Gerard was often a winner at the butts of a Sunday afternoon. Why," he turned to his forester, "do we not see you at the competition now?"

"Me eyes... they've gone cloudy, like."

"Is that why you crept closer to see what we were about?" I asked.

"Aye."

"Hugh, you and Sir John and his squire will come with me to Alvescot. The rest of you," he turned to the silent throng about us, "stay at your work until dark. If you find anything out of place, bring it with you when you leave. There will be food for you all at the castle this night. John," he addressed his reeve, "I leave you in charge. Gerard, come along."

Gerard was the only one of our group not mounted. I offered to seat him behind me on Bruce, but he declined. He was a wirey fellow, and kept good pace, though he limped on the weak left foot he had complained of. We crossed a corner of the woods, thinned where Gerard and his fellows had been at work, and found a track which shortly led us to Alvescot.

The village seemed deserted, but was not. I saw a corner of oiled sheepskin lifted as we passed the first hut. The hamlet comprised but eight or ten occupied dwellings. Alvescot was, I saw, a village the plague had struck hard. There were as many dilapidated, unoccupied huts as those yet tenanted, and the church was in poor repair.

Gerard stopped our party before a domicile which showed signs of occupation and shouted for his son. Walter must have been at the door, for it opened immediately. I recognized the man who stepped out into the dying light as one who had brought Gerard to me and waited outside Galen House for the result of my work.

"The dagger you found in the woods," Lord Gilbert said without introduction. "I would have it."

Walter looked at Gerard, who shrugged, bit his lip, but remained silent.

"Well, go on, man... we know you have it," Lord Gilbert growled.

"Yes, m'lord." Walter bowed and retreated to the dim interior of his hut. I heard a brief conversation, and a woman's muffled cry. There followed the sound of furnishings being moved about, then silence until Walter reappeared. He held a small, jeweled dagger before him in both hands. He lifted it to Lord Gilbert as if in prayer of supplication.

I did not wish to appear overly inquisitive, so restrained my impulse to peer over Lord Gilbert's shoulder at the weapon. But as Bruce sidled forward a step or two, I caught a glimpse of the dagger as Lord Gilbert turned it in his hands. The blade was no more than eight inches long, but appeared sharp and well-kept. The hilt was gilded, and encrusted with jewels: not many, nor did they seem large, but gems on any such weapon pointed to ownership by a gentleman.

"'Tis not Sir Robert's, I think," Lord Gilbert decided as he turned the weapon in his hands. "Mediocre craftsmanship. And the stones are poor."

He turned to Walter, who was rooted in place before Lord Gilbert's horse, his hands yet lifted as if he expected to see the dagger replaced in them. That would not be, but Lord Gilbert was a fair man.

"I will have this," he told the woodcutters. "There is too much puzzle about this business. This," he held the dagger out to me and Sir John that we might have a better view, "must have to do with Sir Robert's cotehardie, but what, no man can tell. But I will not rob you of your find," he said as he turned back to Walter. "I will send my reeve with two shillings. A fair price, I think."

Walter's chin dropped. He had probably thought of no way to turn the dagger to ready cash. Lord Gilbert's offer would both stun and please him. He stammered thanks for the offer. Lord Gilbert cut him off. "And I will pay well for any other articles you may find in that forest... so long as you register the place where it was found and seek me immediately."

"Aye. We will surely do that, m'lord." I thought that promise true enough. When word got through Alvescot of Lord Gilbert's past and promised generosity, the entire ablebodied population of the hamlet would comb the forest for traces of Sir Robert and his squire.

Our small party approached Bampton Castle an hour later from the west road as the search party, wet and cold, straggled through the gatehouse. Some turned to observe our approach, their faces betraying exhaustion and failure. The muddy surface of the castle yard was beginning to freeze. But the snap in the air did not prevent castle inhabitants of all stations from gathering about the hungry search party. Lady Petronilla and Lady Joan were prominent among the crowd. To his wife's question, Lord Gilbert produced the small dagger.

My eyes were attracted to movement as Lord Gilbert displayed the weapon, and I turned in the direction of the motion. It was Lady Joan who attracted my attention, not an unusual event in itself. Her hand had come up to cover an opened mouth. Her eyes were wide, visible in the flickering light of torches. I knew then, before she spoke, that she recognized the dagger.

A sharp intake of breath accompanied Lady Joan's startled expression. I could not hear this from my perch atop Bruce on the fringe of the crowd, but many closer to her turned toward her, including Lord Gilbert.

"Do you know this?" he asked her.

Lady Joan moved toward her brother; the gathering parted to give her a path. "If there is a letter inscribed on the pommel, yes, I know it."

Lord Gilbert bent down from his horse and put the dagger in her hand. She turned it to better see the rounded end of the pommel in the flickering of the nearest torch. There followed another brief gasp, which even I heard, for the throng had fallen silent.

"What letter is there?" Lord Gilbert asked quietly.

"G," Lady Joan replied. "This is Geoffrey's dagger. Sir Robert's squire. I saw him crudely pick his teeth with it at table," she replied with some distaste.

"Then we have discovered foul work this day," Lord Gilbert muttered. He glanced across the heads separating us and spoke: "Master Hugh... attend me in the morning. We have much to consider."

Chapter 8

I gave Bruce over to the marshalsea and made my way through dark, frozen, rutted streets to Galen House. As I approached my door I saw, silhouetted against the whiteness of the snow, what first appeared to be a pile of rags. I nearly stumbled over it, for there was no moon this night and the heap was nearly invisible. But as I approached the bundle moved, and from the folds a slight figure stood to greet me.

"You be the surgeon... Master Hugh?" the now-animate rag-bag said.

"I am. But you have the better of me. Who are you?"

"Alice, sir."

"And why are you at my door in the dark? Curfew bell will sound soon."

"I've come for you. It's me father. He slipped on t'ice this mornin' an' cannot rise. I am sent to fetch you."

"Well, come in for now while I assemble some instruments. How long have you awaited me?"

"Since mid-day, sir."

"Then, here, take this loaf while I am about my work."

The girl gnawed hungrily at the maslin loaf. I could not remember having seen her before, which I thought strange, for there were few young people of her age or younger in the town. Not for nothing was the return of pestilence two years past called the "Children's Plague."

"Where is your father?" I asked as I pulled tight the drawstring of my bag.

"At Weald. He has a quarter yardland of the Dean of Exeter."

That explained why she was unknown to me; her father was a tenant of the Bishop, not Lord Gilbert. A quarter yardland would keep a family alive, with perhaps a small surplus to sell, if it was a small family, and if the land was fertile. "Is your mother attending him?" I asked.

"Got no mum... she died o' plague when I was new-born."

The girl recited her family history as we made our way back across Shill Brook, past the entrance to the castle, where all seemed quiet now, then turned left down a narrow track to a group of small huts. She was, I learned, the only child of her father's second marriage, he having lost two wives. She had two older half-brothers. Two of the huts at Weald belonged to them.

The girl opened the door to her hut and led me inside, announcing to the dark interior the tardy appearance of the town surgeon as she did so.

I could see nothing. There was little enough starlight outside the door. None of that came through the oilskin window or the open door. I asked for light, and after a time of rummaging about in the dark, the girl produced a cresset and lit it from a coal which glowed dully on the hearthstone.

The hut was smoky from the nearly exhausted fire, so the flame from the cresset did not at first illuminate the patient. But I detected the sound of his labored breathing from a dark corner. A haze of stale wood-smoke enveloped everything in the hut. I could not see above, but it was my impression that the thatching of the roof must have begun to collapse over the gable wind-holes, so that fumes had nowhere to go and so filled the small room. I knew I would reek of smoldering fire for hours after this visit.

Alice put sticks on the fire as I made my way, coughing, to the bed. Blessings on the man who invented the fireplace.

I was surprised to see how old the girl's father was. The pain of his injury surely added lines to his face, but even considering that, he was a man of sixty years at least. I asked what had befallen him and learned that it was he I had seen carrying a sack of hides to the tanner across Shill

Brook that very morning. Though but half a day earlier, the event seemed in my mind to have occurred a lifetime ago. His name, he said, was Henry; Henry atte Bridge.

He had fallen, he said, on icy cobbles before the tanner's shop. He had gone there with three hides: he had butchered a boar and two aged sheep of his small flock. He was taking the skins to the tanner when he fell under the load. He could not stand on his leg. The tanner and his apprentice helped him home, where he had awaited me in his bed. I feared a broken leg. No, that was not my greatest fear; a broken leg might mend. I feared a broken hip.

I drew the blankets from the man and went to probing his right hip, where he indicated the greatest pain was located. It took little prodding before I was certain of my diagnosis. A broken hip. I saw no gain to prevarication, so I told him plainly of the nature of his injury.

"As I feared," he said softly. He coughed twice in the smoke, then spoke again. "I'm finished, then."

"Perhaps not. But I will not deceive you. Even young men, hurt in summer, do not easily rise from an injury such as yours."

"What is to be done?" He coughed again.

In Paris I read of an Italian physician who believed he could improve the recovery of his patients with such injuries by raising the head of the victim's bed. For, especially in winter, a man who cannot rise from his bed will soon die as his lungs fill with fluid. It was this physician's belief – I cannot recall his name – that elevating the head might retard injury to the lungs common to a supine position.

I made a poultice of pulped root of comfrey, packed it about the injured limb, then wrapped it in woolen strips. The break was too high, as are most fractures of the hip, to apply a splint. Comfrey is thought to speed healing of broken bones when applied so. In this case I had doubts, but felt no harm in trying. And it gave the man hope that something could be done for him. I am convinced that hope is a curative in the ill and injured, for I have seen those severely

101

wounded recover when they should not have, because they thought they would. And I have seen those ill, but capable of recovery, pass to the next world because they were persuaded they would not recover.

I asked the girl for ale, but she had none. I wished to make a draught to ease her father's pain. I did not bother to ask for wine; in a house that has no ale there will be no wine.

I excused myself, walked the frozen streets back to Galen House, and armed myself with a flagon of ale. It was weak stuff, sold before the village taster had approved it. But for what I intended, it would serve. Alan the beadle accosted me on my return to the Weald cottage, but bid me farewell when in the star-lit gloom he recognized me and learned of my business.

Into the ale I mixed the ground seeds and root of hemp. This concoction would relieve pain and induce sleep. I told Alice that in the morning she must find men who would lift the head of her father's bed, and showed her how high it should be raised. There was nothing more to be done. I promised to return the following evening with another potion, then stumbled home through the cold and dark to an equally cold bed. For all my desire to find a wife to warm it for me, I had made little progress to that end.

The Angelus bell woke me before dawn, but I lay in bed until light streaked my windows. Lord Gilbert had bid me attend him, so shortly after dawn I made my way to the castle. His chamberlain escorted me to the solar, where Lord Gilbert, his wife, Lady Joan, and the guest were seated about a blazing fireplace. I felt warm for the first time in several weeks.

Lord Gilbert bid me be seated. I did so in some embarrassment, for my apparel was plain, and not in the best repair. I noted the hem of my cloak torn out, as it had been for many days, and it seemed to me that Lady Joan's eyes fell also on the offending seam.

"I would hear your opinion of this business. What do

you make of it, Master Hugh? Have you reflected on this matter since we parted last night?"

My thoughts had indeed been swimming through the various interpretations which could be assigned to finding a cotehardie and dagger together in a forest.

"M'lord, I have thought of little else. As the cotehardie and dagger were found some distance from the road, it seems to me likely that Sir Robert and his squire were drawn there as they passed by. Perhaps a call for assistance took them from the road. But someone, I think, wished them away from the path... to a place where what was to happen could not be seen by a traveler."

Lord Gilbert pulled at his chin and nodded agreement. "The cotehardie?" he asked.

"When Sir Robert saw that he had been lured to an ambush, perhaps he threw off the cotehardie, to preserve it, or to escape the restrictions to movement and his own defense that such a close-fitting garment would cause.

"I think the fight went badly. The squire lost his sword, else he would not have been reduced to defending himself with but a small dagger. In time, even this was lost."

"And the fight was over," Lord Gilbert growled. "What then?"

"Death, m'lord."

"But why? You may rob a man without killing him."

"I think this was no robbery. It is as you said. A man may be robbed on the road, not in a forest, if enough strength is presented to him so that he will not challenge his state. It is my belief that Sir Robert's death was desired."

"And the squire?"

"A witness, to be done away with?" I returned his question with another.

"Then we have three murders to resolve. What has become of my estate?"

I did not approve of the "we" of his remark. I thought

Lord Gilbert's assignment to seek out one murderer enough. But I admit my curiosity was aroused, and before I could think of grounds to object, Lady Joan spoke.

"What do you suggest be done, Master Hugh?" she asked softly.

I could not ignore the lady. No man could, but that is a matter best addressed another time. And indeed, I had given the matter some thought.

"Lord Gilbert, you have hounds." It was a statement, not a question. "I think they might serve a useful purpose in this business."

"And what might that be?" he queried.

"I would take the keeper and two of your best hounds, and two grooms, perhaps Arthur and Uctred, and allow the hounds to search where yesterday we found nothing. I will take the cotehardie; there may yet be some scent upon it a hound could trace."

"You would have the hounds search for a grave, then?" Lord Gilbert asked.

"Yes. We must also have shovels."

"Reasonable. Murderers would not bury their prey in a churchyard."

I stood to leave and carry out my task, but Lady Joan spoke before I could turn. "Master Hugh, you need a seamstress to repair your cloak," she remarked, pointing to the undone hem.

"Indeed," Lord Gilbert agreed. "Master Hugh needs care. We must see that he is kept in good repair, body and soul." Then turning to me: "You need a wife, Hugh... and there are other compensations than keeping one's garments mended." He chuckled, and from the corner of my eye I saw Lady Petronilla blush faintly.

"You keep me too busy seeking felons. I have no time to seek a wife."

Lord Gilbert laughed again. "There are females about. Many in Oxford of a certainty, who might seek you if you but gave sign you might be found."

This was news to me. I paid little attention to town gossip, but apparently Lord Gilbert, or his wife, was party to local chatter.

"Shall I wear a notice on my back?"

"That would not be necessary." Lady Petronilla found voice, looked up from her embroidery, and entered the conversation. "A well-directed smile at the appropriate moment will suffice. You seem so sober and businesslike."

"M'lord sets me to sober tasks," I replied.

"I do," Lord Gilbert agreed. "And for that I am sorry. But I have no other to assign to the work. I will send John to the fewterer, and assign Arthur and Uctred to accompany you for the day."

"And I," Lady Joan declared, "will find needle and thread and mend your cloak while John carries out his business. Then you will not catch your foot and stumble in your search."

The guest, Sir John, who had been a silent listener to our conversation, frowned slightly at Lady Joan's offer. Then I understood his presence. Another prospective suitor for Lord Gilbert's sister. I am no keen observer of the human condition, but it seemed to me that, if Sir John was indeed wooing the fair Joan, his suit was not going so well as he might wish.

Lady Joan left the solar for the tools she needed, returned, and demanded my cloak. She was expert with needle and thread, well-practiced in embroidery from her youth, no doubt, and had the hem like new in little time. When she finished her task she rose, held out the cloak, and bade me put it on. She held out the sleeves and settled the cloak on my shoulders with a pat of her delicate fingers. I felt my skin burn through the layers of wool as she adjusted the fit, and my heart burned as she smiled.

"There; we must not have our surgeon going about disheveled. That would reflect badly on us."

The hounds were confused. A hunt would employ the entire pack, not just the two. Still, they were eager to be off, straining at the leash. Forgive me for feeling superior as we set off; I was mounted on Bruce, the others walked.

The old horse was becoming accustomed to the route. He followed the proper turns, took Church View north past St Beornwald's Church, and even turned from the road to the tree where he had been tied the day before.

Uctred and Arthur had participated in the previous day's hunt, so required no explanation of our purpose. I told the fewterer of our previous discoveries, placed the cotehardie before the dogs, and then set off behind them as the keeper put them to their work. Arthur and Uctred followed, shovels over their shoulders.

A weak sun, barely penetrating a hazy, foggy sky, warmed and softened the snow. The dogs ranged far; the keeper was required to call them in often. An hour passed with no signal from the hounds that they had found a scent. I propped myself in the sun against an elm which fringed the coppiced woods, and was near to dozing while standing when from near a hundred paces away, through the forest, I heard first one, then the other, of the hounds bawl out. Over the excited din I heard the keeper shout. Arthur and Uctred followed me as I plunged into the coppicing.

The fewterer had leashed and quieted the hounds when we arrived. The dogs were stiff and alert, their attention focused on a small clearing which they had penetrated in their search. A dense fence of coppiced saplings surrounded this opening, so that to enter we had to pull ourselves through the enclosing scrub. The hem of my cloak caught on a shoot and tore, but not at the place Lady Joan had mended. I resolved to fix the tear myself before Lady Joan might see it and wonder at my careless ways.

I motioned for Arthur and Uctred to begin their work. They scraped snow and leaves from the center of the clearing, then set to work at digging. I traced four lines across the opening with my heel, and directed them to dig along those furrows. The fallen leaves and snow had blanketed the soil, so it was not yet frozen. I could not imagine

106

murderers taking time to bury their victims deeply, so told the men to excavate trenches no more than knee deep.

It seemed Uctred's fate to uncover bones. He was half-way down his second trench when one of the dogs growled and the hackles stood erect on its neck. A few scoops later, Uctred's shovel caught on something at the base of his trench. This did not alarm us, for both he and Arthur had found digging through the forest roots an arduous business. But this time, when he yanked the spade from the tangle, it came up with a shred of linen caught in a split at the point. I directed Arthur to cease work on his trench and join Uctred. In half an hour two moldering corpses lay open to the gray sky in a shallow grave. The dogs would not be silenced, so I ordered the keeper to remove them and wait for us at the road.

I turned to Uctred, he being at my elbow as we peered into the grave. "You saw Sir Robert about the castle when he visited; is this the man?"

"I cannot say. They're too far gone, like..."

I could see he found it irksome to gaze on the decaying bodies. "Was Sir Robert fair?" I asked him.

"Aye, he was," Uctred nodded in agreement.

Removing the bodies would require more labor, and a conveyance. I asked if Arthur or Uctred would stay to guard the grave while I and the other took the news to Lord Gilbert. The men looked sheepishly at each other and I read in their faces dismay at the thought of spending time alone in an empty forest with unquiet cadavers whose spirits might seek revenge on any who disturbed their rest.

So I sent them to give the account of our discovery to Lord Gilbert and request assistance. My wait at the grave gave me opportunity to inspect the bodies. Flesh was nearly gone, but the clothing was yet whole, though filthy and disarranged. The grave, while shallow, was deep enough that no marauding animal had detected and upset it.

The larger of the two bodies was fair-haired, the smaller was dark. The kirtles of both were of fine linen, once white, now stained with earth and, I thought, blood. Gashes disfigured the kirtles, and it seemed to me darker stains surrounded these cuts. The squire would also have worn a cotehardie, though not so fine as Sir Robert's. There was no sign of it in the grave. Where, I wondered, was it?

My last word to Arthur and Uctred was to urge them to haste. This they must have taken to heart. One might suppose that sitting on cold, wet ground in a silent forest accompanied only by the dead would cause time to creep. I did not find it so. The sound of voices from the road soon told me that the grooms had completed their mission in good time.

Arthur pushed into the clearing first, Lord Gilbert at his heels. "You have found Sir Robert?" he asked.

"I fear so."

Lord Gilbert's eyes fell to the excavation before him. He knelt and peered in. The cold of winter had slowed decomposition, so no stink assailed his nostrils as he bent to look at the bodies. He remained motionless for so long that I began to fear that the sight might cause him to become unhinged.

But Lord Gilbert had seen men slain in battle; some were friends, a few were relatives. This apparition could not disturb him much. He rose slowly to his feet. "'Tis Sir Robert. I have no doubt. And his squire. The lad was slight and dark."

Lord Gilbert ordered the exhumation of the bodies, and directed that they be taken to Galen House for my inspection when that work was done. I would have objected to this, had I thought of a reasonable complaint. I thought of many reasonable protests while riding Bruce back to Bampton, but by then it was too late to interfere with Lord Gilbert's command. And he explained himself logically enough as we rode to the town together:

"You are our expert on bones and bodies. This time you will not need to identify the dead. You must tell me and the coroner's jury what you can of how they died, as you did for the girl found in my cesspit."

I thought that clear already, and considered telling Lord Gilbert so, but doubted he would be content with a conclusion based on so cursory an examination.

"That may tell us," he continued, "why they died, though I doubt it. But if you can discover why they died, we may then also know who has done this."

I agreed with that possibility. But I had deep misgivings that I could learn anything past the how of the business. We parted at Galen House. The reeve, riding behind us, took Bruce's reins and led him on while I employed my time making another draught of ale and hemp for Henry atte Bridge.

I found Henry where I left him the night before, not that I expected any different. Pale afternoon sunlight filtered through the single window which illuminated the fuming interior of the hut. A smoldering fire continued to burn, putting some heat, and much smoke into the atmosphere. The bed my patient lay on, I saw, was yet flat on its four legs.

"Could you not find someone to raise the bed?" I asked the girl, rather more sharply than I should have, I fear. She began to cry.

"Nay. Asked me brothers. They would not. Too busy in t'fields."

This seemed unnatural to me. Lifting the head of their father's bed would be but the work of minutes and in no way harm their work for the day. There is, I thought, some family discord lodged in these huts.

"Very well. I will raise him. First, help me prop him up to take this draught."

Henry atte Bridge grunted heavily as we lifted him, but took the ale readily.

"Did the potion give you sleep last night?" I asked him.

"Aye... the pain returned by morning. I've looked for your return, and another draught."

"Send your daughter tomorrow, after the morning

Angelus bell. I will have another draught prepared for the day."

I walked back up the track to the castle, then along Mill Road to the brook. On its banks I found two round, flat stones of likely size, grasped them with wet, frozen fingers, and returned with them to the hut. I placed them on the packed earth floor, one on either side of the bedposts, and instructed Alice to slide them in place as I lifted the bed. I reminded the girl to come to Galen House in the morning for another draught, then made my way home through the gloom of a winter evening. A cart with two bodies, attended by half a dozen cold, impatient men, awaited me.

My table would have to serve again. The toft behind Galen House was enclosed, so I ordered the bodies moved there. The table was long enough to serve the squire, but Sir Robert overhung it head and foot. He would not care.

Chapter 9

There were advantages to residing across from the churchyard. Being awakened before dawn by the Angelus bell was not one of them. I reasoned that I could learn nothing from the corpses until daylight, anyway, so kept to my bed for two more hours. Had I known who lingered at my door I would not have been so sluggardly.

I stumbled down the stairs and lit a cresset to improve the dim glow from my east window. Before I could slice a loaf of barley bread for my breakfast, I heard a soft knock at my door. I opened it and found Alice, bundled against the cold, shivering there. I bade her come in, and asked how long she had waited there.

"Since the Angelus bell, sir," she replied.

"Is your father taken worse?"

"Nay, not worse. But the draught you gave him last night no longer serves. He needs another. You told me to come."

I set about preparing the crushed seeds and root of hemp, added some crushed lettuce for good measure, then mixed the stuff in a pint of ale.

The girl watched me work in silence for a time, then spoke: "He'll not live, will he?" she said softly. It was more a statement than a question.

Not for the last time in my profession, I met an issue for which I had no good answer. Should I destroy all hope, and speak frankly? Should I attempt to preserve hope, especially in a child, when I knew that hope was all that remained? Henry atte Bridge had too many obstacles to overcome: the broken hip, his age, the cold of winter, and the noxious air of his hut among the worst of these. He would not live.

I paused before I answered the girl, sorting these thoughts in my mind. My hesitation was response enough.

"I thought not," she said quietly. I turned to her, the laced ale before me. The girl stood, trembling yet from the cold, with a tear reflecting the lamp as it coursed down her cheek. "What will become of me?"

"You have family. Your brothers live at the Weald, do they not? Surely one will make a place for you?"

"No," she whispered, "they'll not want another mouth to feed. Not mine, 'specially."

I needed ask only a few questions. The girl gave me the story of her life with little prompting. Henry atte Bridge's first wife died twenty years before. His sons were angry when, six years later, he married a widow of the town, Alice's mother. They feared another son who might share Henry's meager possessions at his death. A daughter born of the union should have allayed their fears, but too much anger had passed between the families. The death of Alice's mother eliminated the possibility of more contenders for inheritance. This also should have softened the sons, but did not. Then plague struck again. There was fallow land available across the shire for payment of a small fine and rent. Henry atte Bridge's smallholding might be doubled or tripled by enterprising tenants. But the alienation continued.

I sent the girl back to her father with the draft and what remained of my barley loaf. I had another loaf, of mixed oats and barley, and a finer one of barley and wheat. I feared there might be little to eat in her hut and I had plenty. I must confess that, as I watched her go, I reflected that this child might grow to become a beautiful young woman. Her features were fine, her carriage seemly, and her eyes and hair glistened.

I could put off my repulsive duty no longer. I opened the rear door and approached the bodies. In the light of day I discovered the cause of death quickly. I had not seen this from above the grave, because of the bent position the corpses took in the ground, and in the night, as they were deposited on my table, it was too dark. But now in the day I could see clearly.

There were slashes in both kirtles where blades had wounded the two. These injuries, I thought, did not bring instant death, but the wounds were near enough the heart that whosoever received such a stroke would not live long.

I studied both bodies, but could find no purse, nor were any rings on the fingers or chains about the necks. There had been theft when this murder was done, but I doubted that was the only motive.

Hubert Shillside convened the coroner's jury next day, and I told them what I had learned. This was murder for murder's sake. The slayers were unwilling to bury gold and silver, but did not, in my opinion, kill for it. The jury met in the church nave, as it had done when I presented evidence of the bones of Margaret Smith, then retired briefly to the porch, and returned with a verdict that murder had been committed.

The coroner dismissed the jurymen and Lord Gilbert dismissed the coroner. He did not, however, dismiss me.

"I know," he began as we walked in the churchyard, "that the unraveling of what has happened to Sir Robert should be the duty of a bailiff."

"And revealing the killer of Margaret Smith," I reminded him.

"Indeed." He fell silent for a moment as we walked the path sunk among the graves. How high, I wondered, will the earth over these graves rise? Will my body some day help add another layer to the embanked earth lining this path? Lord Gilbert spoke again, distracting me from my morbid thoughts.

"I must appoint a bailiff before I depart for Goodrich. Tell me... I ask for candor... do you think my reeve, John Holcutt, suitable?"

I did not, but wished to be tactful. It is not easy to criticize a man politely. Once again my hesitation was answer enough.

"I agree," Lord Gilbert punctuated my silence. "John is an excellent husbandman, and manages accounts well enough. My tenants have chosen him three years now to serve. He would decline the position, but I walk softly with him, and permit him more consideration than I might another because of his abilities."

"He seems a competent man," I agreed, "in his management of the manor."

"Indeed. But to place upon him the burden of bailiff? That, I fear, may extend his duties beyond his talents. And I think a bailiff should be one of higher rank, not drawn from tenants or villeins. The younger son of a knight, or from the gentry, perhaps, would serve."

Lord Gilbert had gone to pulling his chin as he spoke. I made no reply, for I feared the direction his words were taking.

"To be brief, Hugh, I would have you serve here as my bailiff." To my raised hand and unvoiced but imminent objection he continued, "No... no... hear me out. You are performing some of the duties of a bailiff already, seeking miscreants in my lands. The townfolk admire you for your service to them. You can continue to perform that duty. John dislikes his position as reeve, which makes him a good man for that work. He will not begrudge me passing over him for bailiff. To the contrary, I think he will be relieved."

"But I know little of managing a manor," I protested.

"You grew up on one, where you observed your father. Did he administer well?"

"He did."

"Then do as you remember him doing, and I will be content. You may safely leave direction of fields and meadows to John. And the tenants here make sensible decisions at bylaw. My steward will preside at hallmote. You need only enforce the decisions of bylaw and hallmote."

"And collect rents and enforce week-work. I will be the most unpopular man in Bampton."

"Perhaps. But if you set a child's broken arm, his father is not likely to deny his half-virgate of week-work on my demesne."

"I should dislike using my competency to enforce a man's obligation."

"He has the obligation whether you serve him or not," Lord Gilbert replied. "I prefer a bailiff who can persuade my villeins and tenants to their duty rather than compel them. And I will make the service worth your while. Thirty shillings a year... no, thirty-two. And you will live in the castle, of course. You will dine at my table, and have a room there, off the hall."

When I made no immediate reply, Lord Gilbert continued, "You force a hard bargain. I see you are the man for the job. I will also give you Bruce, or any horse in the marshalsea but for my dexter or the palfreys Lady Petronilla and Lady Joan employ. And a fur coat." Winter was upon us and Lord Gilbert could see the frayed condition of my cloak and the newly ripped seam. "You will have fodder for Bruce from my stable, and twopence yearly for Christmas oblation."

When again I did not immediately respond to this demonstration of largesse, Lord Gilbert interpreted my hesitation as a demand for more. "All right, then... thirty-four shillings each year, but not a penny more. That's my limit."

"It is not your generosity which troubles me," I answered. "It is my fitness to serve."

"I am a better judge of that than you, I think. Serve me one year. If either of us thinks the bargain a mistake, next year at Michaelmas we will conclude the arrangement. You can go back to being surgeon. I will hold Galen House untenanted for you until then."

With much misgiving I accepted the post.

"Excellent. Now, tell me, what will you do to seek out Sir Robert's killers?"

"I am lost for direction," I admitted. "But I think two things must be done first; I will visit his manor at Northleech to learn of his friends and enemies."

"And the second?" Lord Gilbert asked.

"When we found the squire, he wore no cotehardie. But a search of the forest yielded no other discarded garment."

"You have lost me," he acknowledged.

"Where is the cotehardie? Not abandoned in the forest, or we or the foresters would have found it, I think. It was not in the grave nor on the corpse."

"You think it was taken, with Sir Robert's purse?" Lord Gilbert mused.

"I do. What do you remember of the squire's dress?"

Lord Gilbert was of no help at all. He could remember the gait of a fine horse or the coloring of a bulldog, but another man's clothing made as much impression on him as his chaplain's sermons. Well, as he grows older arthritis will remind him of mortality and he will attend a sermon more thoughtfully. But he will never give attention to wool or silk unless it adorns a shapely female. He and I, I admit, are much alike.

"Come to the castle with me. The women will know, and I must announce your new duties."

The women did know. The squire's cotehardie was green; not a brilliant green, but somewhat faded. It was not a cast-off from some gentleman of greater wealth, for its cut was plain and it boasted no ornamentation.

"Greet my new bailiff," Lord Gilbert announced when the cotehardie was identified.

I cannot well remember the conversation which followed; nearness to Lady Joan often had that effect on my memory. But it revolved around good wishes from both ladies, and plans for improving the apartment off the hall which would be my home; for the next ten months, anyway. The women left us, making animated schemes for my chamber as they departed.

"How far beyond Burford is Northleech?" I asked Lord Gilbert.

"Umm... twelve, perhaps fifteen miles."

"Too much for Bruce in one day, I think."

"Aye," he agreed. "A halt at the inn in Burford would be called for."

Two or three nights at vermin-infested village inns did not provoke joyous thoughts, but I could see no other way to discover the information I required.

"Sir Robert's father is Sir Geoffrey Mallory," Lord Gilbert continued. "When you see him, tell him I travel to Goodrich in a fortnight. I will bring with me the bodies so they may be buried there."

"Lady Joan and Lady Petronilla will not relish the company on that journey," I observed.

"Lady Joan," Lord Gilbert observed with a frown, "did not relish Sir Robert's company when he was alive, so I think his present state will cause little distress."

"Oh... I thought..."

"You and most others, I suppose. I thought so as well... but she would not have him."

"Your sister is a particular woman?" I asked.

"Hah! You are a tactful man when you choose to be, Master Hugh. I see I have chosen well for my bailiff. Yes, particular, that would describe Lady Joan. And, I am sorry to say, Sir Robert's reputation preceded his suit."

"What reputation had he?" I asked, for I knew nothing of the man but his death.

"It was said no man's wife or daughter was safe within his reach."

"But you would have married Joan to him," I protested.

"Perhaps he would have changed. If Joan could not keep a man from wandering, no woman could," he observed.

"I have heard it said that a woman marries a man believing he will change, but he does not, and a man marries a woman believing she will not change, but she does," I remarked.

My words set Lord Gilbert to tugging at his chin again. "Hmm... well... yes, perhaps."

"Now Sir John is a suitor?" I asked.

"Is, or was, I know not. I am not informed of recent developments. I have told my sister that she must soon choose. Her beauty will not last forever. I do not wish her to become my spinster responsibility."

"So even such a one as Sir Robert was preferable to that fate?"

"He was, Master Hugh, he was."

I saw a man, a youth, and a bundle of poles before my door when I returned to Galen House. The man I recognized as one of the woodcutters. My broken-headed patient had paid his debt with a great stack of arm-sized poles I no longer needed. But I knew someone who did. I directed the man to take as much of the wood as he could manage to Henry atte Bridge's hut. I could send a valet from the castle for the rest. I was already beginning to like the idea of being bailiff, directing others to do work I wished done.

The youth at my door was a stranger to me, come to ask my assistance in some injury, I assumed. He asked if I was the surgeon, Master Hugh, so you may understand my error.

He introduced himself and stated his mission: he was Ralph, from Burford, and had a message from Edith Church. She had recent information I might find useful. I would, she had informed the boy, be happy to pay him for his effort to bring to me this news. I gave him three farthings, which did not cause him a surfeit of joy. I might soon be a prosperous man, but Lord Gilbert had not yet filled my purse. And I admit I have always found it difficult to abandon the frugal ways of my youth.

Early next day I prepared a half-dozen hempen drafts for Alice, who was at my door as the last tones of the Angelus bell faded. I was off to the castle yard for Bruce, so accompanied her on her way. She was voluble in her appreciation for the wood delivery, and passed to me her father's gratitude, as well. I knew his injury was one for which my service could avail little, and did not expect to be recompensed in any way but appreciation.

118

I asked how her father did. She tried to feign optimism, but in the half-light of dawn I saw the tear on her cheek. She knew as well as I that her father would soon see God. He had lived many years. This end could not be unexpected. But the girl, I think, grieved for herself as much as for her father. He was, she said, a devout man, who had been diligent to teach her right from wrong and had urged her to live as a good Christian. His future was secure. Hers was not. I said a silent prayer for the child as I turned right into the castle yard and she went left to her father's hut.

The morning was bitter. As I rode Bruce north a low sun gradually peered above leafless trees and illuminated branches glittering with frost. It was a beautiful morning to travel, or would have been had my feet and fingers not stung with cold.

As I passed through Shilton I saw Thomas about his work in his father's toft and gestured a greeting. He did not acknowledge my lifted hand, but stared impassively after me for a time, then went back to his employment, turning the earth with a wooden spade.

Edith was behind her house, feeding her chickens. She greeted me cheerily, and held out her left foot. "I kin walk near good as ever," she proclaimed, and she confirmed this assertion by walking to me with a youthful stride which camouflaged her years. Her recovery was indeed remarkable, for but five days had passed since my work on her toe.

"The lad you sent yesterday said you had news for me."

"Oh... aye. Best come inside," she said, glancing about as if she feared an observer. She sat heavily on a stool and motioned me to take my place on a bench.

"Two days ago, Tuesday, it was, I was takin' eggs to Emma, t'cooper's wife. She lives out on Sheep Street. We had a talk, an' as I was comin' home I saw Matilda atte Water – she's got a hovel an' toft down t'river – widow, she is, an' gone a bit strange."

"Oh?"

119

"Aye. Talks to herself, like, an' wanders about town day an' night. Not so much in winter, mind, but beadle's likely to find her on t'streets at midnight of a summer's eve. I tell her she must not do so... folks'll take her for a witch. But she'll not listen."

"How does she live?" I asked.

"Priest gives her poor money, an' folks give her a loaf now an' then. I give her an egg if I have to spare. An' she grows turnips an' cabbages in her toft, when t'river don't flood it."

I did not think I had been called from Bampton to learn of an eccentric widow's late-night rambles. But I had learned that Edith would not be hurried. I had but to inject the occasional exclamation or question to keep her going.

"Matilda were babblin' to herself as we passed. Barely stopped long enough to greet me. We're of an age, y'see. Grew up together, had children together... lost husbands together."

"And then?" I prompted, as Edith's mind wandered back to lost days.

"Mostly she passes folks by these days. Won't stop to talk. Goes on about her way, whatever that might be. But Tuesday she took me by the arm an' stopped. Looked me right in the eye, she did, an' said, 'Tisn't right, young folks meetin' like that, at midnight.'"

"'Like what?' I says."

"'In t'churchyard,' she said. 'We never met w'lads at night in t'churchyard when we was maids.'"

"I wondered at that," Edith explained. "Who did she see in t'churchyard? I like to know as what's in t'wind, so I asked her who 'twas in t'churchyard."

"Who was it?" I thought I knew the answer.

"'Twas Margaret Smith."

"But it was night. How did this woman know who was there in the dark?"

"Heard 'em over t'wall. Knew Margaret's voice."

"But could not see her?"

"Oh, she did. Said she crept through t'gate an' seen Margaret in t'moonlight."

"Who was she with?"

"Thomas Shilton."

"Did your friend say when this meeting happened? It must have been some time in the past. Would she remember well from so long ago?"

"Aye. 'Twas 'bout Whitsuntide."

"Where may I find your friend? I would speak to her of this."

"I'll take you. She'll not welcome a stranger."

Edith took me to the High Street, turned right a few paces to the river, then left the street before the bridge. We took an obscure path barely above the water. In spring flood it probably would not be. Edith led the way past a dilapidated wharf, then past the smithy across the river. I could hear from across the Windrush the rhythmic swing of Alard's hammer. We were nearly even with the mill when I saw, rising from reeds and brush, a decaying hut. Wisps of smoke trailed from the peaks of the gable ends and wreathed about the frayed thatch of a roof which had seen no repair for many years.

"Stop here," Edith commanded, and went forward alone a few steps. "Matilda...Tildy... S'me, Edith. Will you come out?" she bawled.

The sagging door opened a few inches and an unwashed face peered through the crack. "How ye be, Tildy? I've brought someone t'see you."

"Don't want to see none," a thin, cracking voice replied.

"Tildy, Master Hugh's a surgeon – a doctor. Thought he might help you with your back, you bein' afflicted an' all."

The door opened a little wider, slowly. I stood silently behind Edith, afraid that at any movement of mine the door would shut and Matilda would flee my presence like a doe in the forest.

Edith motioned me to follow her. The bent form I could dimly see at the door retreated to the dark, smoky interior as we approached. It took some time for my eyes to become accustomed to both the gloom and the stinging haze. When I managed to blink my vision clear I saw that we would stand for this interview. The only piece of furniture, if that it could be called, was a low cot strewn with rags which served as bed and bench to the frail, twisted woman before me.

"Come here, Tildy. Let Master Hugh have a look at you."

The woman did as she was bidden, all the while keeping a wary eye on me. She was bent over a stick which she propped before her to support the weight of an upper body warped to a nearly horizontal position. I had seen elderly folk bent like her before, most often old women. The cause eludes me, and physicians who have written of human ills do not remark on the condition. As I do not know the cause of the infirmity, I am unable to assist those afflicted. I told this to the women. They seemed neither surprised nor distressed, for truth be told, we who deal with human ills most often find ourselves incompetent to change the course of human faults. This the two women knew.

I waited for Edith to continue the conversation. An abrupt change of subject from Matilda's ailment to nocturnal activities in the churchyard last spring would likely raise the guard of a woman whose guard was permanently aloft at the best of times. Edith did not disappoint me.

"Have ye been by t'churchyard these days?" Edith asked.

"Aye," the bent woman replied. "Go there most every day an' it's not rain nor snow."

"I think I would see you about more often," Edith replied with some surprise in her tone.

"Oh, I go after curfew bell. Want to be alone, see... account of I talk to my Ralph, an' if folks were about an' heard, they'd think I was daft."

Ralph, I assumed, was Matilda's late husband, resting now in the churchyard until our Lord Jesus should call him forth.

"You see any more suitors with their maids there?" Edith asked calmly.

"Nay. An' them as I saw wasn't suitors. Quarrelin', they was."

"Lovers sometimes quarrel," I said.

Matilda looked up at me from under her hunched posture, as if surprised I was yet present. "Aye. S'pose they do. Not like as them I heard, though."

"Why do you say so?" I asked.

"There was to be no arrangement. 'At's what the lad said. Sounds like no suitor to me."

"You could hear their conversation?"

"Aye, mostly. They was whisperin', but in a wrathful whisper."

"What did the maid say then?" I asked.

"Oh, she were right distressed. Said over and again as how he'd promised care for 'er if she got with child. Said she'd make it hard for him."

"And what did the lad reply?"

"Laughed, he did. Didn't say nothin' more, just laughed."

"And that ended their conversation?"

"Nay. Margaret jumped up on a stump an' said as she'd tell her father. Him bein' a smith, she said, he could make a point to run through the lad's black heart. An' he'd do it too, did he know what the fellow'd promised."

"And then?" I queried.

"The lad began to turn away, laughin' yet, he was. He stopped an' he told her she an' her father'd both regret should she do such a thing. Then he walked away. I had to hide behind the wall. Margaret stayed, cryin'."

"Did she stay long?"

"Don't know. Went home. Couldn't talk to Ralph with all that goin' on."

"No, I expect not. You are sure the girl was Margaret Smith?"

"Aye, saw her plain. Moon were shinin' full on her face."

"And the lad? You saw him, also?"

"Oh... were Thomas Shilton."

"Then you saw him?"

"Not so clear, like Margaret, but were him. Tallish. Fair hair. I'd know him. I ought to, I birthed him."

That caught me off guard, and I looked through the smoky haze of the hut at Edith. "Matilda was midwife to most 'round here twenty years an' more ago," she explained.

I turned back to Matilda. "You know that Margaret was murdered within a few days after you overheard that quarrel?"

"I do now. Didn't 'til Edith told me. Folks don't tell me much, an' I don't ask, 'cept to be left alone. Thought were odd, though."

"What was odd?" I asked.

"After that night I didn't see her at the smithy 'cross the river like I would most days."

I thanked the women for their assistance and paid each a penny. Matilda had probably not seen more than two farthings together for many years, but I was feeling charitable. I chided myself later for giving away my new-found wealth before I possessed it, but the expression on Matilda's wizened features made the expenditure worthwhile.

I decided on another visit to Thomas Shilton on my return, but first I must find shelter at the inn and press on to Northleech.

I found the inn. I also found coarse bread, gristly meat, watered ale, and vermin. I did not find sleep, for it was my lot to share a room with two men who snored through the night like dogs worrying a bone left over from supper.

Chapter 10

Bruce and I ambled into Northleech next day before noon. Sir Geoffrey Mallory heard the news of his son's death with equanimity. He had three other sons, so the loss of one affected him less, perhaps, than a father with but one heir. And he had had five months to prepare himself for the news that his missing offspring might be dead.

I told him that Lord Gilbert would bring Sir Robert's body in his train. Sir Geoffrey nodded, then asked the question I was expecting. "What was the manner of his death?"

I explained, tactfully, what I had learned of Sir Robert's demise, and what Lord Gilbert and I speculated about the event. "Did he," I concluded, "have enemies who might wish him dead?"

Sir Geoffrey chuckled. I was not prepared for this response, although Lord Gilbert's appraisal of Sir Robert's habits should have readied me. I waited for an explanation; certainly he would know such was expected. He did.

"Robert had many friends. He had a winning way about him. But enemies as well. Many husbands 'tween here and London, I expect, would be pleased to see him come to harm. And some fathers, too."

"Sir Robert was fond of the ladies?" I asked.

"He was that," the man chuckled. "I warned him he might play court to the wrong maid some day. What son listens to his father? Especially on the subject of women?"

"You think his... uh... pursuit of a lady might have led to his death?"

"'Twould be my guess. But she wouldn't need to be a lady."

I asked for a list of angry fathers or cuckolded husbands, but Sir Geoffrey fell silent. He would not name any his son might have offended. "I cautioned him," was all he would say. I could get no more from the man. He thought he knew what had happened to his son, and why, and seemed to hold no great grudge against any who had acted against him.

I found the inn at Northleech and settled myself for another long and noisy night. I admit that the table at this inn was better than at Burford, so that my lack of sleep could not be charged to an offended stomach.

I set out for Burford and home at dawn next morning. As Bruce sauntered across the empty marketplace past the church, I noticed the vicar about some morning errand. A question or two could do no harm, I decided.

I reined Bruce to a halt and addressed the man from across the churchyard as he was about to disappear into the porch. He arrested his progress and waited for me under the arch as I tied Bruce to the gate and approached.

I introduced myself as the surgeon from Bampton, uncertain whether my new position as bailiff would generate more consideration than my other occupation. The vicar was tall and angular and well wrapped against the cold. He peered at me from both sides of a truly impressive nose, which he held aloft in such a manner as to indicate that surgeons weighed little on his scale. I should have proclaimed myself bailiff.

I asked if he knew Sir Robert. He nodded. A man of few words. I asked if I could seek information about the man from him. He nodded again, and shrugged his shoulders as if to say, "If you must."

I pointed to the stone benches lining either side of the porch and suggested we sit. He swept his cloak about him and did so. Silently. I sat opposite him and immediately felt the cold of the stone penetrate my clothing. Well, at least we were out of the wind.

The vicar produced another nod as I announced the discovery of Sir Robert's body. This man, I thought, must be a popular priest. I could not imagine his sermons lasting more than a few minutes.

"Can you think of anyone who would harbor enough ill will to lie in ambush and kill Sir Robert?" I asked.

126

"I can." The man could speak.

"Can you name them?"

"No."

"The confessional?"

"Aye."

"I have learned that Sir Robert could be... a difficult man for some to like."

"And easy for some to hate," the vicar replied in a somber tone.

"Then you are not surprised to learn that he was murdered?"

"More surprised the attempt was not made long ago." The man was growing almost voluble.

"Oh?" That one-word question had worked well with Matilda atte Water; I decided to try it with the vicar of Northleech. It was not quite so successful with him, but worked well enough that I resolved to use it more often in the future.

"What have you to do with this matter?" the vicar asked, without malice. He was simply curious. I explained once again the commission Lord Gilbert Talbot had settled on me.

"Murderers must be found out," the vicar said softly when I had finished my report.

"Even those who attack evil men?" I asked.

"Even those," he sighed. "It is for God to judge the deeds of men, evil or good."

"Then we would not prosecute Sir Robert's killer," I responded.

The vicar smiled thinly. "You have studied the trivium, I see. You pose an interesting riddle. We must have law, else men would fall on each other like beasts; some men, at least."

"They would," I agreed.

"So the king must do God's work to enforce justice among men. It is his right and duty. So holy scripture tells us."

It was my turn to nod agreement.

"But men must not take justice to their own hands," he continued.

"What if a king will not do justly?"

The vicar was silent for a moment. "You pose another engaging question," he said, finally. "Is a king who behaves badly nevertheless due homage as king? To say otherwise is to assert that God has made a mistake in placing such a sovereign."

"Does God make kings," I challenged, "or do previous kings and queens?"

"God knows all," the vicar replied, speaking so softly that I could barely hear him over the wind whistling through the porch entrance.

"He does," I agreed. "Does that make him responsible for all, even the deeds of bad kings, or bishops, or any other who may break his laws?"

The vicar's eyebrows raised at that remark, but he was not deterred. "Job would say, no."

"True. We must not blame God when men do wickedness in violation of his law."

It was the vicar's turn to nod agreement. It was warming to find harmony in such a cold place. "What does God require?" the vicar asked. He answered his own question: "To do justice, to love mercy, and to walk humbly with God," he quoted from the prophet. This vicar was no illiterate priest, as were some.

"Micah," I said.

His eyebrows lifted again. Above that nose, it was an impressive feat. "You know the scriptures?" he asked.

I explained that I had studied at Oxford. I generally avoid mentioning that, fearing resentment from village priests, most of whom had studied nowhere but at the feet of some other equally untutored priest. This vicar sighed, and remarked that he would have liked to complete a term or two at university. He was envious, but not jealous.

This philosopher's discussion was entertaining, but

not productive. I am suspicious of philosophers. There is nothing so foolish that, allowing his thoughts freedom, some philosopher has not said. I directed the discussion back to Sir Robert's untimely end.

"Sir Geoffrey gave me to believe that Sir Robert made enemies through his, uh, unwanted attention to ladies."

"They were not all ladies, and the attention was often welcome."

It was my turn again to nod knowingly. Distant witnesses might have thought us two ravens pecking at the ground. When the vicar did not continue, I followed.

"He paid court to wenches?"

"He did."

"From his father's manor?"

"Aye."

"But you will not tell me who?"

"I cannot. My pledge at the confessional screen…"

It was my turn again to nod. "Such maids, I concluded, were foolish to think his court was anything but dalliance."

"They were," he sighed, "but a wench may believe a foolish promise if he who makes it be convincing."

"Sir Robert could be convincing?"

It was the vicar's turn to nod.

"Did he promise marriage to a wench?"

"Nay, not that I know… but promised a lass he'd set her up in comfort as mistress."

"And is her father a man to take action?"

"Dead of plague, two years ago."

"A brother, then?" I wondered aloud.

"All younger, just lads. Probably know nothing but they have a nephew."

"Does Sir Geoffrey know of this grandchild?"

The vicar's turn to nod. "Worst of it is, he demanded leirwite and childwite from the lass. Sixpence, he required of her."

"And he knew the father."

"I'm sure of it."

"Does the child thrive?"

"He survives. Sixpence, from them who had not two farthings to rub together." The man sighed heavily at the injustices of the world.

The conversation continued, but I learned nothing more of Sir Robert. I bid the vicar farewell with the wish that we might meet again, and set Bruce toward home on the Oxford – Gloucester road. I could hear behind me in the distance the vicar ringing the noon Angelus bell, the sound carrying a mile or more on the gale blowing against my back.

It was near dark when I returned to the inn at Burford. I saw Bruce put to the stable and oats, then availed myself of bed and board, although not in that order.

The howling wind did not keep me awake long, but before I fell to sleep I heard, over the snoring of my companions, the hiss of snow driven against the shutters. Next day the snow was so fierce that I determined to spend the day with my thoughts, beside the fire. Bruce was tired from three days of travel and needed rest as well.

Snow continued the second day, but not so severe. One day of idleness might serve a worthwhile purpose; two days would not. Although it was Sunday, I decided to continue my journey. I directed a hearty feeding for Bruce, and ate well of the landlord's unsavory table myself. I lodged a loaf under my cloak for midday, and pointed Bruce south up the hill and into the drifted road leading to Shilton and Bampton.

I saw no living soul, nor beast nor fowl, on the way to Shilton. The road lay unmarred before me. But Bruce was stout and rested, and broke the way with little strain.

Shilton lay buried, roofs white under their load of snow. Smoke wafting from under cottage eves and tracks in the snow where inhabitants had ventured out to the church, or to care for livestock or poultry, indicated that there was life under the white blanket. The house I sought had such footprints at its door. I knocked, and was admitted.

"Who... ah, it is the surgeon of Bampton. Caught in the storm? Where did you spend the night? Come in."

I answered the older man's questions, then turned toward a corner of the room where I saw Thomas at a table, spoon in hand and a bowl of pottage before him. "I would speak to you again of Margaret Smith," I said.

The youth shrugged. My request seemed not to trouble him, but he took no more of his meal.

"Perhaps you will accompany me?" I asked, and motioned toward the door. "'Tis no day to be out," he replied. "You may speak here." He looked at his parents as he spoke. His meaning was clear: "I have nothing to hide." But I knew now he did.

"You know of Matilda atte Water, of Burford?" I asked.

"Aye."

"She prowls about at night, as you may know," I told them.

"Mad as a March hare," the mother interjected.

"She goes to the churchyard, to speak to her husband. Early summer she went one evening, late, after curfew bell, and found two lovers quarreling behind the churchyard wall."

I waited, but this information brought no comment from Thomas Shilton. So I pressed on.

"Matilda says 'twas you and Margaret."

"She is weak in the head," Thomas said evenly, and went back to his cooling bowl of pottage.

Between mouthfuls he spoke again. "Margaret and I quarreled on t'riverbank, as you well know. I never disputed with her in t'churchyard... or any other place but t'river."

"Matilda knows you well?" I asked.

"Aye," his mother entered the conversation again. "She were midwife to many hereabouts, 'till she went soft in t'head. No one'll have her now, nor for ten years past an' more."

"She knows you well, so you say, and says so herself."

"How could she see who was in t'churchyard at night?" Thomas challenged.

"'Twas near full moon. What did you promise Margaret?"

"Promise?" The youth was surprised, or acted so.

"Matilda overheard Margaret protesting your broken promise – to care for her if she was got with child."

"With child?" I saw Thomas' mouth drop, and he laid down the spoon. "I promised Margaret nothing. We – that is, I – assumed I need make no promise."

"Oh?" (This was fast becoming my favorite word.)

"I supposed she knew, so I made no promise."

"Knew what?"

"That when she decided, we should wed."

"Had you asked her?" The light was dim, for the commons will not burn a lamp or candle when daylight, no matter how thin, gives light, but I thought I saw him redden at the question.

"Aye... well... not like askin', actually."

"Then how, actually?"

"Oh, we'd talk about how many children we'd have. What I could do with another yardland; perhaps rise to gentry someday."

I understood why such conversations might lead a man to think the question of marriage had been answered. "You said that when you quarreled at the river she spoke of a gentleman keeping his promise." I added.

"Aye, she did. When was I supposed to have had this dispute in t'churchyard?"

"About Whitsuntide. Matilda does not remember exactly."

Thomas smiled. "She remembers what did not happen, and cannot remember what did."

"You insist you were not there?"

"Yes," he answered with more vehemence than I had yet seen from him. "It may have been Margaret in dispute with a man, but the man was not me."

"He was broad-shouldered and fair, like you. Are there others Margaret knew well who fit such a description?"

"Walter, the hayward's lad," said the father.

Thomas chuckled softly. I turned to him with raised eyebrows. "All the lads knew Margaret, but you're askin', did Margaret know him?" Thomas commented.

"Well, did she?" I asked.

"Knew of him. Would never meet 'im past curfew in t'churchyard."

"Oh?"

"Had no prospects," the father spoke again. "Handsome an' strong as Thomas, but she'd not be interested in a hayward's son."

"I have been trying," I told the three, "to log this churchyard encounter in to the last events of Margaret's life. Matilda's was, I think, the last sight any acquaintance had of her yet alive, but perhaps for her father."

"If such a fool as Matilda heard or saw anyone in t'churchyard at all. Talks to her husband, indeed," the mother exclaimed in a superior tone.

I decided to lay my knowledge out for all to see. "You claim not, but a witness says you quarreled with Margaret Smith but a few days before you took a cartload of oats to Bampton Castle. You returned next day. Margaret was not seen alive again."

"You speak foolishness," Thomas said sharply.

"Put yourself in my place." I wished someone could be in my place, for this work was repugnant to me.

"Put yourself in mine," he replied. "I was to marry a beautiful maid; over-spirited, perhaps. I'd made no promises her father would take amiss. An' should I wish to kill her, why would I put her in Lord Gilbert Talbot's cesspit? There are barren places along the road I could have hid her. What of that?"

What of that, indeed? I did not speak for a time. I remembered well our first meeting, when to spare him sorrow upon sorrow I had refrained from telling Thomas where the girl was found.

133

"How did you know Margaret was found in the cesspit?" I finally asked.

I saw him swallow, but not a mouthful of pottage. That lay cold in his bowl. He replied readily enough, "Roger atte Well told me."

"Who is he?"

"A villager here. Was a villager here. Took ill a fortnight ago; could not rise from his bed after three days, and died six days past."

"How did he know of this?"

"His sister married a cooper in Witney. T'cooper's brother is cooper in Bampton," Thomas replied.

"So gossip spread this far? Has Roger a widow?"

"Aye."

"Where might I find her?"

"She lives in t'house beside t'well," Thomas replied evenly. "If you would speak to her, I will take you there... now, if you wish."

I did wish it. Together we pushed through the snow to the widow's cottage. She answered the knock at her door suspiciously, startled that anyone would call on her on such a day. But at second glance she recognized Thomas and admitted us.

I told the woman that I had learned from Thomas of her husband's death and expressed my sorrow for her loss.

"Got soaked comin' home from Witney," she explained. "Made some staves for 'is brother-in-law; lives in Witney. I told him he should await a better day to take 'em, but he would not delay. Wanted t'money, y'see. Caught a fever two days later, an' now here I am, an' he's gone. Little use a few pence is to me now."

"Did your husband, on his return, speak to you of events in Bampton? About a girl's death there?" I asked.

The woman's eyes narrowed as she tried to divine a motive for my question. She was suspicious, although I tried to make my tone as gentle as possible.

"Nay. Don't recollect he said anythin' 'bout anybody

dyin' in Bampton. I know who you mean, though. Wan't any of our business, was it?"

I turned to peer through the gloomy cottage at Thomas, but directed my words to the woman. "He said nothing about the manner of Margaret's death, or where she was found?"

"Nay. I told you, he said naught about it."

"How much did he receive for his staves? Did he say?"

"Oh, aye. Fourpence for t'bundle."

"Did he learn of other Bampton town gossip on his journey?"

"Aye," she chuckled lowly.

"What did he learn?" I leaned forward as if I was a fascinated co-conspirator in exchanging tales.

"You live there," she replied. "You should know all."

"Perhaps I have missed something? I have no wife to keep me informed."

The woman chuckled again but was otherwise silent, considering, I suppose, whether or not to enlighten this foolish man regarding things he should already know.

"He spoke of Lady Joan," she said finally.

"Oh?' The one-word question worked again, this time assisted by a raised eyebrow. I had seen Lord Gilbert perform this asymmetrical feat and was laboring to perfect it myself. The woman answered readily.

"Word is she traveled to Cornwall to catch a husband, but," she cackled, "he got away."

"Anything else?" I prompted.

"Of Lady Joan? No, not that I recall."

"Of townsfolk, then?"

"Hah. S'pose it'll do no harm, as I don't know the woman, but rumor is there's a wife of the town grown unnatural fond of the smith."

Bampton's smith rarely scrubbed away soot and sweat. On approach he could be smelled from thirty paces. Fondness for him, bachelor though he was, might be construed as unnatural in several ways.

135

I thanked the woman for her time and rose to leave. Both she and Thomas peered quizzically at me. Why should I be satisfied with information so inconsequential and disjointed? When we were well away from the house, Thomas voiced his puzzlement.

"What was that about, then?" he challenged. "Did you not know of Lady Joan, or the smith?"

"Not the smith, no, although I take her story lightly there. Does it not seem odd to you, Thomas, that her husband would speak to her of such ordinary things but not tell her the startling news of a murdered girl found in Lord Gilbert's cesspit? If he would tell you, why not his wife?"

"You doubt my word?" he challenged.

"It had occurred to me."

"No man can say I've been false to him, nor woman, either! Ask any in Shilton. I was not with Margaret in t'churchyard when the crone accuses me, and Roger atte Well did speak to me of Lord Gilbert's men finding my Margaret!"

"Your Margaret?"

"Aye! She would have been. When whoever was misleading her affections tired of her."

"Would a man have grown tired of Margaret?"

"A gentleman might have... would have, surely. I would not."

I thought I heard a choke in his voice. But perhaps it was the wind whipping snow about the eaves of his dwelling as we approached.

He stopped at the door, blocked it, and turned to me. "You think I killed her, then?"

"I am unsure," I replied. "But I will tell you there is no warrant to accuse any other."

"Will Lord Gilbert's bailiff charge me?"

"I do not know." That was no lie. I did not know, and saw no point in yielding more information to him then. "Murder is not business for a manor court, as you well know. The king's sheriff, in Oxford, will take whatever steps he sees fit."

"Aye," he muttered, "at Lord Gilbert's word and the coroner's court."

That, I agreed, was probably true.

Chapter 11

I pointed Bruce toward home. He knew a stable and respite from the snow awaited him, so ploughed resolutely through the drifts.

The spire of the Church of St Beornwald was invisible in the falling snow, but as I approached the town, well past the ninth hour, I heard, over the sighing wind, the slow steady tolling of a passing bell ringing from the tower. Someone in Bampton was dying this cold evening.

Wilfred took Bruce when I entered the castle gatehouse and told me that Lord Gilbert wished to see me immediately upon my return. I walked across the castle yard, ankle deep now in mud and slush. John the Chamberlain set off to seek Lord Gilbert while I brushed snow from my threadbare cloak and stomped my boots clean. As I did so, feeling began to return to my frozen feet.

"Ah... what news, Master Hugh?" Lord Gilbert hailed as he approached across the now-empty hall. He led me to the solar before I could answer and bid me warm myself at the fire. We sat before the blaze, and I related my discoveries to him.

"You are no better informed of Sir Robert's death than before your journey, then?"

"No," I agreed. "I fear not, but those who knew him think it likely his habits had much to do with his death."

"Well, no matter," Lord Gilbert commented. "You have done well on the other business. I think we know what happened to the lass from Burford, and how she came to be here."

"You believe the testimony against Thomas Shilton strong enough to prosecute him?"

"Do you not?" he replied, with one quizzically raised eyebrow. (It was this skill of his I was trying, with little success, to emulate. Perhaps it is a talent inbred only in the nobility.)

"I see no other likely culprit," I agreed, "yet I admit to misgivings."

"Why?" Lord Gilbert was not pulling at his chin. I thought this significant.

"I have met the man. I said once before, you may remember, that he seems incapable of such a crime."

"What do you think me capable of, Hugh?"

He caught me unready for such a question. I was silent.

"I am a calm, reflective man, am I not? Most of the time?"

I agreed that this was so.

"But in battle, when my blood was hot, I have hewed men limb from limb with no regard. Is there a thing which raises a man's blood more than battle?"

"Jealousy, perhaps," I answered.

"Precisely," he said, and smacked me on the knee. "You take my point readily."

"Then what is to be done?" I replied.

"Your discoveries and the verdict of the coroner's court must be presented to the sheriff at Oxford. I have delayed departure for Goodrich long enough. I will leave justice in your hands, Master Hugh. When the weather improves you must go to Oxford.

"I will send Arthur and two others with you. An unaccompanied bailiff is more easily dismissed than a man who commands a retinue. I know Sir Roger."

I nodded understanding of what was expected of me. Indeed, distasteful as I found it to imagine Thomas Shilton performing the sheriff's dance at the end of a rope, I saw no other course. Perhaps the jurors would decide our evidence flimsy and release the fellow.

Then justice for Margaret Smith might not be done. But to hang the wrong man would give no peace to the girl's spirit, either.

I changed the subject. Through the castle walls and muffling snow the dismal ringing of the passing bell could yet be heard. I enquired of Lord Gilbert who was dying.

"Some cotter in the Weald. I know him not. A tenant of the bishop."

"My patient," I said. "I feared this would be the outcome."

"Of what does the man suffer?" Lord Gilbert inquired.

"Old age, and a broken hip."

"Ah... well, either will suffice to end a man's life."

"I must call on him on my way home," I said.

"Home? Oh, you speak of Galen House. Ha... this is now your home," he exclaimed, sweeping his hand about him as he did so. "Galen House will be cold, but I will have a fire laid in your room here, and bread and meat provided."

"I will return shortly. I must visit Galen House for more of the draught I use to ease the man's discomfort."

"You take this man's death hard, I think," he observed.

"Perhaps. More so than some others."

"Why so? You admit little hope of saving one injured such as he, and so far past his prime."

"He has a daughter. She will be orphaned."

"Has she no family to care for her?"

"Half-brothers, but they resent their father's second wife and her offspring, so will have no truck with the girl."

"Hmm." Lord Gilbert went to pulling at his chin, which in this case I thought a good sign.

"She'll be the vicars' responsibility. How old is the lass? It'll be their charge to provide for a ward of the bishop's manor."

"A child, m'lord. She is perhaps twelve or thirteen years, but very slight for her age, I think."

"Old enough to work in the scullery?"

"Yes, I should say."

"Quick-witted? Obedient?" he asked.

"She seems so. Devoted to her father and willing to do all to ease him."

"Then if the vicars will discharge her, and they surely will, as she'll bring them no advantage, you can hire her as scullery maid... if you wish."

"I will tell her so this very evening. She frets of what will become of her. This news will ease her mind when she will be distraught enough that her father is leaving her."

I did not delay taking a draught to Henry atte Bridge by first visiting his bed empty-handed. Rather, I made my way directly to Galen House. It seemed cold and empty. Well, it was cold and empty, but I mean that it seemed already no longer my home. I wondered if it ever would be again. If it was, it would mean that I had failed at my new position. I resolved not to inhabit the place again, although memories of the house remained warm, if the house itself often was not.

Alice answered my knock at the cottage door. It seemed to me I always visited the place in darkness, and once again was compelled to stand within the door, shaking snow from my feet and cloak, while I waited for my eyes to become accustomed to the shadows.

This acclimation took less time than earlier visits, for a fire burned brightly on the hearth-stone, sending light to all corners of the hut. There was a measure of warmth, as well, and I could not help but observe the flames with some surprise.

Alice saw the object of my gaze, and said, "Your wood, sir. Woodman said as 'twas you told him to bring it."

I remembered. Four days ago, had it been?

"Father's near gone. I thought to keep 'im warm."

"You have done well," I told her. "Does he rest easy?"

"Aye. But he'll try to rise now an' again. He conjures my mother, and would go to her."

"I have another draught. Help me raise him and we'll see if he can take some of it."

Alice went to the far side of the bed and together we got her father vertical enough that he could take a few swallows. A brief light of reason flickered in his eyes as he tried to gulp the potion. I believe his wits were active enough that he remembered the relief it brought.

"Has the vicar been here?" I asked the girl when our work was done.

"Aye. Went to him this mornin'. I was sure father would not last 'til sixth hour."

"But he did," I said. "Did Father Thomas offer Extreme Unction?"

"Nay. Said as how father might live an' what sorrow would then follow. I was to send for him if father took worse. I went to t'vicarage just before ninth hour to tell 'im father was failin'. He set t'curate to ringin' t'passin' bell, but he ain't come yet. Will father live the night, Master Hugh?"

I went back to the sleeping figure, now resting quietly, for the draught had done its work, and placed my ear against his chest. His breath came in shallow gasps. I feared briefly that the weight of my inclined head might stop it altogether. A thin rattle in the throat accompanied each choking breath.

I shook my head. "No, I will not give you false hope. He wishes to go to your mother, you say?"

The girl nodded, her throat too full for words.

"God is merciful to those who love Him. He will grant this request soon. I will stay, if you wish it. When the time is near I will fetch Father Thomas or one of the others."

There was nothing to do but wait, and feed the fire. The curfew bell sounded, then the steady reverberation of the passing bell continued, louder now, for the snow had stopped, and the peal was unmuffled. The child sat cross-legged on the ground, gazing into the fire. I saw at intervals the reflection of a tear on her cheek and my heart was heavy for her grief. I sat on a stool across the flames and listened to her father breathe. I have learned that as a man's breath weakens, it becomes more noisesome, like some men; the most clamorous are often least effective at their business.

I heard, over the snapping of fresh wood on the fire,

a sigh. The child was weeping again. "Do you mourn your father," I asked, "or yourself?"

The girl sniffled and rubbed a sleeve against her nose. If she was to work in the castle scullery, that behavior must be changed.

"I know not," she whispered. "I know my father will go to God, so it is unseemly to sorrow overmuch. But he has cared for me. Now I must make my path in the world and I know not how."

"Lord Gilbert," I told her, "has made me bailiff of his manor here. There is work and a place for you at the castle kitchen, if you wish it and the vicars will release you."

This announcement did little to staunch her tears, but she raised her head and looked about rather than stare dimly into the coals, as had been her practice. Then a slight smile turned the corner of her lips, incongruous with the tears which continued to flow.

"My brothers would storm, to see me live at t'castle. Told me yesterday, when father dies I am to leave this house... where I go they care not."

"Then they will not care that you find a place at the castle," I said.

"Oh, they'll care 'bout that," she explained. "They'd not care was I to perish, as how they meant. They'll care was I to prosper."

"Shhh," I said, and listened to Henry atte Bridge's labored breathing. His chest was rising and falling more quickly. I rose from the stool. "It is time... I will fetch Father Thomas."

The sky had cleared while I sat gazing into the fire, waiting with Alice for death. The world was all white and silver, from the ground beneath my feet to the sky and stars and crescent moon above. I might have enjoyed a walk on such a night had my destination been other than it was, and my feet warmer.

It took some time and much thumping at the vicarage door to rouse Father Thomas. He suffers the disease of the

143

ears, which this night was a blessing, for the tolling of the passing bell just outside the vicarage did not much disturb his sleep.

"Master Hugh! What is your need? I did not know of your return."

I explained the reason for my call, and the vicar went immediately about gathering the tools of this unhappy business: his surplice and stole, and the blessed sacrament. Rather than rouse his clerk from bed, he appointed me to attend him as server, so I led him to the Weald ringing a bell and carrying a lantern. As we passed the church I saw a face peer whitely from the porch and a few minutes later, as we turned from Mill Street into the Weald, the passing bell went silent. To the great relief, no doubt, of he who must ring it and his assistant, and the neighbors of the church.

Henry atte Bridge was not conscious when we arrived at his hut, so could not confess his sins. This troubled Alice, but Father Thomas reassured her that the blessed sacrament would suffice for her father's entry to the next world. He then pried open the man's mouth, placed the wafer on his tongue, and clamped it shut. A prayer, and the business was done, which was well, for as the vicar stood, his task complete, Henry atte Bridge produced a great sigh and breathed no more.

"Will you have a wake?" I asked Alice.

"Nay. I've nothing to offer any. My brothers will not provide."

"Have you a shroud… or coffin?"

"I bought a shroud. I've no one to carry 'im to church-yard, though."

"Your brothers will not do even this for their father?" I asked.

"I will not ask them," she replied.

"You will not need to," I told her. Midnight or not, I strode to the first of the brothers' huts and pounded on the door until an angry face appeared. This visage was not, I suspect, any more inflamed than my own.

I told the fellow in few words what I thought of his filial devotion, and in my remarks managed to insert announcement of my new authority as bailiff at Bampton Castle. He was a tenant, as was his father, of the Bishop of Exeter, but I knew he would prefer to be on good terms with Lord Gilbert's bailiff. I ended my tirade by telling him what I expected of him and his brother when the new day dawned. He tugged at his forelock in acquiescence, and I turned and stalked back to the girl and the vicar. I had rather enjoyed telling the fellow what I thought of him, and what I required he do. This, I recognize, showed a lack of humility and is a sin. I enjoyed it, nevertheless, as I think did Father Thomas. It is the nature of sin to be pleasurable, else we would have less trouble avoiding it. The vicar grinned at me as I returned to Alice's door. My words must have carried through the still night, which meant that other cotters in the Weald heard the scolding as well. This, I reasoned, was probably a good thing.

Father Thomas, his work temporarily complete, went out into the snow to the vicarage. I would have stayed to sit up with the girl but she would not hear of it. "I will wash him and stitch him in his shroud. You can do naught for him in death." She did not add, although she might have, that I had done little for him in life, either.

The funeral was set for the sixth hour. I determined to attend: the man had been my charge, and I was eager to learn if Alice's cantankerous brothers accepted my authority.

Late next morning, after a maslin loaf and a pint of ale, I walked out the castle gate, and a few steps later turned from Mill Street to the Weald. Fifty yards down the path I saw mourners preparing for the procession to the church. Henry atte Bridge lay on the ground before his hut, his body sewn into a crude homespun hempen shroud. The plant and its seeds, I mused, had eased the man from this life, and would accompany his bones to the next.

As I approached two men lifted the body to a crude bier: two rough planks supported at either end by two short poles. Two more men stood silently, ready to assist the others at the ends of these shafts. One I recognized as the brother who had received my wrath twelve hours before. He studied the overflowing banks of Shill Brook intently, refusing to meet my eyes.

Alice stood behind the bier, her head high, and as she saw me turn into the lane I thought I saw the flicker of a smile – no, a smirk – cross her lips. Behind her stood Thomas de Bowlegh's curate and a cortege of mourners, including what must have been the brothers' wives and children. The assembly, for a cotter's funeral, was quite acceptable.

I stood away from the lane as the four bearers bent to their burden, then set off for the church. They had, I realized, been waiting for me, on whose orders I know not. I found myself, after Alice, in the position of chief mourner. I dropped in beside her as the bier passed and silently, but for the deceased's frolicking grandchildren, we traveled up Church View Street to the Church of St Beornwald.

The procession stopped at the lych gate for prayers, then entered the church through the porch, and Henry on his planks was laid at the entrance to the chancel. Thomas de Bowlegh said the mass, and preached a brief sermon. This met the approval of most, standing about in the nave on cold feet as we were, but I think Alice was peeved that her father could draw no more from the vicar than a few sentences about the brevity and uncertainty of life.

The grave-diggers had troublesome work until they chopped through the topmost layer of frozen soil, but we eventually got Henry atte Bridge laid properly away, his bones joining the hundreds, perhaps thousands, who went before, each generation raising the level of the churchyard a few more inches above the surrounding soil.

In scattered groups the mourners departed. It was time to speak to Thomas de Bowlegh about the child. I asked first what heriot he would demand of her and the brothers.

"They have little enough," the vicar answered. "A good hen, or perhaps a sheep, will be all I shall get from them."

146

"And what will you do with the child? Her older brother inherits, little as that may be."

"She must be put out to work... somewhere. I have servants enough."

"I will employ her at the castle, if that suits you," I replied.

The vicar was, as I suspected he might be, pleased to have the matter so neatly resolved. He wrung my hand enthusiastically.

Alice observed this conversation from the gate in the churchyard wall, far enough away that she could not hear our words, but close enough that she could read my face as I turned from the vicar and advanced to her place. Tears yet found their way from her eyes, but she smiled through them. "He will release me?" she asked.

"Aye. Now run to your home and gather your possessions, everything you can carry, whether it be yours or your father's. Your brothers will gather their wits soon enough and collect all. You must do so first. Take your goods to the castle straight away. Do not hesitate. Once your chattels are within the castle, your brothers may chafe, but that will gain them nothing. Run, now!"

She did, her feet throwing up fountains of snow as she sped past Galen House and disappeared around the curve of Church View.

I made my own somewhat slower way back to the castle, with more gravity, I hoped, and once there found Cicily and told her to prepare a place for Alice atte Bridge. There! I complimented myself, you have discharged your Christian duty to an orphan, and may now turn with single mind to the business of Thomas Shilton and Sir Robert Mallory.

That business must wait. The sun came out next day, the snow melted, and the road to Oxford turned to mire. I decided on a bath.

I had at Galen House an old barrel I had sawn in half, the seams of which I then smeared with pitch. But at Galen House I had no opportunity to put this tub to use. Now I would. I sent Uctred and his son to retrieve it, and had them place it in the midst of my apartment.

I required of Cicily six buckets of hot water, which, with raised eyebrows, she agreed to provide. Both eyebrows were lifted. It is as I thought: elevating one eyebrow is a noble trait.

Alice was assigned the honor of fetching the buckets. As she hauled the third bucketful through the hall to my room, Lord Gilbert entered from the solar. He watched her labor under the steaming load, then, his curiosity aroused, asked what I was about. I told him.

"A bath?" he said incredulously. "It's winter, man! You'll die of... of... of something."

"I stink," I told him frankly.

"So do we all. What of it?"

"I stayed three nights in verminous inns."

"Ah, yes, I forgot. But still, you will catch your death, bathing in winter. A corpse smells worse, you know, than either you or I alive."

"I will live," I assured him. He flashed the uplifted eyebrow at me, as if to say, "You have been warned."

"Very well, but just in case, who do you recommend as bailiff in your place?"

I laughed. It was a good joke. Lord Gilbert, however, was not laughing. "I will think on it," I replied, "while I soak the dirt away."

Alice had overheard much of the conversation as she made her way between my room and the kitchen. She grinned broadly as she dumped the fourth and fifth buckets into the barrel. I thought to remonstrate with her for lack of respect, but decided against it.

Next day Lord Gilbert and his retinue departed on muddy roads for Goodrich. I was on my own now. I watched the party – Lord Gilbert, Lady Petronilla, Richard, Lady Joan, their valets and grooms, horses, wagons, and carts – pass through the castle yard to Mill Street and east, then north, through the town. There was much jangling of harnesses, squeaking of cart-wheels, and stamping of horses as they got under way. The silence when they were gone was as complete as the noise of their departure.

Lord Gilbert had delayed his move until the issue of the bones found in his cesspit was resolved. Although there had been no trial and no finding yet of guilt, it was clear to me that he assumed these were but a formality. To Lord Gilbert, Thomas Shilton was already a dead man.

Not all the castle residents departed with Lord Gilbert. Some must remain to work the manor in his absence. An hour later I took three of these – John, Arthur, and Uctred – as my escort and we four made our way through the mud to Oxford. The Stag and Hounds was beneath my new position, but I knew the place, and it was convenient. I took rooms there and stabled the horses.

I left Arthur and Uctred with their ale, and with the reeve sought the king's sheriff at Oxford Castle. He did not wish to be found. The evening Angelus bell was ringing from Christchurch Cathedral before, in an exchange of messages, he was convinced that Lord Gilbert's bailiff did indeed have important business with him. By then it was too late to discharge my duty. Sir Roger would see me at the castle at the third hour on the morrow. It was back to the Stag and Hounds for the night; back to cheap ale and miserable fare and verminous beds. I would need another bath.

Oxford castle commands the west side of the town. The old, disused keep rises above the other structures as it has for many centuries. Within the walls are newer buildings, and it was to one of these that I was shown next morning to meet the king's sheriff.

Sir Roger de Cottesford was an orderly fellow. He wanted the particulars of the case and the coroner's verdict in plain language. I presented what I knew, and what I suspected, in unadorned speech. Sir Roger asked few questions. I was done within the hour.

"Lord Gilbert," he said, "has done well to send me this suit. This matter must be for the king's eyre and a jury to

149

decide. I commend you also, Master Hugh, for your diligence in pursuit of justice. Sir William Barnhill is holding court this day, and will do so until the term's work is done."

Sir Roger called a clerk from an anteroom and consulted him briefly. "I will send an officer and company to apprehend this Thomas Shilton tomorrow. His trial will be next week Thursday, if Sir William agrees. You must return to give evidence, of course."

I nodded understanding, bowed, and with John made my way back to the inn. At least I would not need to spend another night in that place. Until the next week.

Six days later, this time with Arthur my only escort, I made my way back to Oxford. I did not sleep well the night before my departure. I reviewed in my mind the evidence I must give, seeking some late insight which might incriminate or reprieve Thomas Shilton.

Next day the trial was done and verdict rendered before the ninth hour. The clerk called for my testimony, which I spoke as concisely as possible. I was nevertheless on the witness stand for more than an hour. The finding of the coroner's jury was read to the court. Then Thomas Shilton was permitted to speak in his own defense. He related the same account he had thrice told me, and again protested his innocence.

I thought that, mindful of his mortal danger, he might offer new proofs of his guiltlessness. He did not, or could not. He did, as was permitted, bring testimony of three men of Shilton to his upright life and blameless character. I watched the jurymen, substantial citizens of Oxford all, lean forward in their box to hear the words of Thomas' advocates. They were successful and prosperous men, who knew when to trust, and when not to trust, the words of another. It seemed to me they gave credence to these witnesses and I thought, from the expressions on the jurymen's faces, that Thomas might soon be on his way back to Shilton, guilty or not.

Some on the jury must have believed Thomas and his

defenders, for it took two hours and more for them to return to court with their verdict: guilty.

Sir William pronounced sentence: Thomas Shilton would be taken from court to his cell at Oxford Castle. On Saturday at the sixth hour he would be hanged in the castle yard. A cloud at that moment obscured the sun and the courtroom went dark.

Chapter 12

I never had much appetite for the fare offered at the Stag and Hounds, and this night less than usual. I desired food for my soul, not my body. I bid Arthur farewell at Cornmarket Street and set my feet for Balliol College while Arthur made his way down the High Street to fill his belly at the Stag and Hounds, a thing he might later regret.

The porter remembered me. It was his business to remember faces of those who had the liberty of Balliol College. I enquired of Master John Wyclif, if he had the same rooms as when I was a student. He did. As I made my way across the college yard I saw a lamp glowing dimly from his window.

Master John remembered me. I was uncertain whether or not this was a good sign. It seems to me that a master must recall most readily those scholars who perform in extraordinary fashion, either well or poorly. I did not want to consider which might be my circumstance.

He bid me enter heartily, and asked if I had supped. I had not, so I lied. I pray God will forgive me this. As He has other, more serious infractions of mine to consider, I think it sure He will.

Master John was finishing his own meal, a bowl of pottage and part of a loaf at one hand, and an open book at the other, beneath his lamp.

"When I saw you last you were considering the profession of surgeon," he said as he brushed crumbs from his beard. "Did you follow that path?"

"Aye. I am practicing surgery... in Bampton. At Lord Gilbert Talbot's request."

"His request for you to practice surgery? Or to do so in Bampton?" Master John inquired.

"Oh, in Bampton. I sought custom here in Oxford for a time."

"Do you find enough work there?" he asked. "'Tis not so large a town, I think."

"Aye, enough. Not overmuch, but I am recently appointed Lord Gilbert's bailiff for the manor there."

"Then you will be well occupied."

"I trust so. It is my employment I would speak to you about."

"Ah, my lad, I know nothing of collecting fines or surgery, and very little of the human body, but that my own seems to perform as God intended... most of the time."

I told him that surgery was not the topic of concern to me, then related the tale of my assignment to identify a decayed body and discover a murderer.

"And so," Master John concluded when my account was done, "you have seen justice done for the girl at the trial today."

I could not answer. To say "no" would be to implicate myself in a great injustice. To say "yes" would be to voice a certainty I did not feel. No fool ever became Master of Balliol College. Well, not to my knowledge, anyway. Master John saw my hesitation and knew what it signified.

"You think this Thomas of Shilton wrongly convicted?"

"No... that is, there is no other who had both cause and opportunity."

"No other you know of," Master John said while he chewed his last bite of bread, "so he must be culpable, in the absence of any other."

"Aye. Lord Gilbert will see justice done for the girl. I would see it done as well."

"And so long as someone hangs, justice will be done?" he asked.

"So all seem to believe."

"And you, Hugh, what do you believe?"

"True justice requires precision, I think. Else when murder was done we should not raise the hue and cry for the guilty. We should simply seize and hang the most

153

convenient sacrifice. A life for a life, who would care which life, unless it was your own?"

"You have sought the truth about this murder for many weeks, yet you cannot be easy in your soul about your conclusion?"

"No," I admitted, "I cannot."

"Why have you come here? You wish me to offer some absolution? To tell you that your good intentions will suffice in exchange for an innocent life... perhaps innocent?"

Master John could be hard when he chose. Not out of disdain or anger, but because he wished his pupils to think for themselves rather than wait upon his wisdom. I knew when I approached the college that such words from him might come. I relished them, as a monk wears a hair shirt. But Master John's harsh questions would not expiate my sin if my error sent an innocent man to the gallows two days hence.

Nevertheless, I complained, "Your words are severe."

"So is hanging. Have you seen a man hang? The lad's face will swell and grow purple. He will kick and struggle while students shout imprecations at him. He will lose control and soil himself. And the last sound he will hear will be accusations of his villainy, as perhaps he should, be he a true villain. But if not, he will die innocent of murder but perchance with another crime on his soul; hate for those who have misused him so. Is it worse to go to God the doer of a foul deed, or the thinker of foul thoughts?"

He awaited my answer in silence. I saw that his was not a rhetorical question. He expected an answer.

"I think there is no difference to God," I said finally.

"You speak the truth. What did our Lord say about speaking ill of another?"

"Those who call their brother 'fool' are in danger of hellfire," I replied.

"A punishment equal to that awarded murderers, regardless of what our brother Dante might say," he added.

"So if Thomas is a guilty man, he will, unless he confess his sin to Christ before the morrow, see the torments of hell," I reflected. "But if he be innocent, but brims with anger for me and others who destroy him, he will also die in sin?"

"I fear so. Unless he can forgive with a noose about his neck."

"Then I have put him in an impossible position. His only escape to heaven may be that he is guilty and will confess it so."

"Or," Master John said softly, "to forgive you your error... if error it was."

"Then I must visit him in the castle jail. Do you suggest it?"

"I think for your good, and the good of his soul, you must. But I would share a pint with you before you go this night."

Master John went to a cupboard, opened it, and drew forth a pitcher which he shook resignedly. "I forgot 'twas empty," he said.

When Master John got his mind into a book, either his own, or another's, he overlooked sometimes both food and drink.

"There is an inn close by on Broad Street. We will go there," he announced.

I asked Master John later, when this business was resolved, if God had a hand in his forgetting to purchase ale that day.

"I am what God made me, and what I have made with the material he provided. But, you ask, can God use my flaws, which he is in no way responsible for? They are my own burden. The answer must be 'yes', if we allow. God will use all we permit him to have. If we give him our weaknesses, he will use them as well as our strengths. The key is in giving them up... as I pray daily I may do."

I resolved to make that prayer for myself. It is difficult to do, for such a prayer reminds a man that a weakness may, with effort, be cured, rather than only used, if God is granted permission to work the remedy. Most, I think, would rather escape the effort and hope that God is satisfied with them as they are.

The inn held a crowd of students from the nearby colleges. Those who took the time to look up from their ale recognized Master John and bowed in greeting. The place smelled of spilled ale, stale food, and unwashed bodies. It was much like the Stag and Hounds. The noisy gathering quieted some as we made our way through the throng to a bench along the opposite wall.

"Would you rather drink in peace?" he asked. "We might take a flagon back to Balliol."

I shook my head "no." The clamorous conversations and conviviality refreshed me for the call I must make on the morrow.

Over the din of contending voices I could occasionally pick out a word. The hanging scheduled for Saturday noon seemed a popular topic. Little did these students know it was me they might thank for their entertainment.

Master John finally caught the wench's eye and asked for a gallon and two tankards. I withdrew my purse to pay, but he would not permit me. "You are my guest. Perhaps some day I shall take a day in the country; you may entertain me at Bampton." I told him this would please me greatly, and meant it so.

Master John thanked the wench, which seemed not to startle her. He must, I thought, frequent the place often, for no one else in the room took notice of her to thank her for her labor. The only comment most made to her was to remark indecently on her condition, which, I could see as she approached with the ale, was advanced pregnancy.

The wench seemed to give as good as she received, although I could hear little of her rejoinders as she passed through the mob about her duties. She responded with saucy air, a shake of her chestnut curls, and a flash of dark and sparkling eyes. "Maggie," one in the crowd named her within my hearing.

I do not remember Master John's topic as we sat in the corner with our ale. Indeed, he did the talking, fleshing out a theological argument he wished to present to his students the next week. I listened, or pretended to. Mainly I thought of what I might say to Thomas Shilton while with dull eyes I observed the carefree students before me.

The wench plied her way busily from counter to tables, but I noted that she did so with a small limp. The strain of her pregnancy, I assumed. Meanwhile Master John rambled on, lost in a proposition.

I was sitting with elbows on my knees, occasionally raising tankard to lips, muttering occasional agreement to Master John's points, when in a lull in the din I heard again a call for the wench's service: "Maggie!"

"Maggie..." Margaret! A broken foot which "troubles her now and again."

I sat up so abruptly that I smote the wall behind me with the back of my head. Master John peered at me across his tankard, hesitating in his conversation. He was puzzled, perhaps, that I should react so vigorously to his logic.

I turned to him: "Do you come here often?" I asked.

"Aye," he answered. "'Tis closest to my rooms."

"The lass; has she served here long?"

"Ah, since Whitsuntide, I think. They come and go. Find a husband and gone... although this girl," he chuckled, "did not find one soon enough, I think."

"You noticed her first about Whitsuntide, or shortly after?"

"Hmm... aye, about then. Why do you ask?"

I did not reply, but rose from the bench and pushed my way across the room. I called the girl's name and asked if she would attend Master John and me when it was convenient. A few minutes later she approached. "More ale?" she asked.

Master John stared quizzically at me, and the girl likewise when I shook my head. I bade her be seated.

"I cannot," she answered. "My master forbids me sitting with patrons. He wishes it known he operates a respectable house."

"Certainly no one will make improper inference from sitting with Master John Wyclif?" I replied.

The girl looked down at the Master of Balliol, and he, as if to answer the question, slid away on the bench to make room for her. She looked at me once again, then sat warily between us.

"What's this about then, if you need no more ale? 'Tis late for the kitchen, but I suppose somethin' might be found."

I decided to voice my suspicion plainly, with no prevarication.

"Margaret Smith, of Burford, your father, Alard, the smith, ages daily, before men's eyes, because he has lost you."

The wench's hand flew to her mouth. She stood and protested my mistaken identification, but I knew from her startled eyes that I was right. So did Master John. She began to move from us, but he reached out a hand to her elbow and gently drew her back to the bench.

"Maggie," he said, "this is Master Hugh de Singleton, surgeon in Bampton and now bailiff to Lord Gilbert Talbot. A body... that of a young woman was found at Bampton Castle these four weeks past. As you disappeared in spring, and no others from the place are missing, 'twas thought to be you."

The girl turned from me to Master John and back again as he, then I, unfolded for her the tale of her disappearance and what came of it.

"And now," I concluded, "you must come with me to the castle tomorrow to set Thomas Shilton free. On my miserable evidence, more than any other, he has been found guilty of your murder."

Her hand went again to her lips.

"He is to hang Saturday morning. You have heard your customers speak of the hanging which is to come? It is of Thomas they speak. He will be pleased to see you."

"I think not so," Margaret whispered. "We quarreled badly when we parted."

"Ah, yes. That night in the churchyard," I remarked.

"Churchyard? Nay, t'were twixt the mill and the smithy... along t'river."

"Well, nevertheless, he will be content. Your appearance means there will be no noose for him."

I wondered who it was that she quarreled with in the churchyard. I was certain it was the father of her child.

Margaret Smith's hair was dark, and flecked with red where candle or fire reflected from it. What sorrow and trouble might I have avoided had I thought just once to ask any who knew her a thing so simple as the color of her hair? The trace of hair clinging to the skull now buried in Burford churchyard was fair. And the broken bone misled me. I resolved that I would make no such foolish omission again should my duties as bailiff ever again present such an opportunity for error.

And I would need to do this work again. Lord Gilbert would not, I knew, permit me to accept failure. My task was not half done, as he had thought, but was now beginning over again. There was the corpse of a girl to identify afresh.

I should have been pleased with my discovery. I was, in that a man I suspected of both guilt and innocence, depending on my mood, was forever proved innocent of murder. But I could not sleep that night for reviewing my past errors and plotting how they might not be repeated.

We bid Margaret farewell after I extracted from her a promise that, when I called in the morning, she would be waiting and would willingly accompany me to the castle. Master John and I parted at the gate to Balliol College. He saw my distress and left me with advice I hope to follow.

"Do not fail to seek justice because you might find flaws in your work. You will recognize them soon enough. If not, others will discover them for you, and willingly, or I mistake my fellow man."

"Is imperfect justice better than no justice?" I asked.

"It must be, else there would be no justice at all. Justice is the work of men, who are imperfect. You must not be content with less than your best work, whether it be in surgery or seeking malefactors. But when you have done your best, put the conclusion of the matter in God's hands and rest content."

"I did not do my best in the matter of Thomas Shilton."

"No; I agree. But I think you will not be inclined to such an error again. Good night, Hugh. Seek me again when you are next in Oxford. I would learn more of these mysteries you must resolve."

Next morning Arthur and I escorted Margaret Smith through the muddy streets of Oxford as terce rang from the priory church of St Frideswide. We passed the marketplace as we approached the castle. There a troop of jugglers and acrobats, with two musicians accompanying, were preparing to begin their entertainments.

Arthur slowed his pace as we passed the outskirts of the throng gathered to watch the performers on their small wooden stage.

"These were at Bampton in t'spring," Arthur remarked. "I remember them well. Watch the juggler, he will toss four daggers in the air and keep them aloft without injury to himself."

Margaret and I stopped in obedience to Arthur's command. It was as he said. The juggler was indeed skillful.

"There are others, also," Arthur advised, "jugglers, and a knife thrower, and a wrestler who is never defeated, and a contortionist. She can twist herself into the most fantastic coils."

The wrestler and contortionist might be entertaining, but Margaret and I had a more immediate duty.

"You may remain, Arthur. There is no obligation for you at the castle, as there is for us. We will seek you here when our task is done."

Sir Roger, as was his custom, did not wish to see me, but I protested with his clerk until the sheriff deigned to permit me entry to his chamber.

"I have," I told him, "a girl waiting in your outer rooms who is thought to be dead." That arrested his attention. "We convicted her killer yesterday, and you have been commanded to hang him tomorrow."

"Thomas Shilton?" Sir Roger said incredulously.

"The same. He has been accused of the death of one who is alive. I found her last night serving at an inn near Balliol College."

"But you had a corpse," he spluttered. "You gave evidence. You specifically mentioned a broken bone, I remember."

"I did. And the lass waiting in your outer room had such a break in her foot long ago. This sorry business is my doing. Now it must be undone."

"You are certain of the wench you found?"

"See for yourself." I nodded toward the entrance. "She stands beyond your door."

The sheriff drew his bulky frame from a creaking chair and followed my gaze to his chamber door. He cracked it and peered through for a moment, then yanked it open and strode into the outer room.

Margaret stood, downcast before Sir Roger, feeling his imposing gaze upon her. Sir Roger in his prime must have been a formidable man; even now I would prefer to have him on my side in a fight rather than against me.

"You are Margaret Smith of Burford?" he rumbled. Even if she were not, she would have wished with every bone in her body that she was.

"Aye, sir... I am," she whispered.

"You have caused me considerable trouble. I sent men ranging across the shire to arrest a man thought to have taken your life. Master Hugh, here, has diligently sought justice for you. All thought you murdered. A man awaits death tomorrow for the deed."

Margaret blanched. "You will set him free?" she asked in quaking voice.

"Sir William must do that. The judge who passed sentence."

"Will you seek him straight away to do so?" Margaret pleaded.

"He is a king's itinerant justice. Yesterday this term of the king's eyre ended its work in Oxford. Today he is to return to London."

"What," I asked, "will you do if he cannot be found to reverse his judgment? Surely you will not carry out the sentence?"

I cannot tell whether or not he would have done, but Margaret surely thought so. She began to weep as the sheriff spoke.

"I have a duty to the law," he said, "and must perform it, unless the law itself requires other."

Margaret produced a great wail and sank to the flagging at his feet. Her words were muffled but through her sobs came a plea that the sheriff do all in his power to see justice done and the verdict overturned. This business was not going at all well. I had thought the matter a simple one; produce Margaret, allow her to tell the sheriff her tale, see Thomas Shilton freed and off to his home, then set off with Arthur for Bampton before the sixth hour. The law, I discovered, was more ponderous than that.

With a few sharp commands Sir Roger sent a sergeant to fetch Sir William – if he was yet at his lodging in the castle. If his party was gone, the sergeant was to take a troop of men to overtake him on the road to London and return him to Oxford. "A matter of life and death," the judge was to be told if he was reluctant to return.

Margaret and I waited, she sniffling, I tapping one foot, then the other, against the stone flagging of the clerk's chamber. It was nearly the sixth hour when the sergeant reappeared, breathless, to tell the clerk that Sir William had been overtaken near Wheatley, persuaded with some difficulty to return, and was at that moment dismounting his horse in the castle yard.

I walked to a window which gave a view over the castle yard. Sir William was striding to the castle entrance accompanied by two grooms and his clerk. His face and manner both indicated a dark mood. Understandable, I thought, for a man who expected to sleep in his own bed on Saturday night and was now prevented from doing so.

The judge disappeared from my view. Moments later heavy footfalls in the outer passage warned of his arrival. The door opened abruptly and banged against the wall. Margaret jumped.

"What's this about, then?" Sir William demanded of the clerk. This minion seemed overjoyed that he would not be required to answer the question. He bowed and announced that Sir Roger would explain all. Then, with a disparaging glance at Margaret and me, he opened the door to Sir Roger's chamber and announced Sir William's arrival.

If the sheriff was awed by the judge's dudgeon, he covered it well. He invited Sir William to his chamber, closed the door behind him, and left me, Margaret, and the clerk gazing at each other. The clerk did most of his gazing at Margaret, who, in spite of her condition, was well worth the occasional glance.

The door to Sir Roger's room was heavy, but I could plainly hear voices in strident conversation behind it. But one of the voices was strident at first, then gradually both were.

The clerk resumed his seat behind a desk, trying to act engaged and unconcerned about the encounter behind the door. Margaret and I remained standing at the window.

The door to the sheriff's chamber opened abruptly and crashed against the wall. The clerk leaped to his feet so abruptly that he rapped a knee smartly against his table. His muffled curse was submerged under Sir William's loud demand.

"Where is this girl, then?"

I should have thought that was obvious. Margaret stepped forward a pace in answer.

"So you have caused this confusion, eh?"

"'Twas not my intention, m'lord."

"Whether or not, I will not see home tomorrow eve."

"I am sorry."

"Sorry won't get me to London. Seven weeks I've been on King Edward's business. Why did you run off and send a youth near to the gallows?"

"I did not want to bring shame to my father," Margaret whispered. Sir William looked down at her belly.

"Ah. You thought he would be better pleased if he thought you were dead, rather than making of him a grandfather before he had a son-in-law? Is that how 'tis?"

The answer to that question, I thought, was that Margaret had fled Burford without thinking at all. Margaret made no reply, but her spirit was returning, for she refused to drop her eyes in some admission of guilt.

"Well," Sir William lifted a document before her, "this business has vexed me, but I'll not see a man hang because some daft wench has fled hearth and home."

He laid the document on the clerk's desk. "A pen," he demanded.

The clerk produced the article and a pot of ink from a shelf behind him. Sir William wrote a sentence on the sheet, then signed his name at the bottom with a flourish.

"There... set the lad free. Now, may I resume my journey?" – this to Sir Roger – "or is there another matter yet to detain me?" This he spoke in a sarcastic tone, intended, I think, to wither Sir Roger. He did not succeed. The sheriff had stood, his arms folded, throughout the exchange between Sir William and Margaret. Now he smiled sweetly, or as sweetly as any king's sheriff is likely ever to smile.

"We will not delay you longer, Sir William. We trust you will have a pleasant journey and find all well at your home. You shall rest easy this night, knowing you have saved a king's loyal subject from death on the scaffold."

There might be, I suppose, some debate about Thomas Shilton's loyalty to King Edward, but this was not the moment to raise the point.

"Harumph... yes... no doubt." And with another "harumph," Sir William stalked from the clerk's chamber. I heard him summon his clerk and grooms, who had remained in the passageway throughout the exchange, and together they stomped off down the hall, their heavy riding boots punctuating Sir William's departure.

Sir Roger handed the release document to his clerk. "Show this to the jailor and release Thomas Shilton, then preserve it in the registry. Bring Thomas here. He is entitled to an explanation," he turned to Margaret and me, "from you!"

I bowed and nodded. There was nothing to be said. The sheriff was correct.

A few minutes later footsteps echoed in the passageway outside the clerk's door. Margaret shrank behind me and glanced at the window as if to measure the possibility of escape. The clerk pushed the door open and motioned Thomas Shilton through it.

Thomas, his eyes blinking in the unaccustomed light, glanced at me, Margaret, and the sheriff with open mouth and stunned expression. Sir Roger, his lips pursed, nodded to me. I recognized the gesture, stood to one side to unshield the cowering Margaret, and began my explanation.

I told him of my misgivings about his guilt, my time with Master John Wyclif, of Margaret's flight and the reason for it, and how I discovered her. I concluded with an apology for the trouble I had brought to him. This was no deception. I trust he felt it sincere.

"And now," I concluded, "Margaret wishes to return to her father." Whether or not this was true I did not know, but I was convinced it should be true, and that at this moment someone needed to push her in that direction. So I did. "Shall I take her to him, or will you?"

Thomas did not speak for a moment. The silence was

165

only for a few seconds, but it seemed hours before he spoke. I was nearly convinced that I would see duty as her escort back to Burford when Thomas finally spoke through thin lips and tight jaw.

"I will see her to her father. We have much to speak of on the way."

From his tone I thought most of the talk would come from him. Margaret remained silent throughout this exchange, but I had seen enough of her spirit to know that had his words displeased her, she would have informed us. I took her silence as acquiescence, which proved to be correct.

"How will you travel?" I asked.

"Walk. 'Tis not so far," Thomas replied.

"The road is mud," I remarked.

Thomas shrugged. "We will keep to the verge. If travel be strenuous, we will seek shelter at Witney and finish the journey tomorrow." He said this with a long glance at Margaret's belly.

"Then be off," Sir Roger commanded. In my apology to Thomas and the further discussion, I had forgotten that the sheriff was an observer. I took his words as a charge to me, as well, and so made to follow Thomas and Margaret out the door. I was mistaken.

"Master Hugh," Sir Roger called as I was about to step into the passageway. "Will you renew your effort to find a murderer?"

"Aye. Lord Gilbert is adamant about the matter. He will surely demand I continue the search. And now it is my bailiwick."

"Quite so... quite so. Well, have you need of my office, send a man and I will provide what aid you require. Murder is the king's business, and in the shire, it becomes my business."

I thanked him for his offer, which I thought generous after the fraud I had put on him. The truth was, at that moment I had no scheme to seek further into the matter of either misplaced bones or buried gentlemen.

I walked from the castle gate to the market, seeking Arthur along the way. I thought he might have tired of the entertainment, but not so. He stood at the fringe of the crowd watching a man throw daggers at a tiny, dark-haired girl who stood unflinching against a panel of boards erected to catch the whirling weapons. The blades fixed themselves to this screen only inches from the girl, who remained immobile, a smile frozen to her face, throughout the display.

The multitude shouted approval when the last dagger was hurled to its target. Then a short, brawny, thick-necked fellow of indeterminate age stepped to the small platform the troupe had erected and challenged all to wrestle. A challenger who could defeat this champion would win sixpence. Others of the troupe circulated through the audience, taking bets and giving odds. I declined the offered wager when it came my turn, not being much of a sporting type.

The wrestler dispatched three opponents in quick succession, then belittled some men in the crowd for refusing his challenge. These smiled sheepishly, shook their heads, and would not be persuaded. They had seen with what ease he conquered those foolish enough to take his dare. His strength was surely great, but it seemed to me as I watched the matches that he won as much through skill and technique as sheer brawn.

The wrestler stepped from the stage and the girl who was the target for the knife-thrower vaulted onto it, flipping head-over-heels from the ground to land on the elevated boards. She proceeded to twist herself into impossible positions, walked about the platform on her hands, then, supported only by her hands, concluded the performance by raising her feet until they were behind her head. The crowd applauded while the knife-thrower and an older woman walked through the mob, baskets in hand, collecting farthings and pennies from the appreciative audience. I threw in a penny and felt myself charitable. Well, Christmas would soon be upon us.

Arthur and I retrieved our horses from the inn stable, and made our way through the inevitable throng on the High Street and New Road to the bridge over the Castle Mill Stream. I turned back at the bridge for a look at the ancient motte and keep of Oxford Castle, rising above the newer fortress. I thanked God that He led me to Margaret Smith in time to prevent a dreadful injustice, and spoke a silent prayer that He would again intercede if in the future I was about to do some similar witless act.

Arthur and I splashed across the river at Swinford, and a half-mile farther on took the track for Bampton. Ahead in the distance, far down the road to Witney and Burford, I saw two brown-clad figures, their cloaks blending with the muddy road and autumn foliage. One was tall, the other short; both were striding purposefully west toward Eynsham. The shorter figure seemed to walk with a limp.

Chapter 13

Arthur chattered on as we rode, pleased to go home, and animated by the performance he had witnessed that morning. He commented on the strength of the wrestler, the skills of the acrobats and jugglers, and the daring of the knife-thrower. I thought he might have mentioned the daring of the girl who served as the fellow's target. He did remark on her ability to wind her slender body into such miraculous shapes.

When he finished his review of the performances he began over again, this time comparing their execution this day with their efforts at Bampton five months before. They had lost none of their abilities, he concluded, but for the girl. Marvelous as her talents were, she could not compare to the lass who had performed even more phenomenal feats of contortion earlier in the year. I paid him little attention. I thought rather of the error I had made which nearly cost a man his life. But when he finished his review a new thought intruded upon my reflection.

"The girl today was not with the troupe at Whitsuntide?" I asked.

"Nay... 'tis another, I think. This lass was dark. The girl with them before was fair, hair the color of barley-straw at harvest."

"'Tis not unknown for a woman to change the color of her hair?"

"Aye," he agreed. "That sort might do so. But 'twas a different lass, all the same."

"You are certain?"

"T'other had pale skin, burned red on her cheeks from the sun. The lass today was dark. She'd not burn red like that."

I agreed such a hue was unlikely for the girl I had seen that day at Oxford. This news unsettled me.

After Arthur reviewed the entertainers' repertoire the second time, he found little more to speak of, so we rode on in silence. There was little to do but sway in synchronization to Bruce's easy gait and think of Arthur's revelation about the other contortionist; the one with barley-straw hair.

"How old would you say the girl was?" I asked.

"Eh? What girl?"

I had forgotten that Arthur was not privy to my thoughts. His mind had wandered in its own directions, which were not the same as mine.

"The other girl with the troupe, the one at Whitsuntide."

"Oh... ah, well, quite young, as was her replacement. Can't imagine any but the young able to do such as that."

"So then, how old did you take her for?"

"Sixteen... seventeen years. No more."

"And how tall was she, do you guess?"

"Oh, like the lass today. Short."

"So she might have been younger than seventeen?" I pressed.

"Might have been. But her face, you know, not the face of a child, nor a child's manner."

"What of her manner?"

"Throwin' glances at the men as was watchin', to get 'em to toss more into t'basket when it come 'round."

"Did it work?"

"Huh?" Arthur feigned ignorance.

"How much did you pitch in, Arthur?"

"I don't remember. I do recall as how Father Simon was that offended, he went to Lord Gilbert and asked for him to send them off, the lot of them."

"And did Lord Gilbert do so?"

"Nay," Arthur chuckled. "He brought them to t'castle to perform in the hall next day. 'Twas a feast for Sir Robert. I helped serve. Thought we'd hear that Lady Joan was betrothed before the festivities was done, but not so."

"And the troupe left the next day?"

"Aye. 'Twas late when supper was done. They stayed t'night in t'castle yard. Set up their own tents. One slept in t'stable. Had horses an' a cart for their stage an' other goods. Was gone next mornin'."

"Did they leave early? At dawn?"

Arthur mulled this over for a minute. "Nay. 'Twas an odd thing 'bout that. 'Twas past third hour when they left. The wrestler – he's leader, I think – was wantin' to see Lord Gilbert, but chamberlain put him off. I was about my duties. Don't know if he ever did see Lord Gilbert. Wanted more coin for his work, I think."

"The contortionist… did she attend Sir Robert while she performed?"

"Can't say. I was in an' out from t'kitchen, you see. I suppose she did. She didn't seem to take notice who she fluttered her eyes at."

We rode on in silence. I thought I now knew who the girl in the cesspit was, and perhaps even how she might have got there. But did Sir Robert's death have to do with the bones in the cesspit? I had been wrong before. I reviewed other possible explanations for the fair-haired skull which had lain on my examination table. None seemed to fit the pattern Arthur had introduced, at least not so well as the solution taking shape in my mind. But how to prove it, and prove it this time without mortal error.

The sun was setting behind the village as we approached Bampton, casting a long shadow from the church spire across the village and fields to the east. Arthur and I rode on silently, pleased to be home. After three days of thaw the weather was turning cold again. I wrapped my cloak about me and thought of the fire I would have laid in my chamber.

I thought also of how I might test my new suspicion regarding the information Arthur had provided since leaving Oxford. By the time I swung stiffly down from Bruce's back and turned him over to the marshalsea, I had a scheme in mind to answer, I hoped, my misgivings. But this plan I would not put into effect soon. I was too unwilling to trust my wits, having failed so badly in the matter of Thomas Shilton. I determined to think through my design for a few days. I had made one serious error already. Delay was preferable to making another.

I left Arthur with instructions for the kitchen for food and a fire, then sought my chamber and peace. There was to be none; peace, I mean. At least, not immediately. I had but settled to a chair when there was a knock at my door: ah, a fire, I thought. As too many times before, I was mistaken. I opened the door to find John Holcutt standing before me. I greeted him and asked his business, and as I did, I guessed it would be no pleasant thing.

"'Tis Walter atte Lane, Master Hugh. He avoids his week-work these last four days. We mend fences, but he will not come."

"He owes two days each week to Lord Gilbert, does he not?" I asked.

"Aye. He has a yardland of Lord Gilbert and for that owes two days from Michaelmas 'til the gules of August."

"Is he ill?"

"He complains so, but he told Alfred that he would try the new bailiff and see had he stomach for the work. I came to you as soon as I heard you had returned."

So that's how it will be, I thought. If Walter atte Lane can shirk and not be held to account, other villeins will hear of it and soon I would be once again Master Hugh, surgeon. Not bailiff.

"Seek Walter tomorrow," I advised John, "and tell him I will call on him should he yet be ill when next week he will owe four days repairing demesnes fences. Perhaps he may need some surgery, which I will be pleased to perform, to cure him of his malaise."

John smiled broadly at my response. "I think Walter will be well next week," he observed.

"I trust it will be so. But you may tell him also that as you left me I was preparing to sharpen my instruments."

"Ha; I will do so!"

The reeve turned to leave my door as a figure approached through the great hall carrying a bundle of wood. The hall was nearly dark, so I could not see that it was the child Alice who approached until she stood before me.

"Cicily says I'm to lay a fire for you, Master Hugh."

"Aye... enter."

The girl busied herself at her work and soon, with a tin box of coals from the kitchen fire to aid her, she had a fire crackling in my fireplace. Heat, and the smell of woodsmoke, slowly permeated my room. Does the smell of smoke also warm a man, I wonder? As the odor is associated with fire, perhaps it is so, that the scent of warmth is of itself warming.

"I'm to return for more wood, an' bring your supper, too," Alice interrupted my thoughts. "I'll be back," she promised, and scurried off.

"A basin," I called after her. "I would have a basin of hot water, also."

The wood, enough for an evening and more, and supper, arrived as planned. And my basin of water. Supper was a rabbit pie and cabbage in marrow sauce. When a man is particularly hungry and cold he is more likely, I think, to remember his meal and the fire that warmed him.

I spent that evening staring into the fire, reflecting on what I had learned these two days. I had learned much, so there was much to ponder. Who had Margaret met in the churchyard? What became of the barley-haired contortionist? Rather than one day, it seemed to me I had lived half a lifetime since morning.

But the meditation of even a wise man, which I do not claim to be, is not always sound. And my experience of the last two days convinced me I was not so wise as I once thought. I stared into the fire for an hour or more, forming, then casting aside, one plan after another. Finally I rose from my chair and knelt before it. I needed guidance. Where better to receive it than from Christ, God's Son?

You may find it odd that I did not beseech Mary, of

the holy well at Bampton, or St Beornwald, to whom the church was dedicated, to intercede in heaven for me and my cause. Most in Bampton will, when trouble comes, go to the church, light a candle, and ask St Beornwald or the mother of Christ to intervene. But I had studied the scriptures as a student at Balliol and sat under the teaching of Master John Wyclif. Theology was not part of the trivium nor the quadrivium, but I read the sacred texts when I could, preparing, as I thought at the time, to study as a Master and spend my life as a clerk. These were not the first, nor the last, of my plans to go awry.

I rented a text of the gospels in my third year and burned many candles low copying the Gospel of St John. I well remember two passages. Actually, I remember more than two passages, but I mean there were in St John's Gospel two verses which stayed in my mind and ever after directed my prayers. In one, Christ told his disciples, "If you ask anything in my name, I will do it." In another, he said to them, "Until now, you have asked nothing in my name. Ask, and you will receive, that your joy may be full."

From my third year at Balliol I dispensed with prayer to the saints as unnecessary and perhaps even useless. Christ himself directed his disciples to ask God for His mercy in Christ's name, not in Mary's name or St Peter's name or the name of any other saint, no matter so holy they might be.

By the time the fire was reduced to embers and my prayers done, I had contrived a plan. I could not put it to purpose 'til morning, so crawled into my bed to sleep on it. I did slumber, eventually, but the cock in the poulterer's yard was considering whether or not it was time to crow before I fell to sleep.

Because of my fitful slumber I was not yet alert when Arthur beat upon my door. I stumbled to it, barely able to see my way in the half-light of dawn. The fire was out, and the stone floor was shockingly cold against my feet. The frigid flagging jolted me awake.

"Master Hugh," Arthur blurted apologetically, "Sir

John Withington is here. He rode yesterday and most of the night to fetch you."

"What does Sir John wish of me?" I stammered.

"He has come to tell you that Lady Joan has broken her wrist and is in great pain. Lord Gilbert would have you attend her."

Those words caused the careful scheme I had devised during the night to fall to pieces. This was excellent, for the unexpected course set before me at that moment brought success. Would my plan have done so? Who can know? I see now that when God answers a prayer, it may not be in the manner we would wish him to. Surely Lady Joan would have chosen another method.

There were few things I would rather do than attend fair Lady Joan. Given the opportunity, I would have selected a different occasion. I do admit, however, to thinking that my skills devoted to her in this trouble of hers might soften her heart to me. Such thoughts were selfish, I know, and beneath the dignity of a charitable man. But I admit to them, anyway.

"Where is Sir John now?" I asked.

"In the kitchen, breaking his fast."

"Tell him I will see him there. Has he had any rest this night?"

"Aye... some. He and his squire sought shelter in a barn at Sherborne."

"We will need bread and meat to sustain us. And ale. 'Tis a hard road to Goodrich this time of year. Tell the cook to prepare food. I will come shortly."

I washed the sleep from my eyes and the dirt from my hands and face in the basin Alice brought. The water was cold, so I was cleansed and completely awakened as well.

I walked across the castle yard to the kitchen, where I knew I would find warmth as well as Sir John, for in the twilight of dawn I saw a vigorous cloud of smoke rise from the kitchen chimney.

Sir John and his squire were chewing on the remains

of the rabbit pies from last night's supper. The pies were cold, but the loaves just set before them were warm, taken from the oven as the morning baking began. I picked a warm loaf from the basket and sat at the table across from Sir John. "Tell me what has happened," I said between mouthfuls of warm bread.

"You know that Lady Joan enjoys the hunt," he commented.

I did.

"And she has a good seat upon a horse... for a lady."

That I also knew.

"Lord Gilbert thinks her over-confident of her skills."

I knew that, as well. And I knew that Lord Gilbert had told her of his opinion. But informing Lady Joan of a conviction which differed from her own was not sure to effect a change in either her views or behavior.

"We were chasing a stag when her horse refused a jump. She was thrown to a wall and put her hands before her to break the fall."

"And broke a wrist?"

"Aye."

"When did this happen?" I asked.

"Two days ago. 'Twas but a few days after they reached Goodrich. Lord Gilbert sent us to fetch you next morning."

"How bad is the fracture? Did you see, or have you been told?"

"'Tis severe. Lady Joan was taken straight away to her chamber. A maid who attends her said the bone broke through the skin."

"Is there no physician nor surgeon near Goodrich?"

"There is," Sir John admitted. "But Lord Gilbert will have you."

Evidently my expression required more from Sir John, for he continued, "There is a man in Gloucester, but Lord Gilbert will not call for him. He is old and knows little of your new knowledge of medicine. And he is reported to be often drunk."

176

"A fracture such as you describe is a serious matter," I admitted.

"Lord Gilbert knows this. That is why he will have you attend Lady Joan and no other."

"And Lady Joan; what does she say?"

"She agrees, and bids you hasten to her."

"I will. I will gather instruments and remedies and meet you at the marshalsea. Oh... tell the boy I'll not take Bruce. The journey to Goodrich will be too hard for the old fellow."

I left Sir John stuffing the last of his rabbit pie into his mouth. Cicily busied herself gathering loaves and two legs of mutton, placing them in a sack.

I would need, in addition to my instruments, salves for healing, potions for relief of pain, and splints and plaster to stabilize the fracture. Egg albumin I could have at Goodrich, other items I must take with me: hemp, willow bark, groundsel, lady's mantle, lettuce, and moneywort would suffice. I stuffed small sacks of each into a leather pouch, along with my implements and a pair of new gloves, wrapped my cloak about me and trotted to the stables.

Castle Goodrich was more than fifty miles from Bampton, but I knew the pain Lady Joan endured and so was determined to be at my destination before evening of the next day. My seat was improving after all my autumn travel, and Sir John and his squire were accustomed to long hours in the saddle. We pushed our horses as hard as we dared and found shelter for the night at St Peter's Abbey in Gloucester. By the sixth hour of the next day, a Sunday, we skirted the Forest of Dean.

Lord Gilbert's castle of Goodrich is built higher and so is more imposing than his residence at Bampton. One enters Goodrich through a gate on the east side in the wall of the barbican, then one must cross the moat, which is cut into the rock of the castle's foundation, on a stone and timber bridge.

We had barely swung from our horses in the barbican

when Lord Gilbert hallowed a greeting from atop the gate-house. Sir John led me across the moat, and Lord Gilbert met me under the raised portcullis, having plunged down the gatehouse stairway.

"How does Lady Joan?" I asked.

Lord Gilbert's face darkened. "Not well. She writhes the night in pain, I am told, and will eat little. Come... see for yourself. She is resting by the fire."

He led me to a small, comfortable, tapestry-hung chamber in the southeast tower. A great blaze warmed and illuminated the room, which was otherwise quite dark, for it was a room low in the tower and so lit only by one narrow, glazed window.

Lady Joan sat between the window and the fire, attended by two maids. I saw in silhouette that her head was thrown back against her chair. Around her neck and right arm a sling of white linen glowed in the firelight. She turned her head as Lord Gilbert closed the door.

"I am sorry," Lady Joan whispered, "to cause you inconvenience. I would have been content with the surgeon from Gloucester, but my brother would have only you."

"To speak truthfully," I replied, "I decided two days past to visit your brother here at my earliest opportunity. I have news of Margaret Smith and the death of Sir Robert Mallory. But first I will deal with your injury."

I turned to Lord Gilbert, who had overheard my words to Lady Joan; he returned my gaze with one uplifted eyebrow. How does he do that, I wondered?

I drew the sling back from Lady Joan's injured wrist and unwrapped the bandage wrapped tightly around it. I was prepared for what I might find, but was not pleased to discover the premonition correct.

The broken bone no longer protruded from the wound, but only because the flesh was purpled and swollen. A mixture of blood and pus stained the bandage as I lifted it from the skin, and Lady Joan drew breath sharply as the removal of the bandage left her hand temporarily unsupported.

"'Tis an evil wound," Lord Gilbert remarked. "I've seen few worse in battle."

I agreed with him absentmindedly while I considered what course I would follow to restore the shattered limb.

"I know," Lord Gilbert spoke again. "You will need wine."

"Aye, that is so, and candles. I must see my work."

"You can set the break?" Lady Joan asked.

I did not know whether I should speak the truth or temporize. I decided on truth. "You have a severe injury. I mean to give you an agent to reduce your suffering and cause drowsiness, but when I attempt to put the break in place you will feel great pain."

Lady Joan nodded, but said nothing.

"It has been four days since you fell from your horse?" I asked. She nodded again.

"A fracture will mend most readily if it is dealt with immediately after the injury. When setting the break is delayed, as in your case, it may be that the bones will refuse to knit, or do so imperfectly." I saw an expression of alarm creep across her face, so I quickly added, "but four days is not so long as to cause serious trouble, I think."

"Imperfectly?" she asked. "What do you mean?"

"The break remains fragile, and easily broken again."

Lady Joan was silent for a moment, then finally spoke again. "And is it possible the break will not join at all?" She cut to the heart of my worry quickly.

"It is... possible... but not likely, I think. You are young and should mend completely." I did not wish to speak of the unsavory potential of such an eventuality.

I ended the conversation and turned to a closer inspection of the injury. I was pleased to see that the swelling and discoloration did not extend past the heel of Lady Joan's hand. I feared the outcome if I found red and purple streaks lacing her palm and fingers. I conducted this examination with as little manipulation of the hand as possible, yet could not prevent inflicting some hurt. Lady Joan winced, and drew a sharp breath, but was otherwise silent. While I worked I heard Lord Gilbert send a serving girl for wine and candles.

"You bear the discomfort well, m'lady," I complimented her.

"'Tis a feature of my sex," she replied with more humor than I could have displayed in the circumstance. "God gave women greater endurance for affliction than men, so we might tolerate bearing children... don't you agree, Master Hugh?"

"Perhaps so you might tolerate the deeds of men, as well," I observed.

"Just so. You speak truth, Master Hugh." I was pleased to hear mirth in her voice.

The servant arrived with wine, and I prepared a draught. I added to the wine ground hemp seeds and root, as I had done for Henry atte Bridge, a pinch of willow, and also added powdered lettuce to bring sleep for Lady Joan when my task was done.

I waited near an hour until I saw her eyes blink to focus and occasionally close, then breathed a prayer for God's guidance and set to my work. Lord Gilbert and Sir John peered over my shoulder as I bathed the oozing wound with wine. Some surgeons might object to close observation of their labor, but I do not. I do good work. I do not care if others wish to observe as I do it.

The swelling of Lady Joan's wrist caused me some difficulty in finding the ends of the fractured bones. I had hoped that only one of the bones of her forearm was broken, but was disappointed to discover that both had been shattered in the fall. Through the injured flesh I sought to position the breaks so that they butted against each other. There would be no healing if I could not do this.

Lady Joan was placid for most of this work. Only when I succeeded in placing bone against bone did she shudder and gasp. I cannot tell if the draught or her nature made her calm. Probably both. Whatever the cause, her tranquility made my task easier.

When the bones were aligned to my satisfaction, I washed the broken skin in wine once more, then stitched closed the wound. You will know I prefer to leave such a wound open to heal, but this I could not do, for a splint was necessary so as to immobilize the wrist until the break should knit. I decided against applying egg albumin to draw pus from the wound. Instead I packed the wrist with moneywort, then wrapped a linen bandage about the sutures.

All that remained was to fix splints about Lady Joan's arm, wrap these in layers of linen strips, then coat the fabric with moistened plaster. Lady Joan had been awake for the procedure to that time, but fell to a restless sleep as I coated the linen with plaster. This was the first use I had made of hemp and lettuce together. I was pleased to see the combination work so well, and determined to use it again when need arose.

"What is your prognosis?" Lord Gilbert asked as I straightened from my work and stretched the tightened muscles of my back.

I watched Lady Joan to be certain that she slept. "She has received a cruel injury," I told him. "There are two dangers we must guard against. We must observe her fingers… if they become streaked with discolor or swollen, I must remove the splints and stiffened linen and deal with the poison."

"And the other danger?"

"The break may not knit. I should not have raised this concern in Lady Joan's hearing."

"Why not? Sir William Caton suffered a broken leg while in my service at Poitiers. He sits a horse today as well as ever he did before."

"Aye, that is common enough, if the fracture is dealt with at once, and by a competent surgeon. But Lady Joan's injury was four days past. Not too long to heal properly, but too far past for me to rest easy until I see signs of success."

"And what if those signs do not come, or her hand becomes discolored and swollen?"

"You ask what is the worst which might occur?"

"I do," Lord Gilbert replied.

"Gangrene. That is the worst."

"Then she would die," Lord Gilbert rubbed his chin, "all because she wished to go a-hunting."

"She might not die."

Lord Gilbert shot me a glance under gathered brows. "How so? 'Tis commonly known to be fatal."

"Unless the gangrenous limb is removed."

"Removed?" he said with incredulity.

"Aye; amputation. If the flesh of Lady Joan's hand should die, that would be the only hope to save her life."

"Might she not die from such surgery?"

"She might. But she would surely die from gangrene. So in such an event she must weigh a certainty against a possibility."

"We must pray," Lord Gilbert sighed, "that such a choice is not presented to us."

"Amen," I agreed. "I have done what I can. Now we must consult your chaplain and have him present the matter to God."

"I will do so. You must stay to watch over Lady Joan, until you are satisfied that great danger is past. I will have a room in the west tower made ready for you. Now, let us withdraw to the solar. I would hear the news of Margaret Smith and Sir Robert."

Lord Gilbert led me through the east range hall and past the chapel to the solar, on the northwest corner of the castle. The east range hall was crowded with poor folk, come to the castle for warmth and food, neither of which they could provide for themselves. There were twenty or more, men and women, old and young, crowded into the hall. Those seated stood, and those standing tugged at their forelocks, as Lord Gilbert strode through the room. He nodded greeting, but otherwise took no notice of his guests. I noticed them, and the smell, which may have been due to the condition of the hall's occupants, or to the proximity to the garderobes.

It was cold in the solar, away from the thin winter sun and with but a small flame on the hearth. Lord Gilbert commanded more fuel be placed on the fire, then dismissed Sir John and bade me sit.

"Now, then, was the lad Thomas Shilton brought to trial?"

"He was, but..."

"Did the king's eyre then find him guilty?"

"Aye, it did so, but..."

"Then he's hung and there's an end to that matter; now, what of Sir Robert?"

"No, m'lord. Thomas Shilton did not hang."

"What?" Then appeared that single lifted eyebrow again. I wondered if others had my success at raising that feature on Lord Gilbert's countenance. "Did he escape? Sir Roger allowed him to escape?"

"No, m'lord. Have patience and I will explain all."

I did. Lord Gilbert did not lift an eyebrow at this tale, but his eyes widened as I related the story.

"So by good fortune you found the lass before Sir Roger could hang a murderer who was not so?"

"Aye; good fortune, or the hand of God in the flawed work of men. A man, I should say, for it was my own flawed work. I thank Him daily that I do not live my life with Thomas Shilton's death troubling my conscience."

"Yes, well, 'tis a good thing to have a conscience susceptible of being troubled."

We sat silently staring into the growing blaze for a moment before Lord Gilbert quietly continued. "Now you must begin this inquiry anew." He went to pulling at his chin. "You must try again to identify the girl found in my castle, and also Sir Robert's murderer."

"I have begun the task already," I told him.

"Oh? Which one?"

"Both, I think, although 'tis hard at present to know of a certainty."

Lord Gilbert caught my meaning. "Ah; you think Sir Robert's death is connected to the body – whoever it was – found in my cesspit?"

"I fear this may be so."

"Then you know who it was found dead in Bampton castle?"

"I suspect. I do not know."

"Who, then? Is she known to me?"

"I have made already one grievous error in your service. I do not wish to make another. For that reason I hope you will, for now, be content with the knowledge I have given you, and the understanding that I will not let the matter rest here."

"You do not trust me with the information," Lord Gilbert frowned. "Then it was someone known to me found in my cesspit?"

"No, trust is not the issue. And no, if the girl was who I think she was, you did not know her, although you have seen her."

"If trust is not at issue, why will you not reveal your suspicions to me?" This Lord Gilbert spoke through pursed lips under a stormy brow. I saw that anger was close under his surface. He was unaccustomed to his employees refusing a request. A lord's request is in fact a demand, as all know who must deal with gentlefolk.

"I beg your leave, m'lord, to withhold my thoughts on the matter a brief time. I fear my own wits may be swayed not by the evidence I uncover, but by the influence of a mind more resolute than my own."

"Hmm... yes, I see. You believe such a thing occurred in the matter of Margaret Smith and Thomas Shilton? That I compelled your mistaken pursuit of the lad?"

"I do not blame you, m'lord. I sought assurance for what I knew otherwise was weak evidence."

"And I was willing to provide it, so that I could then

claim justice done in my demesne. You make a sound argument. Very well, keep your council, but I will be told of your discoveries so soon as you are sure of them!"

"I will do so, m'lord. As soon as I am certain of what I now suspect."

Lord Gilbert dismissed me, and a valet led me through the great hall to the southwest tower, where a circular stairway led to rooms above the pantry and the buttery. "I have laid a fire," he announced as he opened the door.

The room prepared for me was circular, as were others in the towers, and hung with tapestries depicting hunting scenes. There were two glazed windows in this room. It was light and luxurious and warm. A man, I decided, could do worse than spend a fortnight or so in such a place keeping careful watch over a patient like Lady Joan.

Chapter 14

Twice each day I visited Lady Joan in her chamber. For the first two days I left each interview with a sense of optimism, for her progress seemed good. But on the morning of the third day I was alarmed to see what appeared to be reddened stripes on the back of Lady Joan's hand, proceeding from under the stiffened linen.

I tried not to show my unease at this development, and resolved that, three days hence, should the redness increase, I would cut away the plaster and splints to treat the wound with egg albumin so as to draw out the poison.

I was not successful at disguising my concern. On the fourth day, as I inspected her injury late in the afternoon, she confronted me. "You observe something which troubles you, is that not so, Master Hugh?"

"'Tis but a small matter," I lied. "Some discoloration of your hand."

"I saw it appear two days past. I knew it to be worrisome, for I recall your words that discoloration or swelling point to misfortune."

"I thought... I am sorry, m'lady... I thought the draught had done its work, and you were sleeping."

"The draught did cause me to doze, but not so deeply that I could not hear you speak to my brother. I have been watchful since for the signs you warned against. I see but little swelling, and the redness. There has been little change since yesterday."

"I agree. The color does not deepen."

"Is that good, or ill?" she asked.

"Good, m'lady. Very good. It means the toxin does not increase. If it does not advance tomorrow, it will then soon fade."

"I am reassured. Will you take a cup of wine before you go?" she asked. Foolish question. Any excuse to remain longer in her presence was sufficient, a taste of Lord Gilbert's wine all the more so.

"Agnes," Lady Joan turned to her maid. "Fetch wine from the buttery... a flagon... enough for two."

The girl darted off and left us alone. Lady Joan turned in her chair, looked me in the eye, and spoke quietly: "I wish to thank you privily for your care."

I shrugged. "I am pleased to be of service, m'lady." That was no simple pleasantry. I really was.

"A woman of my state is never alone, to speak what she pleases to whom she will and no other."

I knew that was true. Great lords and ladies pay for their position in the coin of privacy. They can neither live nor die alone. Most gentlefolk, I am sure, think this a fair bargain. I could think of no rejoinder to Lady Joan's remark, so remained silent, awaiting illumination. I have learned that when I have nothing to say it is best not to say it.

"My brother would hear of no other surgeon but you to deal with this," she lifted her right arm to punctuate the assertion. "I protested that I wished not to impose such a winter journey on you."

I nodded understanding and said something deprecating the hardships of the journey.

"But," she continued, "my heart was delighted when he insisted, and again when you came."

"I am satisfied if my poor talents may serve you, m'lady."

"Your talents seem to me splendid. Do not belittle yourself so. Modesty is a virtue only when it is honest. I think you know your worth to we who may be ill or injured. And I do not speak only of your talents as a surgeon."

"I have few others," I laughed.

"Ah... you have a talent I think you know not of," she smiled.

This was a puzzle to me. I would have made a witty reply but could think of none. Lady Joan seemed always to have that effect on me. When in her presence I did not think well, and the repartee I should have said came to me only after I was gone from her presence for an hour. "I do?" I muttered.

"Aye. You are a thief of great skill."

"Not so, m'lady. I take from no man what is his," I protested. "Is something from the castle missing? Am I blamed for this? I have heard of no theft!" I protested the accusation with perhaps more warmth than was seemly. She raised the index finger of her uninjured hand to quiet me.

"I do not accuse you of common thievery. Your trespass is of another sort. You steal from ladies."

"But I never... I have not..." I spluttered.

"You mistake me, Master Hugh," she smiled. "You steal only that which they wish to give anon; you steal hearts."

Her words shocked me to renewed silence. I am certain I appeared discomfited. Lady Joan smiled at my stupefaction. I was about to reply when Agnes returned with a tray. Upon it was a pitcher of wine and two goblets. It was well the maid returned just then, else I am sure I should have said something foolish. Why? Because I felt foolish.

Agnes poured wine and we sipped it in silence. I sorted through responses I might make to Lady Joan's assertion but could find none with the combination of wit and solemnity I sought.

"Agnes," Lady Joan called. "Go fetch John and tell him I would have more wood for the fire."

I thought the fire quite suitable, but realized heat was not her goal, although her words warmed me more than the blaze when the girl was again absent.

"You are silent, Master Hugh. Are you offended?"

"Oh, no, m'lady. I... I am often struck dumb in the presence of a beautiful lady."

"You have little opportunity to practice such speech in Bampton," Lady Joan agreed.

"Aye. Nor are scholars at Oxford trained to be students of witty repartee."

"You think my words call for wit," she pouted, "and nothing more?"

"No, m'lady. Such was not my meaning. I..."

"Pray, tell your meaning... your true meaning." She leaned to me as she spoke, and gazed unblinking into my eyes. I blinked.

I thought to change the subject. "Who are these ladies whose hearts I have stolen? None have protested to me, or asked the return."

"They are not few, I am sure, but I know only three of a certainty."

"Are these ladies known to me?" I asked. This was becoming an interesting conversation. I began to see through the fog of metaphor a possible end to my loneliness and single condition.

"They are."

"I would know who I have robbed thusly. Will you tell me?"

"Perhaps I should not. The others might take my words as betrayal." Her hand flew to her lips, and I then realized the significance of the word "others". "And, in truth," she continued, once again composed, "not all are ladies." She smiled at me.

"I am at a loss, and you toy with me," I protested.

"I am sorry," she said. "You would know of whom I speak? Truly?"

"I would, for I have observed no sign of this effect you claim for me over female hearts."

"Well..." she began slowly. "I overheard the new scullery maid say to Cicily that Master Hugh was a grand man and she hoped for a husband like him."

"Alice? A child! And a cotter's daughter. This is a heart I have stolen?"

"Do not belittle her, Master Hugh. A child she may be, but she is woman enough to see what others have seen, but child enough to speak it without reserve."

"I am well rebuked. Alice is a pleasant child... but a child, nonetheless."

"And a cotter's child," Lady Joan reminded me.

"Heaven knows we must not wed outside our station. You, Master Hugh, must find a wife from the gentry, or perhaps the daughter of some landless knight. Is this not so?"

I agreed that convention so limited my choice. "But the others; are they of the station you identified?"

"One is," she admitted. Before I could ask she spoke again.

"There is a merchant in Bampton who has a daughter who thinks highly of you."

I knew of but one merchant in the town who had a daughter of marriageable age. The girl was moderately attractive, but seemed dull of wit. I had never found myself attracted to her.

"And the third lady," I asked, "is she known to me also?"

"She is. She would be better known did not barriers hinder the apprehension."

"And these barriers, may they be overcome?"

Lady Joan sighed. "Perhaps. But the lady cannot surmount such an impediment alone."

"I create no impediment," I protested. "I would seek a consort. I would beat down barriers did I know what they were."

"You are not a bachelor by choice?"

"No, m'lady. I well remember the companionship shared at my parents' hall. I would find the same, but it has eluded me. A solitary life among men and their books holds no attraction."

"You dislike books?" she laughed.

"Not so... but no book will warm a bed of a cold night, nor share my joy and woe."

"Well said, Master Hugh. It is your intent, then, to marry?"

"Aye, should the right lady appear, and she be willing."

"Might the proper lady be unwilling, you think?" she asked.

"I've not found a lady yet, willing or unwilling, so how can I know?"

"How will you recognize this lady?"

"I cannot tell. Until she be known to me, I know not."

"Are you certain?" Lady Joan smiled. "Perhaps she is known to you and you mistake yourself."

"Perhaps. Does love smite a man suddenly, or does it grow slowly, as a vine upon an oak?"

"I have seen men smitten of something all a-sudden," Lady Joan observed.

"Aye. Whatever that is which smites a man has battered me on occasion. But I think 'tis not love."

"Oh? What, then may this be? When did this last occur?"

My face felt warm, but I answered her. "I think, m'lady, it is desire which so attacks a man."

"And when did this fiend last assault you, Master Hugh?"

I stood, took two paces toward the door, then turned and told her truthfully, "When I last entered this room, m'lady."

I walked quickly to the door and escape, but as I approached it swung open and a servant appeared behind an armload of wood.

We startled each other, and he dropped his burden. On my toes. I jumped back in pain and surprise and might have cursed but remembered the presence of a lady.

"Pardon, Master Hugh," John stammered. "Didn't know as you was there. You're all right, then?"

I assured him my toes remained serviceable and helped him gather the scattered logs. While I collected wood I stole a glance at Lady Joan. She grinned at me behind an uplifted hand, and when she saw me peek in her direction, she fluttered her fingers. And then – I am sure of this, though the time was late and the day grew dim – she blew a kiss.

I escaped through the great hall, where Lord Gilbert's valets were erecting trestle tables for supper. I had lost my appetite. I should say I had lost my appetite for food. Nevertheless, I met Lady Joan again an hour later when a horn announced the evening meal.

Since my arrival four days earlier I had been assigned a place at the high table beside Sir John Withington. This was an honor. I was the only layman placed there. My seat was at the far left of the table. On the far right, beyond her brother and next to Lord Gilbert's chaplain, sat Lady Joan.

Some lords use every meal as an opportunity to display their plenty. Not so Lord Gilbert, who, as I have related, could be parsimonious. His dinner table was as lavish as any other, but he thought supper should be a lighter meal. This was acceptable to me that day in particular; my stomach was churning, for reasons you will understand.

I sat before the trencher assigned to me, and washed my hands when servants brought pitcher and towel. Sir John had suffered no event that day to reduce his hunger, so sliced off a large chunk of bread when loaves and butter were brought to the table.

I remember the meal well. Even now, so long after, it is as if I could sit at the table and relive each course. The first dish was a pea soup; hot, to warm a man on a cold winter eve. The second remove was likewise simple; a dish of squabs and eels. The eels were caught fresh in the River Severn and brought to Goodrich that day. I saw the barrels unloaded from a cart that afternoon. There was ale, of course, and cheese, and to conclude, a dish of baked apples and pears freely sprinkled with spices from Lord Gilbert's cellar. At the conclusion of the meal, valets brought goblets of hypocras to us who sat at the high table. Others in the hall, the commons and the poor (who had received no squab, either), had more ale poured into their earthen cups.

During the meal I had opportunity to turn in conversation to Sir John, who sat to my right. When I could do so without his notice, I peered beyond him, past Lady Petronilla and Lord Gilbert, to Lady Joan, who plucked with dainty fingers at her squab.

It seemed to me that each time I stole a glance at her she was aware of it, and lifted her eyes to mine. How she could feel my gaze I cannot tell, for when I bent round Sir John to view her, I never found her already engaged at looking in my direction. She always caught my eyes on her, rather than the other way round. How she contrived to do this I know not. I think it an intuition of the female sex – to know when a man's eyes have fallen on them.

The diners departed the hall when the meal was done, the commons to the east range hall or the huts in the castle yard. We who sat at the high table made our way to the solar, where a great fire had been laid in the fireplace. Lord Gilbert and Sir John fell to conversation about some unrest on the Welsh border. There is always unrest on the Welsh border. It provides ample topic for discourse if no other offers. An outlaw, or patriot, depending on whether one was English or Welsh, was vexing the country to the west of Abergavenny. I listened, half awake, staring into the fire, until Lady Joan addressed me.

"Master Hugh, do scholars from Oxford learn chess?"

"They do, m'lady... some better than others."

"I should like to know how well you were taught. Will you give me a match?"

Chess is a man's diversion. But I was trapped. How could I deny her? I agreed. Lord Gilbert looked up from his conversation with furrowed brow as we began.

She defeated me in the first match. I would go on the attack, about to seize a bishop or rook, when she would find a chink in my defense and capture my attacker.

"'Tis an admirable flaw in a man," she observed after vanquishing me, "to be aggressive in pursuit of a goal. We women, being weak, must always look to our defenses. Would you not agree, Master Hugh?"

I agreed. I would have even had I thought her in error. But she spoke truth, and, I thought, imparted a message. I hoped so.

I won the second match. She seemed close to victory twice, but each time I was able to salvage my position with adroit moves. Whether they were my adroit moves, or hers, I know not. It may be that she allowed me to win.

I thanked Lady Joan for the entertainment and stood to retire. But before I could depart she asked if I thought it not wise to inspect her injured hand and arm once again before withdrawing. I agreed, and we approached the fire, where the blaze would allow more light on her hand. We stood nearly inside the great fireplace. Its warmth was intoxicating. Or was it the nearness of Lady Joan? I know not.

She held her wounded arm out in its sling and I took her hand for a careful and perhaps overlong examination. I was pleased to see that what redness was there seemed more a product of the glow of the fire than any toxin. I held her fingers for this close inspection, but when I had finished she would not be released.

"You will call on me tomorrow? To again measure my recovery?"

"Aye, m'lady... at the third hour, as today, if so be that is well with you."

"Very well, Master Hugh." I felt her gently squeeze my fingers before she dropped her hand. I turned to watch her as she summoned her maid and left the solar.

My eyes followed her form as she faded into the darkened south end of the solar. While my eyes followed her, Lord Gilbert's eyes followed me. I turned from the south door to the settle where he sat with Sir John and saw that, while he listened to Sir John, he observed me.

I nodded and approached. When Sir John finished his point, I spoke: "M'lady's hurt does better, m'lord. I was troubled yesterday... even this morning. But now I think the toxin recedes and we may expect good progress."

"You have been diligent," he said with that eyebrow in upraised position, "in observing your patient."

"It is my duty, and a service to which I am obligated."

"Yes. Onerous, no doubt, but you will perform it nonetheless."

"No, m'lord. Lady Joan is not a troublesome patient."

"No. I have observed. She is troublesome in another fashion."

And with that remark Lord Gilbert turned back to the fire and his conversation with Sir John. I bid him goodnight, but he took no notice. Lady Petronilla sat opposite the men before the fire, her nimble fingers occupied at some work of embroidery. I bid her goodnight also. She replied with a nod and a smile.

I saw Lord Gilbert next morning. We met as I made my way through the castle yard to call on Lady Joan. I think now he watched and waited to catch me there as I passed.

"Ah... Master Hugh. We are well met. You slept well?"

"I did, m'lord." Actually I had not slept well, but to say so might mean having to explain why I had not. As the matter concerned Lady Joan, this I was unwilling to do.

"You go to attend my sister?"

"I do, m'lord."

"I think, if she does well today and the morrow you may be released from duty here and return to Bampton. Do you agree?"

"Aye. If the toxin has gone by tomorrow I will have little work here. Nature must do the work now I have set it in motion."

"And I would have you again employed seeking a murderer... two murderers."

"That is a labor which nature will not accomplish on its own," I agreed.

Lady Joan awaited me in her chamber. I was pleased to see both the lady and her hand. Both looked remarkably well. Almost no discoloration appeared beneath the stiffened linen, and the swelling which had burst up from under the plaster was reduced as well.

"I improve daily, don't you agree, Master Hugh? And the hurt is much reduced. I think I will not need your draught today."

I did agree, although there were certain things about Lady Joan which would have been difficult to improve upon. I thought this, but did not say it, coward that I am.

"I am well pleased. I think you are out of danger. I will return to Bampton on Monday and see to my duties there. You have no more need of surgeon or physician until the splint must be removed."

She looked out the single narrow window of her chamber, across a snow-dusted meadow to the forest beyond. "It is an ill season to travel. I am sorry to have been the cause of your discomfort."

"It has been my pleasure to serve you, m'lady," I replied in my most chivalrous tone. This was not counterfeit. I much enjoyed Lady Joan's company, even if she did vanquish me at chess. Her beauty was surely appealing, but I was learning to admire other qualities as well.

"I think you should remain 'til Christmas is past," she said suddenly. "'Tis but two weeks hence. My brother will offer a feast, and has already procured entertainers. Bampton will be quiet and you will be quite alone there. That should not be at Christmas."

I found the offer appealing, but was not sure Lord Gilbert would.

"I have duties in Bampton which call me, m'lady."

"What is there which cannot wait a fortnight?"

"Your brother has charged me with finding two murderers. Thus far I have failed him."

"Ah, yes. Petronilla told me of the young man you saved from hanging, and the girl who was dead but found alive and well. I congratulate you, Master Hugh. You have skills to save life in many ways."

"I must be frank, m'lady..."

"You generally are, Master Hugh. I find that appealing."

I think I blushed. My face felt suddenly warm. Standing before a draughty window as I was would not be the cause of that.

"The youth... who was to hang... it was my faulty witness which put him near the noose, so 'tis not quite proper to say I saved him. More truthful to say I saved myself from terrible error."

"It is a measure of a man that he is able to see and correct his faults. Many men cannot, or will not." She laughed quietly to herself. "My brother would have me wed one of them anyway, so be it they have lands and a title."

She had steered the conversation in a direction I had no wish to follow. Her remark, however, made it clear that no other direction would be ultimately pleasing, for I had neither lands nor title, and was not likely ever to have either. I admit that since the previous day I had entertained thoughts of Lady Joan as my wife – foolish as I knew that hope to be. I thought her words and behavior indicated a disposition in her to consider it as well, although why such as she would consider a poor surgeon, her brother's bailiff, for a husband I did not understand. I did not want to understand, for then I would recognize the foolish nature of the hope rising in me overnight.

The blast of a horn from the yard indicated a groom calling castle residents to dinner.

"I will speak to my brother... you will remain 'til Christmas." She said this with much assurance. I bowed and followed her out the door into the east range hall. The poor lodged there were arranging themselves to follow us as we passed through the hall. Many spoke soft words of greeting or bowed or curtsied in obeisance as Lady Joan passed.

I noted several times during the meal when Lady Joan was in deep conversation with her brother. A harpist played at the conclusion of the meal to accompany a final goblet of spiced wine.

"Master Hugh!" Lord Gilbert called as I rose from my place. "Will you accompany me to the solar?" Of course I would, but a true gentleman's demand is always voiced as a request.

"Lady Joan," he began, when we entered that small, comfortable room, "castigates me for a lack of hospitality. I am unfair, she complains, to send you back to Bampton when you might remain to celebrate Christmas here."

I made no reply. Lord Gilbert's desire for an employee to return to work and earn his keep did not seem to me unreasonable, yet I did wish to enjoy the holiday at Goodrich.

"I am inclined to agree with her, though I think her concern of another nature than she claimed... do you agree, Master Hugh?"

"I... uh... esteem Lady Joan's thoughtfulness."

"You do, no doubt," he laughed. "A politic answer. By heaven, you should have been a bishop."

"M'lord, I am confused..."

"Aye. Well, so am I. But you may stay, if you wish, 'til St Stephen's Day."

"I am much in your debt, m'lord."

"Hmm... well, you have given me good service and I will expect the more."

"You shall receive all in my poor power to give, m'lord," I replied.

"Spare me your humility," he grunted. "I will be the judge of your poor powers to serve. Modesty becomes a man only when 'tis not hollow.

"There is a service you may perform for me while you linger here," he continued.

"I am at your command," I replied in my most ministerial tone. Lord Gilbert continued as if he had heard nothing.

"A guest will arrive next Wednesday. It is Ember Day,

but there's no helping that. Sir Charles de Burgh will remain through the Feast of the Holy Innocents."

"I will be pleased to do Sir Charles whatever service I can," I replied to this announcement.

"Oh, 'tis not him needs your service. I do, and Lady Joan, although she knows it not… yet. I have invited Sir Charles as I would have him meet Lady Joan. I charge you to observe the man closely; watch if he may make a good husband for my sister."

"You do not know Sir Charles?" I asked.

"Only by reputation."

"And what is that?" I queried.

"He has estates in two shires and is reputed to be a man of valor, although he was too young to serve the king at Poitiers, and since the Treaty of Calais has had no opportunity to show his mettle on the field, or to take profitable hostages."

"A pity," I commiserated.

"Lady Joan," Lord Gilbert continued, "tries me. I cannot force her to marry, and would not if I could, but she will not choose. So where am I, then? What will she have me do? Compel her to choose?"

I thought how unlikely it was that Lady Joan would be compelled in any such matter, but did not need to say so.

"I know, you need not remind me. My sister is not a lady to be coerced to anything, especially marriage. But she seems," he continued, almost plaintively, "to ignore my concern. It is for her benefit. She must find a husband who has lands, for she will inherit none. Where will she go, I ask, if she does not marry well? To an abbey? I would not see my sister a pauper; would you?"

I agreed that such would be a sorry future.

"She thinks not of these practical things," he continued. "But fortunately for her, I am a man of practical notions, else she would, were not someone wiser to guide her, marry some penniless scholar from Oxford or some such foolishness. That would bring her a life of misery and lost rank. She would ever rue her choice. Do you not agree, Master Hugh?"

I agreed, for I received his message clearly. He knew what he had observed, and was not pleased.

I saw Lady Joan twice each day in that week. Our conversations centered on the mending of her fractured wrist, for when I perceived the subject shifting I brought it back to the reason for my visits to her chamber, or devised some appointment which called me away.

Did I think her dull, that she would not remark the change in me and wonder at it? No; I hoped she might rather think me frightened of my quest, or too timid to pursue her.

Wednesday was Ember Day, which made little difference in dinner. Like many in the kingdom, Lord Gilbert and his household always kept Wednesday as a day of abstinence, serving but one dish of meat at midday, and one of fish at supper. This day, fish was offered at both meals, with bread and ale, but no wine.

I peered about cautiously as I entered the hall that noon, searching for the favored Sir Charles, or an extra place at the high table. I saw neither at noon, but in mid-afternoon, as I was about to call again on Lady Joan, I heard a commotion in the barbican and guessed what it might portend.

The noise was due in part to hounds, for Sir Charles arrived with four, a handler, and a brace of squires. Lord Gilbert, I learned later, had praised the hunting in the Forest of Dean, and Sir Charles was keen for hawking and hunting wherever he might travel.

I saw no reason to greet this new guest, so made my way to Lady Joan's chamber. The visit was becoming ritual, as for the past two days there was nothing new to learn of either her wrist or her opinions. I concentrated my attention on the first and avoided as best I could the other.

The window of Lady Joan's chamber looked out over the rock-cut moat. By pressing one's face to the glazing and looking to the left one could just see the barbican gate to the castle and the tumult created by the new guest and his retinue.

Sir Charles de Burgh was a tall man. I could see from even that distance that he was a head taller than his host. When greetings were done Lord Gilbert led him across the moat and out of sight of the narrow window.

"Has my future husband arrived?" Lady Joan asked with a tinge of sarcasm.

"Uh... Sir Charles de Burgh, your brother named him."

"And that is all he told you, Master Hugh?"

I could not look her in the eye, so dropped my gaze to the floor at her feet. "No," I replied, and was silent.

"What did Lord Gilbert say of Sir Charles?"

"Did he not tell you of him, and his visit?" I replied.

"I knew he was coming, and could guess why. He has invited so many men to table that I become acquainted with his purpose."

"Sir Charles has estates in two shires, I am told, and is said to be valorous... and fond of hunting and hawking, as you are, m'lady." I said this with a glance at her sling-supported right arm.

"Ah, estates. Well, then, he must be a suitable husband. Little else matters to my brother."

"He has your interest at heart, m'lady."

"Truly?" She turned on me with flashing eyes. "Does my brother know my interests?"

"He believes so."

"Aye. I suppose he does, in the way powerful men know what is best for others."

"And powerful ladies?" I asked.

"Them, also," she agreed.

"Them?"

"All right... we," she admitted. "But even the weak can know that which others should do before they know themselves."

"They can," I agreed. "But they have not the authority to command others to their will. There is the difference."

"So you," she asked, suddenly very quiet, "know what I should do? But unlike my brother, you will not... cannot... command me."

"Lord Gilbert will not command you to marry."

"I know. But he will make strong suggestion," she smiled.

"There are times when the suggestions of others may help us to see our course more clearly," I observed.

"Perhaps. So I will ask you again, do you know what I should do?"

"I would never direct a lady. Especially when I have made so many mistakes in my own course."

"But you have chosen well," she objected. "You are a surgeon... you give relief and aid to all, as I can attest." She held her right arm before me.

"You forget Thomas Shilton," I replied.

Lady Joan turned from me to peer out the narrow window to the fields and forest beyond. "My brother suggests that if I do not soon choose a husband, I will lose the bait with which I may attract a worthy one."

"You need not worry of that for many years," I assured her.

"You think not? Why, Master Hugh, I believe that was a compliment."

I felt my cheeks go red, and redder yet as she approached me.

"I have heard it said that men fall in love with their eyes. Is this so, Master Hugh?"

"I believe so, m'lady."

"So, then, have you ever been in love?"

"Several times, m'lady. My vision is acute."

"It should be so easy for a woman," Lady Joan remarked pensively. "My brother has sent many comely men for me to consider."

"But you chose none... as yet."

"Nor am I likely to choose among those he has presented."

"How, then, does a lady fall in love?" I asked.

"Does it matter?" she replied. "To love, I mean."

"If not love, what, then?" I wondered aloud.

"Why... lands, of course," she shuddered involuntarily.

"So then a lady falls in love with her purse?"

"You mistake me, Master Hugh, though some ladies do, I think."

"What else, then?"

"Ears, Master Hugh. I think the man I love will be he who speaks the truth to me... and others. He must win my ears."

"Some ladies might prefer not to hear truth on all occasions. Will you find such a man?"

She turned back to the gray view from her window. "I think so," she said. "What good may it do me I know not."

There followed an awkward moment, as Lady Joan made no more comment and I could think of no suitable reply.

"Your wrist does well, m'lady, so I will take my leave. I will call again tomorrow at the third hour."

"You are very kind, Master Hugh." She spoke without turning from the window. Over her shoulder, in the twilight of late afternoon, I saw snow begin to drift across the meadow from a pewter sky.

Lady Joan was, of course, seated next to Sir Charles de Burgh at that Ember Day supper. As it was a fast day, the meal was simple: bread, fish, glazed eggs, and a tart of currants. I peeked at Lady Joan and her companion frequently during the meal and was annoyed to see them apparently enjoying each other's company.

Chapter 15

I visited Lady Joan twice each day, as was my practice, Thursday, Friday, and Saturday, but saw Sir Charles only rarely. When I did converse with him I discovered that his conversation was pleasing, his manner polite, his face handsome, and his shape manly. I began to dislike him.

As I was Lord Gilbert's guest, I attended mass with him and his family, rather than attending his nearby Walford village church. Sir Charles and Lady Joan sat together – Lord Gilbert had installed benches in his chapel – and conversed rather more freely than I thought meet throughout the service. This they continued at dinner. They were yet deep in conversation when I called at Lady Joan's chamber at the ninth hour to again inspect her wrist. What they found to speak of I know not, but truth to say, Sir Charles surely had Lady Joan's ear.

While I attended Lady Joan, Sir Charles busied himself at the window which looked out across the meadow and the barbican. A distant ruckus penetrated the apartment, and Sir Charles craned his neck so as to look to his left and observe the barbican and the tumult there. Lady Joan and I looked up from her wrist as Sir Charles turned from the window.

"The entertainers have arrived, I think," he said.

"Ah... yes..." Lady Joan responded. "My brother was so taken with their performance last spring that he engaged them for the feast tomorrow."

"These entertainers," I asked, "what do they do? Are they musicians?"

"Oh, no... well, one plays a pipe. They are acrobats and jugglers and the like."

"When did Lord Gilbert see them first?"

"'Twas Whitsuntide, I think. They set up in Bampton

town market. Lord Gilbert brought them to the castle next day."

Sir Charles had left the window, so I replaced him there and bent my head so as to see the barbican and the bridge. I caught a glimpse of the thick-necked wrestler as he disappeared from view across the moat, leading a horse which pulled a cart full of the troupe's possessions. The horse was large and strong, a destrier worth £40 or more. Tossing knives into the air, wrestling all comers, and doing marvelous acrobatic tricks must pay well, I reflected.

"I was told," I remarked with as little concern in my voice as I could restrain, "that there was some unpleasantness when this troupe left Bampton."

Lady Joan seemed surprised at my remark, but answered plainly enough. "The leader lost two of his performers, I think. In the morning, as they were to depart, a lad and a lass were gone; they had run off in the night, I believe. The lass was said to be the leader's daughter."

"They ran off together?" I asked.

"'Twould seem so."

"I wonder how they escaped the castle at night, with the gate closed and the portcullis down. The porter heard nothing?"

"No. My brother questioned him quite sharply, but he was not found to be at fault in his duty. He was old, and could neither hear nor see so well as a youth."

"Hmmm... is that why Lord Gilbert put Wilfred in the post?"

"I think so, perhaps."

"They are not the first," Sir Charles chuckled, "nor will they be the last, to run off to begin a life together."

I agreed, excused myself, and wondered if there was yet another set of bones to discover.

A horn awakened me at midnight and I tottered sleepily to the chapel for Angel's Mass. It seemed to me I had barely returned to sleep when another blast awakened me for Shepherd's Mass, at dawn.

The dawn was foggy and dim, but by the fifth hour an occasional glimpse of blue promised clearing sky and a fine day to celebrate our Savior's birth. I looked forward to the feasting which would come, but not, I admit, to the other business now thrust upon me.

For without my contrivance Lord Gilbert had set before me the opportunity, if I acted wisely, to settle the business of three murders; or four, if the missing lad be added to the list.

I spent most of Christmas morning inventing and casting aside stratagems while staring out my chamber window. Once, through the fog, I watched a doe step from the forest to test the misty meadow. She found it unsatisfactory, and soon turned back into the trees and was gone from sight.

Shortly after the cautious doe slipped back into the forest I heard the horn again, this time announcing dinner. The great hall was filled when the company was gathered, warmed by both the Yule log blazing behind Lord Gilbert, and the swarm of guests. The hall was hung with holly, ivy, and pine boughs from the nearby forest. Indeed, these decorations had been accumulating since St Catherine's Day, before I arrived at Goodrich. Although, of course, no holly was permitted in the hall 'til Christmas Eve, when the great Yule log was lit.

I wished to enjoy myself, but my stomach was knotted, for at the far end of the high table Lady Joan and Sir Charles were in animated conversation, oblivious to all others in the hall. This time she did not look up to observe me when my eyes fell on her. And at the far end of the hall, seated with invited tenants of Lord Gilbert's Goodrich holdings, I saw the troupe of entertainers.

The wonderful feast and convivial atmosphere were lost on me. Wherever I looked there was a scene to cause me disquiet. Should I gaze to my right, past the Christmas Candle placed before Lord Gilbert and Lady Petronilla, I saw Lady Joan and Sir Charles. When I looked out across the hall I saw the entertainers. So I spent most of the meal turned to my left, observing closely the stonework of the inner wall.

But I do remember the meal. No worry puts me off my hunger for long, and Lord Gilbert's cooks excelled in their work for the holy day. Lord Gilbert's chaplain began with the Pater Noster, and a page entered carrying aloft a boar's head on a platter. This he set before Lord Gilbert and Lady Petronilla, to much mirth and applause.

The first remove followed, and I permitted myself a portion of each dish: there was beef in pepper sauce, roasted capon, a pea and barley soup, and Lombardy custard. The subtlety was a miniature forest of whipped butter and honey.

My table companion, Sir John Withington, proposed a toast to Lord Gilbert between the first and second removes. His words met with hearty approval, for the largesse shown, and yet to come. Those at the high table lifted cups of wine, and the commons in the hall raised their mugs of ale, to drink to the health and long life of Lord Gilbert Talbot.

The second remove included venison, both roasted and in frumenty, roasted cranes and peacocks, a meat and fruit tart, and leech custard of dates and wine. I do not remember the subtlety, because of what occurred next.

Between the second and third removes Lord Gilbert made a dignified speech welcoming all to his table and celebration. It was a speech he had made many times at Christmases past, and it evoked little comment, but polite applause when he had done.

I was idly gazing out over the throng – the high table was on a platform raised perhaps one foot above the floor of the hall, permitting anyone seated there to see and be seen – when the applause for Lord Gilbert's oration, which had nearly died, rose to a new crescendo. All eyes seemed directed to the opposite end of the high table, so mine were drawn there also. Sir Charles de Burgh was standing at his place. As I watched, he smiled and held before him a pear studded with cloves. All who saw this act, including me, knew what it meant, and what he would do with it next.

He turned to Lady Joan, bowed, and presented the fruit to her. She smiled, took the pear, lifted it to her mouth, and with her teeth extracted a clove. The laughter and applause thundered to a climax. Lord Gilbert was particularly enthusiastic. I feigned delight and clapped loudly with the others. What else could I do? I knew then that I would soon wear the willow.

My mind drifted back to the vision of Father Aymer bending over my dying brother, his spice bag swaying out from his chest as he spoke the words of extreme unction. The smell of cloves within the bag had permeated the air then, and I caught a whiff of the pungent odor as the pear was placed on the high table before the smiling couple. The smell of cloves has since reminded me of loss and I like not a dish prepared with this seasoning.

The third remove seemed not so tasty as the first two; perhaps I had eaten enough and lost my appetite. There was fruit in comfit, partridge, glazed meat apples, rabbits, and the pièce de résistance, the roasted boar. So great was this beast that four grooms were required to bring it from the kitchen. Even when all had eaten their fill, there would be plenty to distribute to the poor this day. The subtlety was a glazed copy of Goodrich castle, made of gingerbread.

For the last remove, by which time I was unable to consume more than a few bites, there were glazed eggs, doves, custard and marrow tarts, a quiche with currants and dates, and for the last subtlety a pie, which when opened revealed four and twenty blackbirds molded of dates, apples, and honey. This was for the high table; there was also a cherry pottage for the others in the hall.

It was well past the ninth hour when the final remove was taken away and the table cleared. Torches were lighted and fixed to the walls to assist the dying afternoon sun.

The first entertainers were a group of mummers from

Walford and Coughton, who portrayed St George, the slain dragon, and the villainous Turk with amateurish enthusiasm. Then came the wrestler's troupe. The jugglers amazed all, as did the knife-thrower and the contortionist. The wrestler did not voice a challenge this day, but directed his entourage from the side of the great hall. As at Oxford three weeks before, the contortionist finished the program. I thought she seemed a little more capable, supple and smooth in her manipulations, than a month before.

It was the twelfth hour, and time for the Mass of the Divine Word, when the girl completed her last pose – to the accompaniment of more booming applause and shouts of approval.

When mass was done, the gentlefolk repaired to the solar for games and conversation, and though I am but of the middling sort, Lord Gilbert invited me to join them. He was, I think, feeling especially expansive after what he had seen between the second and third removes. Because I had observed the same scene, I had no great desire to attend the group. I wished rather to speak to the bull-necked wrestler.

I found him in the marshalsea, attending his horses, requesting they be made ready at dawn of the morrow. One of the beasts, I have noted, was an uncommonly fine animal, large and strong. A dexter, certainly, suitable for a knight more than a troupe of itinerant jugglers and acrobats.

"You are off to another engagement, then?" I asked.

The wrestler turned to peer at me through the dim light provided by the two cressets which lit the stables through the night.

I introduced myself as Lord Gilbert's surgeon – not his bailiff – as I wanted no hint of my purpose to put the fellow on his guard. One did not labor long at his business without learning to be on guard. And I was not bailiff at Goodrich, anyway.

"Not an engagement, like... not like as this. We're off to Gloucester, an' maybe Bristol. Set up in t'marketplace an' the town'll allow."

"Do some not permit?"

"Oh, aye... there's some. But we had success at Gloucester last year. Never tried Bristol, but there'll be money to be made there, I think."

"Sailors will challenge you."

"I trust so," he grinned.

"Some will be stout lads," I remarked.

"All the better. Better odds when t'others take bets."

"You've a new girl... since you were at Bampton at Whitsuntide."

The wrestler's demeanor changed, as I knew it would. "Aye," was all he replied.

"I was not in Bampton then. I saw you first at Oxford a month ago. The new girl, she performs amazing feats."

"Aye, she does well."

"But not so good as the other girl, I am told."

"No, not yet, but she learns. By summer she will do as well... for a few years."

"A few years?" I questioned.

"Aye. No wench lasts long at her trade. They become women and can no longer bend as when they were but children."

"The other girl; I was told she was your daughter."

The wrestler was silent for a moment, turned to inspect his horse, then replied, "Aye... she was."

"And she ran off with a lad you wished her not to marry?"

The wrestler's eyes narrowed. He hesitated again. "That's so. You know much about me and mine."

"Local gossip," I shrugged. "Have you news of your daughter since that day?"

"Nay. Perhaps one day she will find me."

"But you travel about. How will she do that?"

It was his turn to shrug. "She'll find a way."

"When you left Bampton, at Whitsuntide, where did you travel next?"

He turned to inspect a harness, then said, "Can't recall... 'twas six months and more past."

"Did you travel the north road, perhaps to Witney?"

"Might have done. We played at Witney, I think. Did not do well there, so went on directly... went to Banbury. Did well there."

"Did you find a new contortionist soon?"

"Nay. 'Twas a month an' more afore we found Agnes."

"How old is the girl?"

"She knows not... fourteen, perhaps fifteen."

"How old was your daughter... when she ran off?"

He turned back to me, his voice softer. "Seventeen, she was... an' a mind of her own."

"On your way from Bampton, the day you left for the north, did you notice along the road any sign of conflict... of a fight?"

I watched carefully for any sign that the question was uncomfortable for him, and was rewarded. I saw, in the light from the cressets, his back stiffen and the muscles of his jaw go tight.

"Nay. Saw nothin' like that. Why do you ask?"

"A gentleman's cotehardie, and a dagger, were found along the track north from Bampton some months ago. The look of things seemed to betoken a struggle, in which the cotehardie was discarded and the dagger lost."

"Nay. Saw no fight, or hint of one," he said, and to end the conversation he turned to the harness and began to rub tallow into the leather.

As I left the stable I passed an occupied stall from which came a muffled whinny and a stamping of hoofs. I peered through the dark over the half-door and saw two large eyes looking back at me from either side of a white blaze which ran from between the animal's ears to its nose. It was the great horse I had seen from Lady Joan's window when the wrestler's troupe arrived on Christmas Eve.

As I studied the beast the wrestler passed me on his way to the castle yard and his tent.

"A fine animal," I commented.

"Aye, he is that. Too fine for me, you think?" The wrestler seemed agitated at my observation and I looked about to see if any were near enough to hear, should I need help. And if the man took offense at my words and decided to attack, I would certainly need help. I tried to soothe him.

"Not at all... I... I think you and your cohorts are much skilled at what you do. You must reap great rewards. Enough to buy a fine animal such as this."

"Won 'im," the man said gruffly.

"Oh?" My favorite question, again.

"We was in Winchester at Corpus Christi. A young gentleman brought his villein to challenge me. Big, strong lad. The young lord bet large, but I defeated his man. He could not pay, so I took his horse in fee."

"I see. A valuable animal, worth forty pounds, perhaps more," I calculated.

"Aye. He be an insurance policy, like. An' we hit a streak o' bad luck, I can sell 'im an' keep us fed 'til better days."

With that the wrestler turned and left the marshalsea. I followed him out, but we turned in opposite directions. He joined the tents of his troupe in the northwest corner of the castle yard. I directed my feet to the inner yard, and found Lord Gilbert's chamberlain. I told him I wished a word with Lord Gilbert on a matter of some importance.

Lord Gilbert appeared at the door to the solar a few minutes later. He seemed a bit unsteady and quite jovial.

"What? Master Hugh! You will not join us?"

"I thank you, m'lord, but I wished to be about other business this night."

"Business? What business? It's Christmas; a time for pleasure, not business."

"Yes, and so this day has been..."

"It has, indeed," he interrupted.

"But I wished to be about some tasks I owe you before the day passes."

"Eh? What work do you owe me which cannot wait until the morrow?"

"I wish for you to look at a horse, then I will tell you."

"A horse? Where? When?"

"Here, in the marshalsea... and now, if you will."

"Is a horse of mine ill? Surely the farrier will deal with it?"

"No, not that. I would have you view a horse belonging to the acrobats. To learn if you have seen it before."

Lord Gilbert, like most of his class, considered himself a judge of horses, hounds, and falcons, and in his case there was justification for his attitude. He gave as much attention to a fine horse as to a fair lass.

He followed me, a bit unsteadily, across the muddy yard to the marshalsea. I led him to the stall containing the wrestler's fine beast. The horse had withdrawn to a far corner of the stall, but when we stopped before the door he moved to face us. Perhaps he expected a carrot, or a measure of oats.

"Should I have seen this animal before?" Lord Gilbert asked. "'Tis an uncommon fine one, for such as have it, don't you think?"

I agreed. I did not wish to sow a seed of suspicion in Lord Gilbert which might grow to a plant with bitter fruit, so I did not voice the apprehension I felt about the horse's history.

Lord Gilbert opened the stall door and approached the animal. He inspected the white blaze down its forehead, then bent to the left foreleg and hoof, also white.

"A fine beast. But, you ask, have I seen it before? I cannot say with a surety. I think I may have done. What is your interest in this horse, Master Hugh?"

"I would not like to say yet... only to know if you have seen the animal before."

I feared that, in his condition, Lord Gilbert might not remember well. Or that he might recall that which never occurred. There was much good wine in the solar this night, I felt certain.

"I have," he said finally, and with some conviction. "The blaze and hoof I know. This is Sir Robert Mallory's horse, or its twin."

The wine-induced haze which had afflicted him seemed abruptly gone. Lord Gilbert's eye was sharp and his speech suddenly clear. "These jugglers and acrobats know something of Sir Robert. Perhaps they came on his murder and drove off the thieves."

"Perhaps," I agreed.

"Ah... yes..." Lord Gilbert continued, pulling on his chin, an arm draped over the stall door, "I see how it might have happened. The thieves attacking Sir Robert suddenly found themselves outnumbered and ran off. These jongleurs found themselves in possession of the field, and so, poor men that they are, seized the spoil.

"But," he continued, "if so be it happened that way, who buried poor Sir Robert and his squire?" Lord Gilbert answered his own question. "Thieves would not return to do so. The wrestler's men must have done it. They surely believed the taking of dead men's goods to be criminal, and wished to avoid discovery. What think you, Master Hugh? Mayhap the affair followed that course?"

"Perhaps," I agreed. "But it would be well not to speak of this to anyone. I wish to question their leader, the wrestler, more closely on this matter. I would not have him aware of our suspicion and so prepare a fable to divert our pursuit of truth.

"I believe," I continued, "that the troupe might be persuaded to remain here another day. The wrestler told me they have no appointment. They will go to Gloucester to seek profit in the market there. Direct your chamberlain to retain them for another performance for St Stephen's Day. Offer them good pay and I'm certain the troupe will stay."

"You are free with my money, Master Hugh. But I will

do it. One day will be enough to get to the truth of the matter, you think?"

"If I seek truth properly, with true questions, one hour will suffice. If I do not, the next year will not be time enough."

"Then, Master Hugh, think carefully how you will proceed. I will send the chamberlain to do as you ask."

"Direct him to do so now, and report the wrestler's answer to me this night. I will await his tidings in my chamber."

"Very well. Good night, then, Master Hugh. And may the saints attend you on the morrow."

I lit a candle from coals in my chamber fireplace and waited for news from the chamberlain. The wrestler must have accepted Lord Gilbert's offer readily, for the chamberlain rapped at my door but half an hour later with word that the troupe would be pleased to perform again on St Stephen's Day.

Lord Gilbert was firm that those in his household observe the liturgical hours. So I arose before the first hour, while it was yet dark – though a faint glow above the eastern forest showed that day was not far off – washed myself, and made my way to the chapel. Phillip, the chaplain, and Ralph, the clerk, were already at their preparations for matins, and others of the household filed sleepily in after me, with much yawning and staring at the candle flames. The Christmas festivities, I guessed, went on late into the night. Lady Joan and Sir Charles de Burgh contrived to enter the chapel together, though how this adroit timing was managed I know not.

Lady Joan's arrival, and her greeting, distracted me. I did not attend the liturgy of the mass, may God forgive me. Soon, however, my mind wandered from Lady Joan, who was again in occasional dialog with Sir Charles, to the entertainers I must deal with this day. I resolved to seek out some member of the troupe other than their leader for my first questions.

The knife-thrower was a young man, or so he appeared. He was short and solid of body, with muscular arms and wrists. On observation of his build and skills, I would not wish to be one to quarrel with him, even without his daggers. He wore a pale green cotehardie and I found him readily when I approached the tents where he and his cohorts had spent a chilly night.

The knife-thrower had erected two planks against the castle wall and was about to practice his craft when I approached. A human figure was carved on the boards, and the youth began to throw his knives at the fringes of the outlined body. He saw me approach, but continued to hurl his blades until he had surrounded the effigy with eight daggers.

"Do you ever miss?" I asked him.

"Nay," he replied, and strode to the planks to retrieve his weapons.

"The girl who is your target, did she require much persuading to serve you so?"

The youth turned to me and smiled. "Some, but we showed her what I could do, and offered fair pay... a poor lass will do more than that for a silver penny."

He said this as he walked back to his mark and prepared to toss the knives again.

"If you chose to pierce a man's heart, I suppose you could aim to strike as well as miss?"

The youth said nothing, but threw his first weapon with some vehemence. The blade stuck and vibrated squarely in the center of the outlined form.

"I am Hugh," I said, "surgeon to Lord Gilbert on his estate in Bampton." I extended my hand. The youth took it and replied, "I am Walter." He grinned, "surgeon to any who step foolishly before me."

"Hah. Just so. I shall heed where I place my foot. Have you traveled long with the troupe?"

"All my days," he answered. "I was born to the life."

"Your parents are among the entertainers?"

"Aye," he answered. "The wrestler, Hamo Tanner, is my father."

"Ah, I see. It was your sister, then, who ran off with her lad when you were at Bampton."

At this Walter Tanner started and stepped back from his mark. "'Tis common knowledge at Bampton," I continued, "that she did so."

At this remark he seemed to relax, and turned from me to resume his practice. But his aim seemed less sure than before, and two of his throws would have drawn blood from under the arm of the girl had it been her at the planks rather than a tracing.

I remained at the mark as Walter retrieved his blades. As I watched him tug his knives loose from the plank, it struck me, so that my hand sought my forehead: Walter Tanner wore a pale green cotehardie.

I recovered from the shock of this discovery before Walter turned to resume his place at the mark. He scuffed the line deeper in the mud and began his third practice round.

"Was your sister the object of your blades before she ran off?"

"Aye," he replied, without turning from his occupation.

"You did not fear to wound your own sister with a misplaced throw?"

"I know my competence."

"But did not a thought of what a slip of your hand might do never shake your aim before a throw?" I asked.

"Oh, I thought of it," he admitted, "but such musing never displaced my aim."

"Your work must take great courage," I complimented him, "to perform with the life of another in peril."

"There is no peril," Walter scoffed. "I have said, I do not miss my mark." He hesitated briefly, and I knew a disquiet thought had crossed his mind.

"And courage for the lass who faces your blades as they whirl toward her."

Aye. Some we've tried who cannot do it. They scream and run when I launch the first dagger."

"But not the maid you have now?"

"Nay. She's not fearful, now she sees what I can do; she will even keep her eyes open and smile to the throng."

"Others... your sister... would shut their eyes?" I asked.

"Aye. 'Twas the cause of her only wound."

"Oh?"

"Aye. She took her place at the boards, an' as I released the first dagger she moved her hand – her eyes bein' fastened shut, she saw not the blade on its way."

"It struck her, then?" I asked.

"Aye," he admitted, pursing his lips. "The blade pierced her hand and pinned it to the plank. But when we released her and bandaged the wound she wished to continue the performance. What applause she gained, and coin also, when I had done."

"Was she much injured?"

"Aye. Could not carry on her act for the pain in her hand. Not able to do handstands or such for a month and more. But she was sound again, an' could do all after three months. She never again moved when she'd got in place, so such a thing never happened again."

"The knife may have shattered a bone in her hand as it passed through," I mused.

"I thought so," Walter agreed. "Else she would have been whole the sooner."

As we spoke I noted a seam in Walter's cotehardie where a tear had been repaired. It was much like the unmended cut in Sir Robert's blue cotehardie found in the coppiced woods. But torn and mended garments are common enough among the poor. I wear such myself.

"I will disturb your training no longer," I promised. "I look forward to your performance this day."

Walter Tanner went back to his practice and I sauntered off between the tents, seeking some other member of the troupe. I found one. One of the jugglers was stretching and scratching himself, standing between his tent and a fire on which a kettle of pottage was steaming.

"Breakfast?" I asked.

"And supper," he replied.

"Well... Lord Gilbert will feed you well at dinner for your performance again this day."

"I trust so. He did so yesterday. It is well to dine at a lord's table rather than on fare one must catch out of hand."

I sniffed the vapor rising from the pottage and the juggler laughed. "Pork; rare enough in our pot. A bit o' the boar Lord Gilbert's kitchen gave us yestere'en."

"This life you lead is a hard one, then?"

"Life is hard for all, 'cept lords an' ladies, I suppose. An' even them, sometimes. 'Tis better, what I do, than livin' as villein at some lord's pleasure an' owin' work week an' all."

"You will be another day here, then off to Gloucester and perhaps Bristol, I am told."

"Aye," he replied, holding his hands to the fire. "Might be some warmer there... closer to t'sea."

I agreed that might be so, as the juggler moved even closer to the fire and turned his hands to the flames.

"'Tis hard to do what I do an' my hands be cold. I'm not so young; my fingers grow stiff when winter comes."

"Lord Gilbert's hall will be warm."

"Aye," he agreed. "It would be well to toss the balls an' knives there 'til sun returns," he grinned ruefully, "'specially t'knives."

"Have you ever caught a knife wrong?" I asked. In answer he drew his hands from the fire and lifted his palms to me. I saw the scars of several wounds across his hands – one fairly new, and yet red.

"Ah, I see. And this is more likely to happen when 'tis cold?" I asked.

"It is," he nodded in agreement.

219

"Then I shall ask Lord Gilbert to provide a warm blaze in the great hall," I smiled. "I am Hugh de Singleton, surgeon in Lord Gilbert's service on his lands in Bampton."

"Oh... I remember Bampton. We did well there."

"But for losing your contortionist and her lad," I finished his remark for him.

"Aye, we did so," he muttered.

"She was Hamo's daughter, I heard."

"She was. A pert lass."

"She was, you say. But surely she is living yet... somewhere?"

I watched closely for the juggler's reaction to my assertion. He shrugged and looked away. "'Twas but a manner of speakin'. Hamo says she'll come round when she thinks time an' enough has passed an' he won't throttle the lad."

"Will that time come soon?"

"Aye. It has already," the juggler sighed.

"Hamo misses his daughter greatly, then?"

"He does. I've heard 'im call her name in the night... when he thinks all asleep."

"How old was the girl?"

"Ah... seventeen, perhaps."

"And the lad?" I asked.

"They were of an age. Grew up together," he replied.

"The boy was part of your company when a child?"

"Aye. Father juggled, like me, an' 'is ma was acrobat 'til he come 'long. But she stood for the knife-thrower we had then 'til she perished of t'black death when first it came on t'land." He crossed himself as memory of that time rolled across him.

"The lad's father perished then, also?"

"Nay. Took to his bed six, seven years ago just after Candlemas an' never rose from it. He was older, like."

"So Hamo let the boy stay on? What did he do to earn his keep?"

"'Bout anything Hamo'd ask; he was right willin' to

220

please. Saw to t'horses and carts, mostly. He was learnin' to juggle; maybe take my place when I lose my competence."

"Will that be soon?" I asked.

"Nay," he chuckled. "So long as I keep me hands warm."

"Was Hamo surprised," I asked, "when they left the troupe together?"

"Aye. We all was."

"Why so? Did they give no sign of fondness for each other?"

"Nay, I saw no sign. Oh, the lad was fond enough of Eleanor – Hamo's daughter was named Eleanor, for the great queen, y'know – but she'd not return any suit of his... so I thought."

"Why so? Was the lad ill-formed, or dull of wit?" I asked.

"Not more so than t'rest of us," he smiled. "But Eleanor had lads in every town would have offered marriage. A young burgher of Winchester would have had her for wife when we were last there."

"What," I wondered aloud, "did Hamo think of that?"

"Oh," the juggler paused, "he was torn, I'll tell you."

"How so?"

"Every father wishes his daughter well wed, an' Hamo had little enough for Eleanor's dowry. But no man wishes to lose his daughter, 'specially as how he'd need to find another acrobat. A man can do that, replace a servant. Not so easy to replace a daughter... what with Hamo's wife dead an' gone these nine years now."

"Did Hamo forbid her to wed the burgher of Winchester, or did Eleanor so choose?"

The juggler shrugged. "'Twas the lass, I think. Had Hamo forbid it, she'd have wed to spite him. She was of that age."

"She was a troublesome maid, then?"

221

"Aye; could be. Not much more than many of her years," he replied.

"But you were surprised, then, that she stole away with the boy?"

"Aye, that's so. So were we all, I think."

"How do you know of a certainty that she did?" I asked.

That question seemed to take the juggler by surprise. He stammered a moment, then held his hands to the fire again before he answered. "Well... uh... 'twas plain enough. Both gone of t'same night."

"But no one saw them together... that day, or in their flight?"

"Nay. But it adds up, wouldn't you say?"

I was not so sure of that, but decided I would get no other tale from any in the troupe unless I could convince them I knew their story false. But I did not know this, only suspected it so. The juggler seemed, of the three I had chatted with, the most likely to yield the truth when pressed. He had looked away often, avoiding my eyes. So I pressed him.

"Walter Tanner has a fine green cotehardie; how long has he owned the garment?"

"Huh... how... what has that to do with me?" the juggler stammered.

"Perhaps nothing, but one much like it was taken from a corpse near Bampton some months ago, and about the time you were there."

"'Twas not Walter. I remember now. He bought it in London... aye, London."

"When were you there?" I pressed further.

"Uh... 'twas Shrove Tuesday, two years, nearly, now."

"The tear he received in it – a misfortune, surely. How did that happen?"

"'Tis torn?" he replied. "I knew not."

"Come, man. 'Tis at the front, just below the heart. You could not stand before it and the slit escape notice, no matter how well mended it is."

"Oh, that... uh, 'twas mischance," he hesitated, "when 'twas packed in saddle bags with t'knives, I think. Yes, that was the cause. Right woeful Walter was, too."

I thought perhaps I had disconcerted the juggler, and that with another sally he might break, but as he replied I saw confidence return to his gaze and his spine stiffen. I tried again, anyway.

"The cut is in a perilous place, were a man wearing the cotehardie when a fellow skilled as Walter, let us say, might hurl a knife at him."

"Aye, but was Walter wearing it, who would throw the blade?" he countered.

"Perhaps another had donned it," I asserted through stiff lips, "and Walter was free to fling the dagger?"

"Walter is no murderer," the juggler retorted with acrimony.

"But is he a man-slayer?" I replied.

"What say you, that a man can slay another but not be a murderer?"

"Some," I responded, "might say so, if they think slaying a miscreant be justice rather than murder."

"You go too deep for me," the juggler complained nervously. "An' I have business to attend before Lord Gilbert calls. Good day, Master... Hugh." And with that he dismissed me and retreated to his tent. I admit my interview technique was crude, but even a dull blade will cut if applied firmly.

I turned from the tents, uncertain of my course, and saw the new contortionist approach from around the northeast tower. There was a raised, dry path through the mud of the yard, and she picked her way across the mire on it. I directed my feet to the same trail, and we met in the middle of the yard, between the castle wall and the marshalsea. Her eyes were fixed on her course, so I caused her to start when finally she perceived me before her, blocking her way lest she choose to step into the muck.

The girl stepped back, as if she feared I would thrust her into the mud. This, I admit, would have been a simple matter, for the lass was tiny – little bigger than Alice. She could not have weighed more than six stone.

"Good day. Forgive me... I had no wish to alarm you," I reassured the girl. "I am Master Hugh, surgeon to Lord Gilbert at his Bampton estate."

The girl smiled shyly. "I am Agnes, sir."

"Well, Agnes, I marvel at your talent. I am told that you are newly brought to this work."

"'Tis so, sir."

"You have learnt quickly, then. It must be difficult for you... to replace Hamo's daughter, who was so practiced at the art."

"Uh... aye. Uh, I mean, no. Hamo says I do well."

"He speaks truth. I did not see his daughter perform, but I cannot think she could surpass you in facility."

"I thank you, sir."

"Of course, you would not have seen Eleanor perform, either."

"Oh, yes, sir. Hamo brought his company to Banbury when I was but a wee lass. I saw her tricks, and copied as best I could. When Hamo brought his band again to Banbury and I saw he'd no lass for acrobat, I sought him out and showed what I had mastered."

"And now you travel with him. Has he taught you more?" I inquired.

"Aye. Much more; I practice new tricks every week. Some Hamo has taught me, and some I devise."

"No doubt Hamo misses his daughter. Does he seek news of her as you journey?"

The girl was silent and thoughtful for a moment. "Nay," she finally replied.

"He does not wish to find her?" I wondered aloud. "He must be very angry."

"'Tis a puzzle," she agreed. "I was told she fled with a lad of the company. But one night in autumn I was sleepless and lay in my tent listening to Hamo and Walter as they talked by the fire late into the night. They spoke of her as

224

dead, and perhaps the lad too. Perhaps it was but a manner of speaking," she added.

"Did they give opinion how this might be known to them?" I asked.

The girl's tone became conspiratorial, and she stepped closer. "Nay, sir. They spoke softly, and the fire crackled; I did not hear all."

"An accident, or illness, mayhap, took the two lives?"

"No," she frowned. "I think not. 'Twas an evil deed, I think. They spoke of justice for Eleanor."

"Hmm... yes. One would not seek justice if death was a result of mischance or malady. Was this justice they sought, or justice done?"

The girl pressed closer yet, and whispered, "Justice done, sir, I think."

As the girl spoke Hamo Tanner appeared at a stable door. He glanced in our direction as he strode toward his tents, then hesitated in mid-stride and peered under narrowed brows at Agnes and me. It was clear he found our conversation disquieting. He turned from his course and approached us.

"Agnes, don't be takin' up Master Hugh's time. An' you must be limber for your performance this day. Off with you, now."

Agnes fled, and Hamo turned to me apologetically. "She's a good lass, an' does her work well, but dim, she is."

"Dim?" I questioned.

"Not right in t'head, you know."

"Ah... I understand."

"Fancies odd things. Pretends herself a fine lady, she does."

"She has imagination?"

"That's it, sir... the very word. Imagines all sorts of strange things what never was nor never will be. A fine lady, indeed," he scoffed.

"Aye," I agreed. "Her words did drift to strange and unusual events. I see your point."

225

"Good day, Master Hugh. I must see to my band. We need to make ready for Lord Gilbert."

I bid Hamo Tanner good day, and retired to my chamber, where I reflected on the morning's conversations. There were yet gaps in my knowledge, but those were smaller than before. It is the trivial particulars of comprehension, however, which are most difficult to grasp. The general understanding of a riddle comes more easily. Those petty particulars create the details of an image which is otherwise but shadow.

Chapter 16

While I pondered these things the horn sounded for dinner. I hurried to take my place beside Sir John, and while washing and drying my hands managed to steal a glimpse of Lady Joan. A servant also attended that end of the high table with ewer and towel. As she rinsed and dried her hands Lady Joan looked up and caught me observing her. It was that sixth sense again, I suppose, which gives a woman the wit to catch a man so. She smiled, but immediately turned back to Sir Charles and smiled at him as well.

The meal this day was nearly as elaborate as the Christmas feast, but served in three courses, and missing the great roasted boar of the previous day.

This day minstrels played upon tambour and lutes and sang between removes. When the third remove was cleared and the musicians were again at their work, I saw the juggler to whom I had spoken that morning rise from his place at the far end of the hall and leave the room. Perhaps he required a visit to the garderobe before his performance. Whatever the cause, his departure lent credence to the plot I had already formed, and to work his absence into the scheme would require little modification. I left my place and spoke softly in Lord Gilbert's ear. Music covered our conversation. Lord Gilbert at first questioned the plan, but eventually accepted the idea and agreed to fulfill his part.

Hamo Tanner and his troupe rose from their places at the far end of the hall when the musicians were done. The juggler had by this time returned to his place, and so joined his cohorts to begin the performance. He was near the age, I think, when visits to the garderobe become frequent. While all eyes in the hall were on the jugglers, I leaned over to whisper to Sir John. Lord Gilbert, I told him, wished to speak to him this moment on a serious matter.

Sir John bent over Lord Gilbert's shoulder, listened intently as Lord Gilbert spoke softly to him behind an upraised hand, then hurried out of the hall. A few minutes later, as Walter was enclosing Agnes in a ring of quivering blades, I saw valets in Lord Gilbert's colors of blue and black positioned at the exits of the great hall. My plot was begun. If it concluded well, I should receive much honor. If not... well, I tried to dismiss that thought.

When Agnes began her display of acrobatics, tumbling, and contortion, I saw Sir John return and again speak briefly to Lord Gilbert. Lord Gilbert then leaned to his wife and spoke briefly to her. His words brought a shocked expression to Lady Petronilla's face, which abruptly faded to surprise and then puzzlement. Onlookers, and I was desirous that there should be some who would take their eyes from Agnes for a moment, would think she had been given a startling revelation. She had.

Agnes received her usual ovation when she finished her exhibition. Lord Gilbert then stood, as all in the hall expected him to do. But what came next they did not expect.

There was no pleasure in Lord Gilbert's face. Rather, his brows were wrinkled in a scowl. Those in the hall who had been conversing with their neighbors and preparing to rise from their bench were suddenly silent. Lord Gilbert gazed with thin lips and lowered brows across his guests, then spoke.

"Sir John," he began, "has returned from an errand I assigned him. He reports that he found the Lady Petronilla's chamber door ajar. This should not be. I will have everyone remain in the hall 'til it be known if some thief has plundered her possessions."

Audible gasps went round the hall, and hands were raised to lips. Then, as the occupants of the hall digested his words, they began to peer from the corners of their eyes at one another, wondering who might be a thief.

Lord Gilbert turned and spoke to his wife. "You must

inspect your chamber and see if aught be missing. Sir John... I will have you and Master Hugh accompany her and her ladies."

Something was missing, I knew, for I had it hidden under my cloak as Lord Gilbert spoke. Lady Petronilla's casket, a gold and red enameled wood and metal box, in which Lord Gilbert's lady kept her jewels, would not be found. Sir John had seized it from Lady Petronilla's chamber and slipped it to me while all eyes in the hall followed Agnes.

Lady Petronilla and her two maids followed Sir John past the guard and out the door. I followed the others. The casket was large, but my cloak was voluminous and I was able to keep the box concealed. That corner of the hall was dark, as was my cloak, which also served to conceal the lump under my arm.

Lady Petronilla led the way to her chamber in the northwest tower. I allowed myself to fall farther to the rear of the hurrying party. At the door to the tower I turned away. The castle yard was unoccupied, as I knew it must be. It was possible a stable boy might see me if he looked up from his work, but by the time he told any of what he had seen my mission would have failed or succeeded of its own merit.

I ran through the mud of the yard, past the marshalsea, to the jugglers' tent. I drew the flap aside, found a pile of bedclothes, and hurriedly concealed the casket between them. Then I was off again at a run across the yard, into the tower. I heard Lady Petronilla's shrieks before I entered her chamber. She had discovered her casket missing.

We hurried to take this melancholy news to Lord Gilbert, for whom, of course, it would not be news at all. Lady Petronilla was disconsolate, and I was, for a moment, uncertain I was doing the proper thing. The end does not always justify the means, but occasionally it does.

Lord Gilbert banged the table with his cup and demanded silence in the hall, then announced the reason for his wife's grief. Another cycle of gasps and guarded looks filled the hall.

"Sir John," he concluded, "see that no one leaves this place 'til I return. Master Hugh," he turned to me, "come with me. We will find whosoever has done this thing."

Lord Gilbert motioned to four grooms who stood against the inner wall and they took place in line behind us as we left the hall.

"Where is it?" Lord Gilbert whispered when we were in the inner yard.

"Peace, m'lord. The search must not end too soon. Set your men to search the east range hall first. Instruct them to overturn the possessions of the poor – but only a little. Enough to make our hunt seemly without troubling those who have enough trouble already."

Lord Gilbert so ordered, and we stood together in the entry as the searchers overturned the hall. Half an hour later they had done. There was, of course, no casket.

"Where now, m'lord?" a groom asked. Lord Gilbert cocked his head and peered at me, but I looked away, as if examining the carpenters' art in the trusses of the hammer-beam roof.

"Uh... the marshalsea next. Find rods to poke through the straw."

The grooms darted off to the other side of the castle and Lord Gilbert and I followed in their wake. "Is it there?" he whispered.

"No... but next have the acrobats' tents searched."

The sun was low over the bare west woods when the grooms finished their work in the marshalsea. Lord Gilbert set them off to the tents and but three or four minutes later a cry of success rose from the jugglers' tent. I was relieved. I had in the preceding hour suffered visions of some other felon discovering the casket and making off with it.

We approached the tent and peered through the flap. A groom held the casket aloft, bedclothes strewn about at his feet.

"You found it there?" Lord Gilbert asked, pointing to the disarray.

"Aye, m'lord. The very place, under that lot, hidden-like, it was."

"What say you, Master Hugh?" Lord Gilbert turned to me.

"Send two... no, three men to bring Hamo Tanner here."

"It might take three to compel him," Lord Gilbert smiled, "should he wish not to come."

The wrestler came readily enough, his face marked with a combination of anger, fear, and curiosity. A groom pulled back the tent flap, and bade him enter. The light was failing, but there was yet enough to see the casket at our feet.

"We have found that which was stolen," Lord Gilbert thundered. I have said before, thundering was a thing Lord Gilbert did well. Hamo blanched and started as if a groom had struck him from behind with a timber. "Is this how your company repays my favor?"

"N... n... no, m'lord... not me... my tent is next..."

"Then whose is this?"

"The jugglers, m'lord. Roger and John and Robert."

"And whose place is that... whose bedclothes be those?" He pointed sternly at the place where the casket lay.

"Roger's, m'lord, I think."

Lord Gilbert turned to the grooms. "Take this man back to the hall. Bring Roger the juggler."

When Hamo and the grooms were out of earshot Lord Gilbert turned to me. "What now, Master Hugh? I am in the dark. What say we to this juggler?"

"I will question him. You stand by and fix him with an angry eye. Follow my lead when you see my way."

The juggler appeared a few minutes later, quivering so I thought his legs might fail. A groom walked on either arm, ready to steady him should he totter, and another walked behind, should he turn to run. This I thought unlikely as he seemed barely able to place one foot before the other. What I was about to do troubled me some, and has since, for although I did not lie to the juggler, I certainly intended him to believe a thing which was not true.

"You are called Roger?" Lord Gilbert asked the fellow, quietly this time, but with undisguised wrath lurking in his voice. He folded his arms across his chest and scowled so that his brows nearly met above his nose.

"Aye, m'lord," Roger quivered. He looked at the casket. "I did not do this."

"Why," I asked, "was it then discovered here?"

"Some other has placed it here."

"And why would another do such a thing?" Lord Gilbert glowered. "Have you enemies who wish to see you hang?"

At that word Roger blanched and seemed to stagger, as if struck at the knees with an oaken staff.

"A man might hang for such a theft," I reminded him. "It will go hard for you if you will not give us the truth."

"I... I speak truth, m'lord. I have not before seen this box. I know not how it came here."

"Hmm," Lord Gilbert grunted, his face and voice projecting disbelief.

"We must have truth from you, Roger," I pressed. "No guile; your life may depend on it."

"I speak truth... I..."

I interrupted the man's stuttering: "We must have truth about this, and other matters. Shall we have it, or shall Lord Gilbert convene a court for the morrow and send a groom for rope?"

The juggler's shoulders sagged, and his head fell. "I will speak truth... as I have already," he turned to protest to Lord Gilbert.

"We shall see," Lord Gilbert rumbled, then glanced at me with that raised eyebrow, as if to say, "Well, where do you go from here?"

"I would have answers to another matter, before we

learn how this casket came to be in your possessions," I said. "Hamo's daughter, Eleanor... she did not run off with a lad, did she? She is dead, is that not so?"

Roger cast about him as if seeking a means of escape. I thought it wise to remind him of the threat he thought hanging over him. "We will have truth, remember, or you may see the consequences." Roger wilted again; I thought I should permit him to sit before he collapsed. I drew up a stool and motioned him to it. This proved a useful ploy, for it forced him to look up to us, while Lord Gilbert and I stood in authority above him.

"We have found her, you should know, so lying will gain you nothing."

He looked up quizzically from his seat. Then silently he nodded his head, as if he could not bear to speak the words.

"Speak up, man," Lord Gilbert demanded.

"Aye... she is dead," Roger admitted.

"And the lad she was to have gone off with? He, I think, is alive. Is this not so?" I asked.

To speak truth seemed to come easier for Roger now that we had forced the first confession from him. "Aye, he is... so far as I know. We left him stabbed, in the care of his grandmother at Abingdon. I know not if he yet lives."

"Pierced by Sir Robert Mallory or his squire, I think," I asserted. "Is this not so?"

"Aye, 'tis so," Roger agreed.

Now it was Lord Gilbert's turn to stammer in surprise. "What... why should he do so?" he demanded.

"The lad saw Sir Robert with Eleanor. She was not seen again," Roger sighed.

"How is this known to you?" Lord Gilbert demanded, having regained his poise.

"The truth, remember," I reminded him.

"Hamo could not find the two when we were to leave Bampton. None could credit they'd run off together. But what other account could answer?" Roger explained.

"I remember him seeking them," Lord Gilbert remarked, tugging now on his chin.

"We were but two miles from town, speaking loudly of our loss, when Walter heard a weak cry from near t'road. He went to the sound and found Ralph pierced near the heart, but no sign of Eleanor.

"Ralph was near to food for worms, but yet able to speak if one came close to his lips. And all bloody-like they were, too. Told Hamo that Sir Robert had killed him, an' Eleanor as well. Sir Robert, he said, took him from the castle bundled on his pack-horse an' dumped him in a thicket when he thought himself safely away from town."

"And this happened only a few minutes before you came... is this not so?" I asked.

"Aye. Ralph played dead, like, as was near to bein' so, for fear they'd run 'im through again an' they knew he yet lived."

"As Sir Robert surely would have," I agreed. "I will finish your tale. A few of your party unhitched the horses from cart and wagon and rode ahead to accost Sir Robert – Hamo, Walter, surely and as many others as could fit on the backs of three horses?"

"Aye," he agreed. "We were six."

"You caught them a few miles on, near a coppiced woods. Hamo demanded of Sir Robert the whereabouts of his daughter. Sir Robert, I think, would not answer."

"Oh, he answered," Roger replied. "Laughed at Hamo, he did, an' said as how he wouldn't know where to find such a trollop... had they searched the beds of villeins hereabouts?"

"Words became heated, and led to a brawl?" I asked.

"Aye. Somethin' like that," Roger agreed.

I continued the tale for him. "When Hamo pressed close Sir Robert drew his sword, I think. Walter, seeing his father about to be struck down, drew a dagger from his saddle-bag and threw it at Sir Robert. Is this how it happened?'

234

"Aye," Roger sighed.

"Then," I continued, "the squire drew, and made for Walter, so Walter delivered a blade at him, also?"

Roger nodded his head, barely visible now in the gloom. Another sigh.

"Sir Robert and the squire made to ride off," I resumed the tale, "but soon fell from their horses, being struck at the heart. Is this not so?"

Roger sat in silence for a moment, then replied. "They'd murdered Eleanor... least Sir Robert did so, an' the squire was his man an' helped murder poor Ralph."

"How did Ralph know Eleanor was dead?" I asked. "Where did he see her with Sir Robert, and when?"

"'Twas near dawn, like. Ralph was sleepin' in t'stable, as was his work to care for t'horses, an' rose to relieve himself. He saw Eleanor wi' Sir Robert creepin' 'long the castle wall. 'Twas full moon, an' before he thought to hide in t'shadows Sir Robert saw 'im. In t'mornin', afore dawn, before we was about, Ralph said Sir Robert an' t'squire come to marshalsea like to make an early start. Squire caught Ralph from behind an' Sir Robert put his dagger to his heart."

"And this was done while all others slept?" Lord Gilbert exclaimed incredulously.

"Aye. Ralph was only one who slept in t'marshalsea. An' he feared to cry out lest Sir Robert see he yet lived and wound him again."

"And they thought to strike him down because they knew he had seen Sir Robert with Eleanor?"

"Aye. Squire said as he'd put Ralph in t'same place, but Sir Robert said there was no time – folks would be stirring. Best to take him with 'em and leave his body in t'forest."

"What then?" I asked.

"They threw Ralph on t'pack-horse, covered him, an' set off while light was dim an' t'porter could not see the shape of a man laid across the horse. 'At way they got poor

Ralph out of t'marshalsea with no one t'wiser," Roger explained.

"Ralph heard 'em speak of Eleanor dead," he continued, "they thinkin' he was, so didn't mind their tongues."

"What did they say of her?" I asked. "How she was killed? Where they hid the corpse?"

"Ralph did not say," Roger continued, twisting his hands before him as he sat on the stool. "Hamo put his ear to Ralph's lips to hear aught. Ralph said as t'squire was fearful, like, but Sir Robert told 'im not to vex himself wi' worry; none would find her."

"Well... we did," I told him. But I did not say where.

"Then Sir Robert says, 'Foolish wench. Had she not cried out she would yet live,'" Roger added.

"Why did she cry out?" I wondered aloud.

"Sir Robert promised to provide for 'er as his mistress. Ralph 'eard Sir Robert laugh 'bout it. When he'd had 'is way with her he made to send her off. She was not a lass to be put off so. Made such noise about it that Sir Robert slew her to silence her. So Ralph heard Sir Robert say."

Roger, Lord Gilbert, and I were silent for a moment. What Roger said made sense, for Sir Robert had used a similar ploy with another. And with a third and more, I guessed.

"You took Sir Robert and the squire to the coppiced woods to bury them," I said, "but stripped the bodies of valuables first. Is this not so?"

"Aye. But when we had done, we cast away some we'd taken."

"Sir Robert's blue cotehardie," I completed his story, "and the squire's dagger. You thought them too obvious for a troupe of jugglers and such."

"Aye. An' Sir Robert's sword an' dagger as well we abandoned in the forest."

Lord Gilbert looked at me through the gloom. "The foresters?" he questioned.

"Them, or those weapons lay yet under the leaves," I agreed.

"We have found the missing casket," I concluded, "but as you have told us truthfully of this other matter, I recommend to Lord Gilbert that you be released. I believe you say honestly that you did not rob Lady Petronilla of her jewels. You would not, I think, be so foolish to hide the chest here had you done so."

I looked to Lord Gilbert, whose face was now nearly invisible in the shadows. "I consent," he agreed. Then, to the grooms, who had stood by the tent-flap and heard all, Lord Gilbert said, "You will speak of this to no one, until I release you of your oath. Take this fellow back, but hold him outside the hall. Do not permit him to speak to any of his fellows."

"They will tell this tale before the morrow," I advised Lord Gilbert when they had gone.

"Aye, they will... that I know. But they may yet hold their peace an hour or two, 'til we decide what must be done."

"We, m'lord?"

"Aye. You have found a murderer. No... you have found out two murderers. And you are my bailiff. This business is now become your bailiwick as well as mine."

"Hamo and Walter must be charged with Sir Robert's death, and that of the squire," I advised.

"Aye. You think the charge just?" he replied.

"A jury might say 'twas self-defense," I answered, "and but justice done for Eleanor and the lad, but the charge must be made, I think."

"What is your opinion of this business, Hugh? Will a jury release them? Do you wish that may be so?"

My mind had turned this very question for several minutes, so I could answer without hesitation. "I do, m'lord. I see no malice in Hamo or Walter, and I found nothing virtuous in Sir Robert."

"Yet I would have welcomed him as brother-in-law," Lord Gilbert mused. "My sister had better sense of the man than I." He was silent briefly, then continued, "I hope her

237

judgment of Sir Charles de Burgh is as valid, for she seems agreeable to his suit.

"I wish," Lord Gilbert confided, "that when Hamo found his man left to die along the way he had returned and asked justice of me. This matter might have been resolved with less disorder and perplexity."

"That is so. But you must understand that Hamo would fear miscarriage of justice."

"How so?" Lord Gilbert frowned.

"You are a gentleman, as was Sir Robert. Hamo would fear a coroner's jury – your men, all – might bend to your will and vindicate Sir Robert, heedless of the proofs against him."

"He would mistrust me so?" Lord Gilbert muttered incredulously.

"He would mistrust any gentleman to find against another of his rank in favor of the commons."

"Well, not so. But 'tis too late to persuade him of that. We must return to the hall and Sir John. I will place him in charge of the arrest."

We did so. Sir John assembled a company of Lord Gilbert's grooms and footmen, and together we entered the hall. Hamo, from a bench along the east wall, stood to his feet as we assembled. I think he suspected then that his deed was uncovered.

Had Hamo chosen to contest his arrest, I think the dozen men Sir John collected would have barely sufficed. But he did not resist, and so was seized there in the hall, with his son. Lord Gilbert approached from the high table and told him why. To this Hamo replied only, "He slew my daughter, and I repaid him in like coin." Sir John took him and Walter to the keep. They offered no struggle, but neither did they leave the hall with bowed head or back bent in shame.

"I will release the others of Hamo's company," Lord Gilbert advised when the hall was finally cleared. "But not 'til you and Sir John have had time to return to Bampton with the prisoners. 'Tis an ill thing to travel in winter, but I would have you leave tomorrow. The weather remains clement, but who can judge when 'twill turn?

"Seek Hubert Shillside so soon as you reach Bampton. He must convene his jury. Roger the juggler must accompany you and the prisoners. Require of him that he tell the jurymen what he has told us. Should he resist, remind him of where the casket was found, and imply that I am of changeable passions.

"If the coroner's jury charge Hamo and Walter, Sir John will conduct them and Roger to Oxford and put them in the hands of the sheriff."

"And my work," I sighed, "will be done."

"Well... as regards this mystery you have revealed, aye. But my steward, Geoffrey Thirwall, will visit Bampton after Twelfth Night to hold hallmote. You and John Holcutt must have the manor accounts ready for his inspection."

Lord Gilbert wished to be certain that Hamo Tanner would not flee justice. His thick wrists were bound securely, as were those of his son. Roger was permitted to travel unencumbered. Six grooms accompanied Sir John and me as we made ready to depart Goodrich Castle so soon as there was light enough to travel.

"Ah... Master Hugh," Lord Gilbert called as we made ready at the marshalsea to set off. "I forget me, with all that's passed since Christmas. Wait a moment."

He turned to speak to a valet, who immediately scurried across the muddy yard to the castle gatehouse and disappeared within. While the valet was off on his errand I remembered the business which brought me to Goodrich Castle.

"Lady Joan's arm; she must seek the surgeon in Gloucester to remove the plaster."

"When?" Lord Gilbert asked.

"Not before St Valentine's Day. Even a week after if she does not chafe over the inconvenience."

"St Valentine's Day! Hah! Sir Charles will be pleased, I think."

239

To this remark I made no reply. How could I?

At that moment the valet returned, a large, dark object I could not identify in the dim morning twilight slung over his shoulder.

"'Twas not ready 'til yesterday. The tailor would not be pressed," Lord Gilbert explained.

I was confused and stood before him with empty expression. This he observed.

"Your cloak, man. I promised you a fur cloak as part of your wages. Here 'tis."

I took the garment from the panting valet, who seemed for the briefest moment unwilling to give it up. It was soft and luxuriant and I understood his reluctance.

"Put it on... don't just stand there," Lord Gilbert demanded. I did so.

"I thank you, m'lord. 'Tis true you promised such a garment. I had forgot. But I did not expect such as this. 'Tis worthy of a duke."

"Well, if you see one and he would have it, do not give it up to him," Lord Gilbert jested.

I mounted my horse, last of the party to put foot to stirrup, wrapped in my new cloak. As we passed through the outer yard to the barbican I turned to look back at the castle and saw, through the gathering light, Lady Joan and a maid watching our departure from atop the gatehouse. She saw me turn, and waved her uninjured hand, then lifted it to her lips and blew a kiss. I turned in my saddle to wave farewell, but as I did so she was gone. I wondered if I would ever see Lady Joan again.

The cloak was as warm as it was soft, and protected me well from the gale which swept from the Forest of Dean across our path. We arrived in Gloucester before nightfall and again sought shelter with the monks of St Peter's Abbey. The abbot seemed displeased to provide bed and board for miscreants, but as Hamo and Walter were not yet judged guilty of a crime he swallowed his objection and remained true to the rules of his order.

This abbot would have seen us on our way next morning, but the wind howled down from the mountains of Wales – better a wind should do so than the Welsh, Sir John remarked – and snow spattered the cobbles of the monastery yard. Sir John and I were uneasy, so elected to remain within the monastery's hospitable walls another day. We did not wish to be caught on the way in a great snow.

The next day dawned bright and cold, the snow of the previous day leaving but a dusting on our path. The mud of the road froze in the night, so the road was firm beneath the horses' hooves. But it was cold. Sir John gazed often at me that day, snug in my cloak, before, as the sun sank beneath the bare trees at our backs, we reached Bampton and shelter.

Chapter 17

This tale has grown longer than I intended. My parchment is nearly consumed, and it will be many weeks before I can visit Oxford to replenish my supply. Your candle no doubt burns low and a warm bed calls. So I will conclude this account.

Hubert Shillside convened the coroner's jury in the Church of St Beornwald on a bitterly cold first day of January. Twelve townsmen listened as Roger and I gave evidence. The juggler did not prevaricate, and needed no prodding from me to present a full report of all he knew. There was no reason he should not, for when the coroner questioned Hamo Tanner, the wrestler freely admitted his deed. His emotions came near the surface – remarkable in so sturdy a man – when he justified the revenge he had taken against his daughter's slayer.

Nevertheless, the jury brought a charge of murder against Hamo and his son. Sir John and the grooms took Hamo to Oxford and the sheriff while I kept Roger with me at Bampton, where I could be certain he would not flee before we should be called to give witness at the trial.

Sir John returned two days later from his mission to the sheriff and reported that the king's eyre would meet the next week. Sir Roger would send for me when a day was set for the trial. That week passed quickly, for there was much work on the manor for a new bailiff to learn.

Geoffrey Thirwall, the steward, arrived in Bampton two days before Twelfth Night. He searched diligently for some flaw in my work, or that of John, the reeve, but found only minor complaints to issue against us. Well, it is his business to root out that which is wrong and right it.

I was some worried that tenants and villeins might discover some defect in my labor and protest against me at hallmote. But none did. Perhaps because I had done so little on the estate that I had few opportunities to blunder. Given a full year before next hallmote, I was sure I could err often enough that some would find reason to complain of me.

Two days after Epiphany, Sir Roger sent a messenger to summon witnesses to the trials of Hamo and Walter Tanner. I was nearly as reluctant to attend as I had been for the trial of Thomas Shilton. In the days before Roger and I were summoned, I tried to think what I, had I been a father in Hamo's place, would have done. I fear I would have acted no differently. This is not to say I justify the murder Hamo did. But any might be capable of the same crime in the circumstance.

I will say that I was not sorry when the jury made of my labors no consequence. The burghers of Oxford were mostly men who rose from the commons, and they understood Hamo's remark that he did not trust gentlemen to do justice for him against one of their own. They brought a verdict of not guilty. As Sir Robert drew first, Walter and Hamo were justified in defending themselves.

The judge, Sir William Barnhill, was the same I had caused to interrupt his journey home two months earlier. He recognized me, I knew, when I was called to the stand to testify, for he glared at me through narrowed eyes all the while I spoke, as if to say, "You'd better have it right this time."

When he dismissed jury and defendants, I watched to see how Hamo and Walter would receive Roger. I was too far away to hear their words, but they walked from the room in seemingly amicable conversation. Perhaps a good juggler was hard enough to find that Roger could be forgiven his disloyal truth.

I had no wish to return to Bampton that evening in the dark, so returned to my inn for another night. I stayed this occasion at the Foxes' Lair, a more substantial place than the Stag and Hounds, suitable to my rising position in the world. The soup and ale were thicker, as well as the beds, at the Foxes' Lair.

I retrieved my old friend, Bruce, from the inn stable at dawn and set out across Castle Mill Stream Bridge. But not for Bampton. There was another question I must ask before I could be satisfied that I knew all there was of the events I had seen and probed since St Michael's Day. At Eynsham I took the road to Witney and on to Burford. Bruce would have turned for Bampton at Eynsham; it took a strong hand on the reins to persuade him that we could not yet go home.

I guided Bruce down Burford High Street, to the bridge across the Windrush. Ice clogged the riverbanks. The cold current flowed only in the middle of the stream. I turned from the road to the path which led to the smith and the mill.

Smoke rose from Alard's forge, and I heard once again the clang of his hammer as I approached. But 'twas not the smith I sought. My question was for his daughter. As I drew near the building Bruce neighed. He was heard between the strokes of the hammer, for the tolling of the blows ceased and Alard appeared in the opening door. Behind him, craning her head to see past his broad shoulders, I saw Margaret.

I thought – perhaps I hoped – that I might not find her there. Perhaps, I mused, Thomas Shilton would take her for wife yet, and I would need to seek her in Shilton village. But not so. She pressed past her father to greet me, her belly large beneath her surcoat, her time near come.

"Master Hugh," she greeted me. "Who do you seek?"

"You. I have news, and a question," I replied.

Alard peered beneath bushy eyebrows from Margaret to me, then grunted and returned to his work. I was pleased, for I wished Margaret to speak freely and thought my question might be too raw for her to wish to answer before her father.

I left Bruce tied to a willow, where he began to munch contentedly on the stems. I led Margaret along the river while I told her of Eleanor and Sir Robert, of Hamo and

Walter and the trial. She shuddered when I told her of Sir Robert's death.

"And now," I said, "I wish one thing of you. I have a question... I believe I know the answer, but I desire confirmation. The night last spring, when you were heard quarreling in the churchyard late at night with a man thought to be Thomas Shilton: that man was Sir Robert Mallory, was it not?"

She hesitated, then nodded "yes."

"Do others know of this?" I asked.

"Aye. Thomas would be told... but no other."

"Your father?"

"Nay. He has not asked. I have not volunteered."

"Your words, in the churchyard; did you believe Sir Robert would make place for you?"

"Aye," she hesitated. "He promised... if I was got with child, to provide. He promised a life of ease, would I be 'is mistress." Margaret spoke in a whisper, a tear in her voice if not yet on her cheek. Perhaps there were in her no more tears to shed for this misery.

"What of Thomas?" I asked.

"You said, 'one question,'" she replied. "That is a second. But I will answer. If the child be a girl, he will have me and rear it as his own. He will forgive my foolishness. If it be a boy, he will not. He will have only his own son inherit his holding, not another man's offspring."

"You are content with this bargain?" I questioned.

"Aye," she whispered. "I betrayed him for riches and place I thought I might win with my appearance. How can I begrudge his wish for an heir of his own?"

We turned from our way at the mill. The grinding wheel and stone made continued conversation difficult, and there was little more to say. We returned in silence to the forge, where the rhythmic clang of the hammer proclaimed her father still at work.

I wished her well, retrieved Bruce from the willow he had munched so far as he could reach, and set off for the

245

Windrush bridge and home. It was near dark when I arrived at Bampton Castle. Wilfred had closed the gate, and had to leave his quarters to heave up the bar and shove the gates open to admit me. He said he was pleased to see me home again. This I doubt, as my arrival took him from his fire into a cold January night.

A week later an ironmonger called at Bampton Castle. His was a regular visit, for he supplied Lord Gilbert's farrier and the town smith from the stock in his heavily weighted wagon. I asked if he supplied stock to Alard, the Burford smith. He did.

"How does he?" I asked. "And his daughter, is she well?"

"Oh, aye," he replied. "An' Alard's a grandfather. Margaret had a babe four days past. A fine, healthy little lass, too, she is."

Afterword

The Unquiet Bones is a work of fiction. But some of the characters in the tale were real people. The Lord of Bampton Castle in the 1360s was indeed Gilbert Talbot, and his wife was Petronilla. Alas, he had no sister named Joan.

John Wyclif was real, as was his service as Master of Balliol College. Only scholars will know the small liberty I have taken with the dates of his career there. Roger de Cottesford was High Sheriff of Oxford from 1362 to 1365. Thomas de Bowlegh was one of three vicars assigned to the Church of St Beornwald in the mid-fourteenth century. All other characters and the events portrayed are fictional.

Bampton Castle was enlarged in the early fourteenth century by Aymer de Valence, Earl of Pembroke. It was for several centuries one of the largest castles in England in terms of area surrounded by the curtain wall. By the mid-seventeenth century it was largely in ruins. All that remains in 2008 is a part of the west gatehouse and a ten-meter length of the curtain wall, now incorporated into a farm called Ham Court.

Lady Petronilla's enameled jewel box may be seen in the Victoria and Albert Museum.

The Church of St Beornwald was renamed in the sixteenth century and since then has been called the Church of St Mary the Virgin. It is essentially unchanged since the thirteenth century, except in name.

Time has not been kind to the old church. Time is hardly ever kind to anything. The town is currently attempting to raise £390,000 to replace the roof. The need is urgent, as the safety of the current roof – and therefore the entire church – cannot be assured after 2009. As of February 2008, £170,000 has been raised. £220,000 more is needed to prevent the church from closing permanently. Contributions to this project will be gratefully accepted. Checks should be made out to "Bampton CCC Church Roof Appeal" and sent to Mr Chris Ruck, Oban House, Bridge Street, Bampton, Oxon, OX18 2HA. To see photos of this wonderful medieval church visit the author's website: www.melstarr.net

Schoolcraft, MI
July 2008

A Corpse at St Andrew's Chapel

An extract from the second chronicle of

Hugh de Singleton, surgeon

Chapter 1

I awoke at dawn on the ninth day of April, 1365. Unlike French Malmsey, the day did not improve with age.

There have been many days when I have awoken at dawn but have remembered not the circumstances three weeks hence. I remember this day not because of when I awoke, but why, and what I was compelled to do after. Odd, is it not, how one extraordinary event will burn even the mundane surrounding it into a man's memory.

I have seen other memorable days in my twenty-five years. I recall the day my brother Henry died of plague. I was a child, but I remember well Father Aymer administering extreme unction. Father Aymer wore a spice bag about his neck to protect him from the malady. It did not, and he also succumbed within a fortnight. I can see the pouch yet, in my mind's eye, swinging from the priest's neck on a hempen cord as he bent over my stricken brother.

I remember clearly the day in 1361 when William of

Garstang died. William and I and two others shared a room on St Michael's Street, Oxford, while we studied at Baliol College. I comforted William as the returning plague covered his body with erupting buboes. For my small service he gave me, with his last breaths, his three books. One of two these volumes was *Surgery* by Henry de Mondeville. How William came by this book I know not. But I see now in this gift the hand of God, for I read de Mondeville's work and changed my vocation.

Was it then God's will that William die a miserable death so that I might find God's vision for my life? This I cannot accept, for I saw William's body covered with oozing pustules. I will not believe such a death is God's choice for any man. Here I must admit a disagreement with Master Wyclif, who believes that all is foreordained. But out of evil God may draw good, as I believe He did when he introduced me to the practice of surgery. Perhaps the good I have done with my skills balances the torment William suffered in his death. But not for William.

I remember well the day I met Lord Gilbert Talbot. I stitched him up after his leg was opened by a kick from a groom's horse on Oxford High Street. This needlework opened my life to service to Lord Gilbert and the townsmen of Bampton, and brought me also the post of bailiff on Lord Gilbert's manor at Bampton.

Other days return to my mind with less pleasure. I will not soon forget Christmas Day 1363, and the feast that day at Lord Gilbert's Goodrich Castle hall. I had traveled there from Bampton to attend Lord Gilbert's sister, the Lady Joan. The fair Joan had broken a wrist in a fall from a horse. I was summoned to set the break. It was foolish of me to think I might win this lady, but love has hoped more foolishness than that. A few days before Christmas a guest, Sir Charles de Burgh, arrived at Goodrich. Lord Gilbert invited him knowing well he might be a thief. Indeed, he stole Lady Joan's heart. Between the second and third removes of the Christmas feast he stood and, for all in the hall to see, offered Lady Joan a clove-studded pear. She took the fruit and with a smile delicately drew a clove from the pear with her teeth. They married in September, a few days before Michaelmas, last year.

I digress. I awoke at dawn to thumping on my chamber door. I blinked sleep from my eyes, crawled from my bed, and stumbled to the door. I opened it as Wilfred the porter was about to rap on it again.

"It's Alan... the beadle. He's found."

Alan had left his home to seek those who would violate curfew two days earlier. He never returned. His young wife came to me in alarm the morning of the next day. I sent John Holcutt, the reeve, to gather a party of searchers, but they found no trace of the man. John was not pleased to lose a day of work from six men. Plowing of fallow fields was not yet finished. Before I retired on Wednesday evening, John sought me out and begged not to resume the search the next day. I agreed. If Alan could not be found with the entire town aware of his absence, another day of poking into haymows and barns seemed likely also to be fruitless. It was not necessary.

"Has he come home?" I asked.

"Nay. An' not likely to, but on a hurdle."

"He's dead?"

"Aye."

"Where was he found?"

"Aside the way near to St Andrew's Chapel."

It was no wonder the searchers had not found him. St Andrew's Chapel was near half a mile to the east. What, I wondered, drew him away from the town on his duties?

"Hubert Shillside has been told. He would have you accompany him to the place."

"Send word I will see him straight away."

I suppose I was suspicious already that this death was not natural. I believe it to be a character flaw if a man be too mistrustful. But there are occasions in my professions – surgery and bailiff – when it is good to doubt a first impression. Alan was not yet thirty years old. He had a half-yardland of Lord Gilbert Talbot and was so well thought of that despite his youth, Lord Gilbert's tenants had at hallmote chosen him beadle these three years. He worked diligently, and bragged all winter that his four acres of oats had brought him nearly five bushels for every bushel of seed. A remarkable accomplishment, for his land was no better than any other surrounding Bampton. This success brought also some envy, I think, and perhaps there were wives who contrasted his achievement to the work of their husbands. But this, I thought, was no reason to kill a man.

I suppose a man may have enemies which even his friends know not of. I did consider Alan a friend, as did most others of the town. On my walk from Bampton Castle to Hubert Shillside's shop and house on Church View Street, I persuaded myself that this must be a natural death. Of course, when a corpse is found in open country, the hue and cry must be raised even if the body be stiff and cold. So Hubert, the town coroner, and I, bailiff and surgeon, must do our work.

Alan was found but a few minutes from the town. Down Rosemary Lane to the High Street, then left on Bushey Row to the path to St Andrew's Chapel. We saw – Hubert and I, and John Holcutt, who came also – where the body lay while we were yet far off. As we passed the last house on the lane east from Bampton to the chapel, we saw a group of men standing in the track at a place where last year's fallow was being plowed for spring planting. They saw us approach, and stepped back respectfully as we reached them.

A hedgerow had grown up among rocks between the lane and the field. New leaves of pale green decorated stalks of nettles, thistles and wild roses. Had the foliage matured for another fortnight Alan might have gone undiscovered. But two plowmen, getting an early start on their day's labor, found the corpse as they turned the oxen at the end of their first furrow. It had been barely light enough to see the white foot protruding from the hedgerow. The plowman who goaded the team saw it as he prodded the lead beasts to turn.

Alan's body was invisible from the road, but by pushing back nettles and thorns – carefully – we could see him curled as if asleep amongst the brambles. I directed two onlookers to retrieve the body. Rank has its privileges. Better they be nettle-stung than we. A few minutes later Alan the beadle lay stretched out on the path.

Lying in the open, on the road, the beadle did not seem so at peace as in the hedgerow. Deep scratches lacerated his face, hands and forearms. His clothes were torn, his feet bare, and a great wound bloodied his neck where flesh had been torn away. The coroner bent to examine this injury more closely.

"Some beast has done this, I think," he muttered as he stood. "See how his surcoat is torn at the arms, as if he tried to defend himself from fangs."

I knelt on the opposite side of the corpse to view in my turn the wound which took the life of Alan the beadle. It seemed as Hubert Shillside said. Puncture wounds spread across neck and arms, and rips on surcoat and flesh indicated where claws and fangs had made their mark. I sent the reeve back to Bampton Castle for a horse on which to transport Alan back to the town and to his wife. The others who stood in the path began to drift away. The plowmen who found him returned to their team. Soon only the coroner and I remained to guard the corpse. It needed guarding. Already a flock of carrion crows flapped high above the path.

I could not put my unease into words, so spoke nothing of my suspicion to Shillside. But I was not satisfied that some wild beast had done this thing. I believe the coroner was apprehensive of this explanation as well, for it was he who broke the silence.

"There have been no wolves hereabouts in my lifetime," he mused, "nor wild dogs, I think."

"I have heard," I replied, "Lord Gilbert speak of wolves near Goodrich. And Pembroke. Those castles are near to the Forest of Dean and the Welsh mountains. But even there, in such wild country, they are seldom seen."

Shillside was silent again as we studied the body at our feet. My eyes wandered to the path where Alan lay. When I did not find what I sought, I walked a few paces toward the town, then reversed my path and inspected the track in the direction of St Andrew's Chapel. My search was fruitless.

Hubert watched my movements with growing interest. "What do you seek?" he finally asked. It was clear to him I looked for something in the road.

"Tracks. If an animal did this, there should be some sign, I think. The mud is soft."

"Perhaps," the coroner replied. "But we and many others have stood about near an hour. Any marks a beast might have made have surely been trampled underfoot."

I agreed that might be. But another thought also troubled me. "There should be much blood," I said, "but I see little."

"Why so?" Shillside asked.

"When a man's neck is torn as Alan's is, there is much blood lost. It is the cause of death. Do you see much blood hereabouts?"

"Perhaps the ground absorbed it?"

"Perhaps... let us look in the hedgerow, where we found him."

We did, carefully prying the nettles apart. The foliage was depressed where Alan lay, but only a trace of blood could be seen on the occasional new leaf or rock or blade of grass.

"There is blood here," I announced, "but not much. Not enough."

"Enough for what?" the coroner asked with furrowed brow.

"Enough that the loss of blood would kill a man."

254

Shillside was silent for a moment. "Your words trouble me," he said finally. "If this wound" – he looked to Alan's neck – "did not kill him, what did?"

"'Tis a puzzle," I agreed.

"And see how we found him amongst the nettles. Perhaps he dragged himself there to escape the beasts, if more than one set upon him."

"Or perhaps the animal dragged him there," I added. But I did not believe this, for reasons I could not explain.

It was the coroner's turn to cast his eyes about. "His shoes and staff," Shillside mused. "I wonder where they might be?"

I remembered the staff. Whenever the beadle went out of an evening to watch and warn, he carried with him a yew pole taller than himself and thick as a man's forearm. I spoke to him of this weapon once. A whack from it, he said, would convince the most unruly drunk to leave the streets and seek his bed.

"He was proud of that cudgel," Hubert remarked as we combed the hedgerow in search of it. "He carved an 'A' on it so all would know 'twas his."

"I didn't know he could write."

"Oh, he could not," Shillside explained. "Father Thomas showed him the mark and Alan inscribed it. Right proud of it, he was."

We found the staff far off the path, where some waste land verged on to a wood just behind St Andrew's Chapel. It lay thirty paces or more from the place where Alan's body had lain in the hedgerow. But our search yielded no shoes.

"How did it come to be here?" Shillside asked. As if I would know. He examined the club. "There is his mark – see?" He pointed to the "A" inscribed with some artistry into the tough wood.

As the coroner held the staff before me, I inspected it closely and was troubled. Shillside saw my frown.

"What perplexes you, Hugh?"

"The staff is unmarked. Were I carrying such a

weapon and a wolf set upon me, I would flail it about to defend myself; perhaps hold it before me so the beast caught it in his teeth rather than my arm."

Shillside peered at the pole and turned it to view all sides. Its surface was smooth and unmarred. "Perhaps," he said thoughtfully, "Alan swung it at the beast and lost his grip. See how polished smooth it is... and it flew from his grasp to land here."

"That might be how it was," I agreed, for I had no better explanation.

As we returned to the path we saw the reeve approach with Bruce, the old horse who saw me about the countryside when I found it necessary to travel. He would be a calm and dignified platform on which to transport a corpse.

We bent to lift Alan to Bruce's back, John at the feet and Shillside and me at the shoulders. As we swung him up, Alan's head fell back. So much of his neck was shredded that it provided little support. I reached out a hand to steady the head and felt a thing which made my hackles rise.